PRAISE FOR ALLEN ESKENS'S

NOTHING
MORE
DANGEROUS

ONE OF THE YEAR'S BEST BOOKS

Florida Sun-Sentinel • Library Journal

"*Nothing More Dangerous* works well as a mystery, a dissection of hatred and racial prejudice, and a coming-of-age novel...Eskens gracefully moves the novel through the little moments that help to shape people and see the world with a different attitude."

—Oline H. Cogdill, Associated Press

"A stunning small-town mystery...Eskens clearly has an affinity for clever boys like Boady and Thomas; but he also has lovely visions of the mighty trees and secret swimming holes that make them long for summer—and mysteries to solve."

—Marilyn Stasio, *New York Times Book Review*

"The story is gripping...The characters are intriguing...Eskens weaves a fine mystery that involves layers of racial intro-spection...Eskens tells us in an author's note that he started this book in 1991 and kept putting it away, never quite feeling it was ready. He can proudly pronounce it ready now."

—Ginny Greene, *Minneapolis Star Tribune*

"Allen Eskens hits it out of the park with his new novel... More relevant than ever in this divided country... This is a story of hope through an act of love... It would be a fine supplementary text for high schoolers, especially the discussions of prejudice and where it comes from." —Mary Ann Grossman, *Pioneer Press*

"This powerful, unforgettable crime novel is a coming-of-age book to rival some of the best, such as William Kent Krueger's *Ordinary Grace* or Larry Watson's *Montana 1948*... This timely stand-alone is a must-read for followers of the best in crime fiction."

—*Library Journal* (starred review)

"Allen Eskens doesn't just tap into the experience of growing up in a rural Southern town; *Nothing More Dangerous* dissects the inner life of a teen forced to confront prejudice and persecution... Eskens has the skill to make readers cry... and then cheer."

—Paul Dinh-McCrillis, *Shelf Awareness*

"Magnificent... *Nothing More Dangerous* is the next best thing to Harper Lee's *To Kill a Mockingbird*... Setting, plot, and characterization are masterfully woven together to create a tapestry of a small town as a tinderbox of prejudice, fear, friendship, and dark secrets." —D. R. Meredith, *New York Journal of Books*

"Eskens does an excellent job of weaving the disparate threads together into a fine blend of mystery and coming-of-age novel. The setting is spot-on, the characters are empathetic and well realized, and the plot is clever and compelling, building suspense until a harrowing denouement reveals all."

—*Booklist*

"Both heartwarming and hard-nosed, *Nothing More Dangerous* is a coming-of-age page-turner that probes the dark heart of small towns and the resilient strength that keeps families together."

—Thomas Mullen, author of *Darktown*

The Shadows We Hide
The Deep Dark Descending
The Heavens May Fall
The Guise of Another
The Life We Bury

NOTHING MORE DANGEROUS

A NOVEL

ALLEN ESKENS

MULHOLLAND BOOKS

Little, Brown and Company
New York Boston London

Mulholland Books / Little, Brown and Company
Hachette Book Group
1290 Avenue of the Americas, New York, NY 10104
mulhollandbooks.com

Originally published in hardcover by Mulholland Books, November 2019
First Mulholland trade paperback edition, November 2020

Mulholland Books is an imprint of Little, Brown and Company, a division of Hachette Book Group, Inc. The Mulholland Books name and logo are trademarks of Hachette Book Group, Inc.

The publisher is not responsible for websites (or their content) that are not owned by the publisher.

The Hachette Speakers Bureau provides a wide range of authors for speaking events. To find out more, go to hachettespeakersbureau.com or call (866) 376-6591.

ISBN 978-0-316-50972-5 (hc) / 978-0-316-50973-2 (pb)
Library of Congress Control Number: 2019949856

10 9 8 7 6 5 4 3 2 1

LSC-C

Printed in the United States of America

*I dedicate this book to my beloved wife, Joely,
my partner on this wonderful journey.
I also dedicate it to my parents, Bill and Pat,
and to my siblings, Dave, Joyce, Don, Bob,
and Susan, whose adventures in the woods of
Missouri gave rise to some of the vignettes in
this novel. And I would like to thank my
daughter, Mikayla, for pushing for me to finish
this story after twenty-eight years of messing
around with it.*

AUTHOR'S NOTE

I began this novel, *Nothing More Dangerous,* in 1991 as a way to explore my own failing regarding notions of prejudice and racism. The characters and story line intrigued me, and I worked on the novel for twenty years before setting it aside. It wasn't ready, and I knew it. I then wrote five other novels, including *The Life We Bury,* which became my first bestseller. My experience in writing those novels led me back to *Nothing More Dangerous* with renewed focus and enthusiasm. I am pleased that this novel is finally ready, and I hope you enjoy it.

NOTHING

MORE

DANGEROUS

CHAPTER

1

I WAS FIFTEEN YEARS OLD THE DAY I LEARNED THAT Ms. LIDA POE had gone missing. Her name meant nothing to me at the time, but I repeated it under my breath just for the way it felt on my tongue. *Lida Poe*—it sounded whimsical yet stern, the kind of name that should belong to a saloon keeper or stunt pilot—not someone who scribbled numbers at a plastics factory. Her disappearance was a topic of discussion in my Current Events class that late-spring morning, and would have soon been lost to my many other distractions had everything else not gone to hell that day.

I never really understood the point of that Current Events class. It went like this: Mrs. Shaw had us read that day's newspaper for the first half of the hour—keeping us busy while she scrolled through her gossip magazines. Then she used the second half of the hour to discuss what we'd read, but those discussions never seemed to dig much past the surface, using a hoe when what you really needed was a shovel. For example, I knew that a guy named Jimmy Carter won a bunch of primaries, surprising every-body, and I knew that President Ford had his hands full trying to beat out an actor named Ronald Reagan for the Republican nomination, but what any of it had to do with the price of a turnip down at the IGA I couldn't tell you.

Ms. Poe wasn't the headline that day. In fact, her story didn't show up until page three. The headline, and most of the front page, was devoted to the American Freedom Train, or what we locals called the Bicentennial Train, which stopped in Jessup earlier that week, inviting students from every corner of Caulfield County to walk in lockstep through a celebration of the nation's two hundredth birthday. It was the biggest thing to hit Jessup, Missouri, since the *Apollo 11* capsule drove through on the back of a flatbed tractor-trailer.

Because I had already experienced the Freedom Train, I saw no need to read about it all over again, so I turned my attention to the open window next to me and let my thoughts drift in the breeze. Soon I found myself sitting in the crux of my favorite oak tree, watching the afternoon sun ripple across the surface of Dixon's pond, the smell of mud and water in my nose, the feel of tree bark under my bare feet. I could hear the zip of dragonflies and the rustle of an old turtle in the reeds. A sense of relaxation washed over me as I settled into my daydream—the only part of school that I found the least bit tolerable.

I would have stayed in that lull until the bell rang had I not been pulled back to the classroom by the sarcasm in Mrs. Shaw's voice when the discussion turned to the missing woman. The way Mrs. Shaw went on you'd think that Lida Poe spent her evenings dancing naked in her front yard under the glow of a red porch light. "Lida Poe," Mrs. Shaw said, "was thirty-five, colored, and a...*divorcée*"—that last word dripping with such a thick tang of ruination that you were just sure that all of Ms. Poe's hardships could be traced back to that one original sin.

The article didn't mention that Ms. Poe was a divorcée. Mrs. Shaw added that tidbit herself. And her tone suggested that she knew Lida Poe on a personal level—or more likely, she knew someone who knew someone who heard something. Back then, Jessup was big enough that you passed strangers on the street every day, but at the same time, if someone went missing, everybody seemed to know a little something about it.

The newspaper article pointed out that Poe worked in the purchasing department at Ryke Manufacturing, the largest employer in Jessup. Ryke molded plastics for use in everything from sunglasses to car dashboards. Those plastic phones that hung on everyone's wall, the ones with the long cord that came in every color of the rainbow, they all started out there in Jessup, Missouri. Shaw had once mentioned that her husband worked at Ryke, which might have explained the connection. Whatever the reason, Mrs. Shaw didn't much care for the missing woman.

The article gave little information as to why Ms. Lida Poe went missing. It merely reported that someone stopped by her house and found her gone. It had been two weeks, and no one had seen hide nor hair of the woman. Personally, I didn't find it hard to believe that someone had up and left Jessup; what baffled *me* was why more people *didn't* do it.

I looked out the window again and tried to get back to Dixon's pond, hoping to stay there until the bell rang. I conjured up bits and pieces of the daydream, but they came and went like a candle that just wouldn't stay lit. Mrs. Shaw had moved on to another article, but something about Lida Poe's story kept me away from my daydream. I remember thinking that when the time came for me to run away from Jessup, I would be sure to leave a note. I didn't want students in some Current Events class reading about me going missing—not that they would have cared.

When the bell rang, kids poured out of their classrooms with the force of a river breaking through its levee. I headed down the main stairs, which opened into a hallway lined with mildew-green lockers, where I dumped my morning books into my locker, grabbed a yellow notebook, and headed to the cafeteria for lunch.

I hated the lunch hour.

Unlike most kids, I didn't mind the food. I mean, how bad can you screw up a hot dog? No, I hated lunch because I had no regular place to sit. Cafeteria politics dictated that I wait until the various cliques settled into their seats before I claimed a chair, my daily reminder of just how much of an outsider I remained after almost a full year at St. Ignatius Catholic High School. I told my mother that I had been making friends at my new school—I didn't want her to worry—but I think she knew that I made it all up, because she never asked for their names, and I never offered them.

Up until the end of eighth grade, I had attended a small country school in Dry Creek, a town a little closer to my home out in the woods. That all changed when I decided to take up smoking. Back then, the IGA sold cigarettes in the checkout lane, right next to the candy bars and tabloid magazines. It was easy to take a pack. I just stood with my back to the rack and slipped the smokes into my pocket. Once I got out of the store, I moved them into my sock so that my mom wouldn't see them.

At home, after I helped Mom carry in the groceries, I ran out to my tree at the edge of Dixon's pond, climbed onto my favorite limb, and lit my first cigarette. I can't say that I particularly liked the experience; truth be told, I felt like I coughed up half a lung that day.

I took up smoking to try to fit in with a loose collection of misfits from Dry Creek who smoked cigarettes after school and called themselves the Rowdies. Smoking was kind of like their secret handshake; it made them different from other kids, and that difference gave them something they could share. Theirs was a least-common-denominator basis for friendship, and I thought that by learning to smoke I could be one of them.

But just as I was making inroads with the group, we got busted. One of the teachers spotted us sneaking down to the train trestle during recess. When the dust of that particular flap settled, my mother decided to enroll me at St. Ignatius in the fall instead of Jessup High, where the rest of those guys went. As far as I knew, I wasn't even Catholic before that. St. Ignatius had no rowdies, at least not the type that I knew in Dry Creek. The rowdies at St. Ignatius were dentists' and bankers' sons who dressed sharp, drove jacked-up trucks and Camaros, and beat up freshmen like me for fun.

I hated St. Ignatius.

I got to the cafeteria that day, waited in line, and bought my lunch: two hot dogs, two milks, and a bag of chips, the same lunch I ate every day. I grabbed an empty chair at the end of a row of tables and opened my yellow notebook, flipping past page after page of rock band logos that I had drawn, or attempted to draw. I had no talent—not even a little bit—but drawing gave me something to do so that I didn't have to stare at the empty chair across from me for an hour. I drew a lot of KISS and Lynyrd Skynyrd stuff, but that day I worked to perfect the wings of my Aerosmith logo. That's what I was doing when I heard Lida Poe's name again.

I hadn't noticed, but a group of seniors had taken seats at the table behind me—Jarvis Halcomb and his boys, Beef and Bob. Beef and Bob weren't related, but because they shared the letter B as their first initial, most underclassmen took to calling them the Boob Brothers, a silly alliteration born of adolescent swagger—a name that could be whispered from a distance but never spoken loud enough for one of them to hear it.

You rarely saw Jarvis without the Boob Brothers at his side, laughing at his jokes and pretty much agreeing with anything he said; such was the privilege afforded those deemed popular. Jarvis had been the first wrestler from St. Ignatius to go to the state tournament in over a decade, and he had been voted prom king even though most of the kids in my class thought he was a jerk. And he drove a four-wheel-drive truck that he'd jacked up so high that he had to weld an extra step below his running boards so he could climb up into the cab.

I'm pretty sure Jarvis Halcomb had no idea that I existed before that day—though I made sure to fix that. I hadn't planned on butting in on their business, but I couldn't help eavesdropping once I heard Jarvis mention the name Lida Poe.

"We just have to wait until this whole thing with Lida Poe blows over," Jarvis said to the Boobs.

Beef spoke. "You said your old man would hire me. I told Mom I got a job already."

"He'll hire you. We just have to wait a bit. The jackasses up in Minneapolis are sendin' down some guy to look into what happened to Poe. Dad can't do nothin' till he's gone."

"But your dad's the boss," Beef said. "Why can't he do what he wants?"

"Dad's only the boss here in Jessup," Jarvis said. "They all gotta answer to the head office in Minneapolis. And what's worse, the guy they're sendin' down...he's a coon."

"Bullshit," Beef said.

"As God is my witness, that's what Dad said."

Bob said, "Every time you turn around there's another one getting moved up the ladder for no good reason. It ain't right."

"There's a reckonin' on the way," Jarvis said. "That's for damn sure."

"Maybe we should do some reckonin' of our own," Bob said. "Maybe take a drive through Goat Hill tonight."

Beef said, "I don't know, boys."

"Gonna chicken out again?" Bob asked.

"It ain't chickenin' out. I just don't see the point of it."

"The point of it is, we're sendin' a message," Bob said.

"We don't need to go to Goat Hill to send a message," Jarvis said. "We can do that right here. Where's that little black girl sittin'?"

I knew who they were talking about. A freshman, like me, she too ate her lunches alone, being the only black kid in the whole school. She sat next to me in my history class, although I don't recall ever talking to her. Her name was Diana and her mother worked in the cafeteria, which gave Diana free tuition—at least that's what I'd heard—which made sense, because why else would someone like her go to St. Ignatius?

"How 'bout we just eat in peace," Beef said.

"God, Beef, stop bein' such a wuss," Jarvis said. "We ain't gonna hit her or nothin'."

"Whatcha gonna do?" Bob asked.

"I ain't doin' nothin'—you are. You're gonna...you're gonna take my puddin' and dump it on her. Pretend it's an accident."

"Come on, Jarvis," Beef said. "Numb-nuts here might take you serious."

"I am serious," Jarvis said. "Bob talks big, but I wanna see if he's got any grit to him."

"Why me? It's your idea."

"Bob, are you suggesting that I'm not the kind of guy that would do what needs doin'?" A low snarl had found its way into Jarvis's voice and seemed to turn the room cold. "Is that what you're sayin', Bob? Cuz I think you know better."

"No, I ain't sayin' that." I could hear backtracking in Bob's tone as he answered.

Jarvis continued, "Between the two of us, you're the one that still has somethin' to prove."

I peeked over my shoulder, pretending to look at the clock on the wall, and saw Jarvis slide a bowl of chocolate pudding onto the tray in front of Bob. Beef stared at his lunch tray lightly shaking his head.

As the plot coiled up behind me, I scanned the lunchroom and spotted the monitors, Brother Evan and Brother Bart, lost in a conversation on the far side of the room. I thought about running over and alerting them to Jarvis's scheme, but by the time I'd get there, it would be too late. All I'd be doing is snitching after the fact, doing no good for either Diana or myself.

Like most things Catholic, the dress code at St. Ignatius favored us boys over the girls. We were allowed to wear knit pants and shirts of any color, as long as the shirt had a collar. The girls, on the other hand, could only wear white blouses with either navy blue pants or navy blue skirts, hemmed at the knee of course. I looked at Diana and pictured the mess of pudding on her nice white blouse, and I felt bad for her.

"No problem," Bob said.

I tucked my elbows into my ribs, shrinking in my seat as I tried to convince myself that this wasn't my fight. I had no part in it. I was a freshman—a weak and bony one at that, and they were seniors. Freshmen don't stick their noses into such places or they'd get those noses broken. If anything, Brothers Bart and Evan were at fault for what was about to happen. They were supposed to be watching out for problems like this, not gabbing away. The blame lay with them, not me.

Yet, try as I might, I couldn't talk myself into minding my own business. I looked at the unfolding situation and could see only one option, and if I'd had more time to think about it, I'm sure that I would have chickened out.

I heard the squeak of Bob's chair as he stood up.

Stupid. Stupid. Stupid. Those words clanged in my brain.

Bob began walking, coming from behind me and to my right.

Stupid. Stupid.

As he passed, I swung my foot out, catching his left heel and sending that foot into the back of his right knee.

Stupid!

Bob splayed out as he crashed to the floor, his tray and flatware slamming into the tile with a clamor that echoed off the walls—a gong to focus all eyes on Bob's humiliation.

I stopped breathing. What *had* I done?

Bob turned to look at me, rage boiling red on his face, a cow-pie of pudding smeared across his cheek and on his shirt. It's possible that Brothers Evan and Bart might have been able to break up the fight before Beef and Bob and Jarvis did too much damage to me, but I didn't stick around to see. I grabbed my yellow notebook and ran.

"The little puke tripped me!" Bob shouted.

There seemed to be a moment of confusion for Jarvis and Beef, because they didn't grab me as I shot past them. When Bob yelled a second time, he just said, "Get him!"

I had gone out for track that year—my mom's suggestion—the idea being that I might be able to survive St. Ignatius if I had some kind of extracurricular hobby to distract me. But I only lasted one day. It wasn't that I couldn't run fast; I could. No, I dropped out of track because Brock Nance, the Jarvis Halcomb of my grade, and his little band of suck-ups made fun of me for wearing black socks with my gym clothes instead of the knee-high white socks like everyone else had on. They called me Boady Bumpkin, a name I didn't want catching on, so I quit going to track. Besides, I didn't need to race other boys to know that I was fast.

The cafeteria had a courtyard where kids could eat outside. I made it halfway across that space, heading for grass and the path around the back side of the gymnasium, before Jarvis and Beef got out of their chairs. I crossed the point of no return before I realized my mistake; I'd turned right when I should have turned left. Left would have taken me to the main part of the school, where there'd be windows and teachers and help. The gym had no windows. If Jarvis caught me back there, no one would hear my screams. There'd be no rescue.

I kicked it up a gear, my feet clapping hard on the packed dirt of the path. I glanced back to see Jarvis gaining. Beef, our school's top heavyweight wrestler and offensive tackle, lagged well back, although he had impressive speed for a big guy. Straight ahead of me lay an open field where the marching band usually practiced. If I ran out there, I'd be tackled like a baby wildebeest. My only hope was to boomerang around the gym and try to make it back to the front of the school, maybe catch the eye of a teacher before Jarvis caught me.

My fingers scraped along the rough brick as I cut close to the building to make my first turn. I could feel my adrenaline wearing off and fear taking its place. Faster. I had to run faster. Forget about pacing myself—it made no sense to save fuel for later.

As I approached the next corner, I heard Jarvis's steps pounding closer. Again I looked back to see that Jarvis had gained another thirty feet on me. I wouldn't be able to make it to the front of the school before he caught me.

I thought about shooting left and heading for the student parking lot, where I could dodge around cars until they gave up, but with two of them and only one of me, they'd be able to trap me. I was almost out of ideas when I saw the back door of the cafeteria's kitchen. Students weren't allowed in there, but I hit that door anyway.

A stocky woman, standing at a sink hosing off a stack of plastic trays, saw me stumble in, and her face took on a perplexed expression. I bent down, hands on my knees, and gulped in big chunks of air, doing my best not to puke. I expected a hassle, but the woman made no move to shoo me out of her kitchen.

Peering over a stack of dirty pans, I saw that both Brother Bart and Brother Evan had left their post, probably making their way toward the back side of the gym, their keen senses having finally figured out that something was amiss. I thought about slipping back into the cafeteria, but saw Bob leaning against a table, wiping pudding off his shirt with a stack of napkins. With no teachers in the room, I couldn't go there.

Then I heard the beat of Jarvis's shoes coming to a stop outside, followed a few seconds later by Beef, so out of breath that his wheezing penetrated the door. The woman at the sink pointed to an empty space below one of the countertops. She nodded to tell me to hide there, so I did.

No sooner did I get my feet tucked up under me than Jarvis pulled the kitchen door open. From my hiding spot, I could see the woman's shoes, brown leather with small holes in the toes, as she scurried to intercept my pursuers. "Students ain't allowed in the kitchen," she said.

"We're lookin' for someone," Jarvis said. "We think he might be in there."

"Students ain't allowed in the kitchen," she repeated, giving a punch to each word.

"We just wanna take a quick look," Jarvis said. "It won't take a second."

I could see Jarvis attempting to wedge his way past the woman, and I watched her feet move to block him.

"Son, if you don't get outta my kitchen right now, I'll get one of the brothers to haul ya out."

"Boys, what seems to be the problem here?" It was Brother Bart's voice, deep and resonant, the kind of voice that belonged on the radio or doing movie trailers. I watched Jarvis back out of the kitchen, the door closing behind him.

A few seconds later the woman walked to where I hid and bent down so I could see her face. "You can come out now."

I wiggled my way out of the cubbyhole.

"What's your name, son?"

I hesitated, and then said, "Boady Sanden."

"Well, Boady Sanden, I'm Mrs. Lathem, and this is my kitchen. So you wanna tell me why you're pickin' fights you can't win? You got rocks in that head of yours or somethin'?"

"Excuse me?"

"I saw you trip that big fella. What in the Sam Hill were you thinkin'?"

"He was gonna dump puddin' on this girl named Diana and I—"

"Diana Jackson? Evelyn's girl?"

"I guess." I brushed some dirt and an old french fry off my pants.

"Principal Rutgers is gonna hear about this," she said.

"No. Please. I don't wanna make a big deal of it. I gotta go to school here, and I don't need people callin' me a snitch. It's over. I just wanna go to class and forget about it."

The woman chewed on the inside of her cheek for a bit, then said, "Okay. I won't tell if that's what you want, but you'd better stay here until the bell rings. It ain't gonna be safe out there."

"Thanks."

"And, Boady?"

"Yes, ma'am?"

"Mind you, this little tussle ain't over for them, not by a long shot. So you best grow a pair of eyes in the back of your head."

"Yes, ma'am."

CHAPTER

2

THAT FRACAS WITH THE PUDDING HAPPENED ON A FRIDAY. I remember because having dodged Jarvis and the Boob Brothers for the last three class periods, I figured I'd have all weekend to come up with a plan to steer clear of them for the remaining few weeks of my miserable freshman year. But sometimes fate has a way of putting your plans—even something as life-and-death important as getting thrashed by seniors—on the back burner.

The school bus dropped me off at the top of my dead-end gravel road, and as it pulled away, the bus kicked up a cloud of exhaust and limestone dust that drifted my way. I stood motionless, my eyes closed, my breath held, until the spring breeze cleared the offending cloud. When I opened my eyes again, Frog Hollow Road—my road—snaked its way along the side of a modest Ozark ridge, dipping and twisting like a discarded ribbon.

I gripped my gym bag handle with both hands, spun in a circle the way I'd seen Olympic hammer throwers do, and heaved the bag—with my algebra and Spanish textbooks inside—as far down the road as I could, watching it tumble and skid to a stop in the loose gravel. I was on the cusp of flunking both classes, and found the books themselves an easier target for my frustration than, say, my reluctance to crack them open.

I shuffled to the side of the road and climbed atop an old,

cedar corner post, a log almost as big around as me, which didn't mean much since I was a fairly skinny kid at fifteen. I stood on that pedestal, my size-tens overlapping its flat crown, and my thin frame, all five-eight of it, stretching up like an extension of the post itself. Out in front of me, the Ozark hills rolled along like a lumpy quilt on an unmade bed, the land all wrinkled and twisted like God had casually dropped it there as he passed by. I traced the long meandering line of the valley in front of me until my eyes came to rest on the hazy outline of a water tower eight miles away, proof of civilization beyond my woods.

It used to be that I would stand on that fence post and feel like a king, with miles of trees stretching out all around me. I knew every path, pond, creek and cave in those woods. I wandered over that terrain during endless summer days, inventing games that I could play by myself, cutting trails with my machete, and making elaborate campsites complete with fire pits and twine-string hammocks. I dug mud from the floors of rock outcroppings looking for abandoned treasure but finding only more mud. I made boats out of sun-dried turtle shells and floated them down the creek with crawdads for skippers. Those woods had been a nest that I once thought I would never want to leave.

But around the time I first stepped through the doors of St. Ignatius High School, my beloved woods began to change, the hills growing tall and foreboding—walls cutting me off from the rest of the world. I became preoccupied with thoughts of city-scapes and oceans, and the enormity of life beyond Jessup. What started out as an itch in my chest had festered to the point of near suffocation, and I knew that I had to get out of that town and away from the hell that was St. Ignatius. All I needed was a driver's license and a car—and I had a plan to get both of those.

When I tired of my daydreaming, I jumped off the post and began my walk home. Frog Hollow Road was only half a mile long, with no place to so much as pitch a tent for the first half of the way—the land rising at a hostile slope on the left and falling into a deep valley on the right. But near the halfway point, the road took a sharp turn and the land flattened out level enough for a few houses.

I lived in the first house on the left, just around that bend—my mother and me and Grover, our redbone coonhound. I took solace in knowing that Grover would be there to comfort Mom after I lit out to make my mark on the world. I told myself that she'd be okay as long as she had Grover. But then again, Judas probably had the same notion as he filled his pockets with those silver pieces. I pictured Mom and Grover sitting on the back porch, Mom's hand resting on the dog's head as she read my letter—the one explaining why I had to leave.

In my mind's eye, she'd wear a wistful smile in that moment, but deep down I knew there'd be no smile, no comfort born of a faithful dog. She would cry and her heart would break—again—but this time it would be my fault. Every time that thought came to haunt me, I'd shove it away with feckless excuses of how she should have seen it coming. Kids grow up, they leave home—even at sixteen. She'd understand eventually. I used those excuses to tamp down the truth. I knew the darkness my leaving would bring to my mother, the hole she'd climb into once she found me gone, but I saw no other way.

I also eased my conscience by pointing out that she wouldn't be completely alone after I left home. Hoke Gardner lived right next door to us, so close, I could sometimes hear jazz music from his hi-fi late at night as it climbed through my bedroom window. She also had Wally Schenicker, her boss who ran a drywall company down at the tail end of the road. It wasn't like I'd be leaving her all alone in those woods.

Other than Wally Schenicker, Hoke Gardner, and us, Frog

Hollow had only one other house, the Dixon place, which stood vacant and quiet across the road from Mom and me. Over the years, I had grown used to the emptiness of the Dixon house, the fall of moonshadows outside my window at night where Tilly Dixon's porch light used to glow, the unraked leaves on shaggy grass where her manicured lawn had once been. We still called it the Dixon place even though it had been five years since Matilda Dixon—Tilly as we knew her—died there in her sleep. The house fell empty on the night of her death and had remained so ever since.

As I walked home that Friday, the Dixon house looked the same as it did every day. Set back a ways from the road, it had a large porch that stretched across its entire front, steep gables that wore the delicate woodwork lace of an era that had never heard of plastic, and a turret on one end with a pointy rooftop that gave it a castle-like quality. The genteel old Victorian stood two stories tall, although it had always seemed so much larger than that to me.

But as I got closer that day, a glimmer of light caught my eye, a reflection flashing through the grove of cedars where there should have been no reflection at all. I crouched on the road to peer between the trees and saw some pickup trucks parked in the driveway. I continued down the road with my eyes fixed on the trucks until I found myself standing in front of the house, its screen door standing open, and men moving in and out with drop cloths and ladders and buckets of paint.

After Tilly died, I would sometimes see a repair truck drop by to do a little upkeep on the place, work paid for by some distant niece who lived in Philadelphia and had inherited the property. But what I saw that day wasn't upkeep—it was full-blown transformation, with men scurrying around as though some deadline nipped at their heels. They were hard at work trying to improve on what was already one of the nicest houses in the county, a prince separated from us paupers by a mere gravel road.

My house, on the other hand, was a small rambler so simple and boxy that if it weren't for the carport on the side, it'd almost look like a dressed-up shed. Years of wear and neglect had taken their toll on the old place: blue siding dulled to an ugly gray, gutters sagging with dead leaves, shingles bubbling with age. Like a small child clomping along in his father's shoes, I stepped clumsily into my role as man of the house, repairing what I could, things like loose screws and blown fuses. But fixes that required an experienced hand, those I put on a list that I kept in my head, tucked far away so that I didn't have to admit that I was not yet my father.

As I stood in the road, looking back and forth between the two houses, Grover lumbered out to welcome me home. My hand found the top of his head without my eyes having to look for it. There had been a time when he used to charge up the road to greet me as soon as I rounded the bend. It took me until fourth grade before I was big enough that he didn't knock me down. But sometime this past year, about the time he turned nine, he gave up that routine, preferring instead to wait for me in the carport.

As I petted Grover, I heard Hoke Gardner's screen door flop shut and saw him step onto his porch, taking a seat in one of the two rocking chairs he kept there. I nodded to him, and he gave a small wave back. One of the workers came out of the Dixon house, dug through the back of his truck, and returned to the house carrying an extension cord. I looked again at Hoke, who had opened a book on his lap, seemingly paying little mind to the goings-on across the road. He would know something about all this, so I took Grover back to the carport, checked his water bowl, and made my way to Hoke's porch.

"Hey, Hoke," I said, planting myself in the second rocker.

"Hey," he answered back.

A lanky man with mostly gray hair, Hoke wore his sixty-plus years like an old boot. He seldom smiled, but when he did it could warm you up like hot cocoa. Sitting close to him, you could see the loose ends of a past that Hoke never talked about. His left arm hung lifeless at his side when he walked, and lay on his lap like a wet towel when he sat. He had a finger-length scar extending up his right temple, giving an unnatural part to his thin hair. He also had burn scars that covered the back of his hands and snaked up his pale forearms. He made it clear early on that his scars were a subject he preferred not to discuss, so we didn't.

Hoke put down his book as I settled into my rocking chair. Then he picked up his pipe, wedged it between his thighs, opened a pouch of tobacco, and began packing leaves into the bowl with his pinky finger. I waited patiently as he finished tamping the pipe, struck a match, and took a pull. I liked the smell of his tobacco. I still think of Hoke whenever I catch a whiff of pipe smoke. If I had a choice in the matter, that's how I would remember Hoke Gardner—sitting on his porch, a book on his lap, a pipe in his mouth, and his feet propped up on the rail—but life doesn't always give us that choice.

"What's goin' on over there?" I asked, pointing across the road.

"The house finally sold."

"No way?"

"They're fixing it up for the new folks. The owners might be moving in as soon as next week."

"Really? You know anything about 'em?"

"The realtor came out earlier. Said they're a family by the name of Elgin. That's about all I know."

"Must be a big family...with that house..."

"He didn't say."

"Pro'bly at least a couple kids, don't ya think?"

Hoke glanced at me and gave half a smile, but said nothing. In the distance, I could hear the crunch of gravel from around the bend. Over the years, I had developed a pretty good sense of gravel sound, and I measured this one to most likely be a car or one of those small pickups. It definitely wasn't Schenicker's flatbed or his one-ton.

"I've never been upstairs in the Dixon house," I said. "How many bedrooms ya think they got up there?"

Hoke squinted and nodded slightly as he counted windows. "My bet...I'd guess at least four."

"Plus the bedroom downstairs," I added.

The sound of crunching gravel drew closer, and we both turned to look as the car came into view, long and white, with a light bar across the top and the Caulfield County Sheriff's emblem on the door. I had never seen the sheriff's car on Frog Hollow before. I looked at Hoke for a reaction, but all he did was take his pipe from his mouth and puff out a thin plume of smoke.

The car slowed to a crawl, and I could see the man inside leaning his face out the window, examining my house. He slowed almost to a stop before he noticed me and Hoke on the porch, and the man rolled on until he came to a stop in front of us.

"I'm looking for a Hoke Gardner," the sheriff said.

"I'm Hoke Gardner." Hoke pointed at his chest with the stem of his pipe.

The man in the car shifted into park, killed the engine, and stepped out, fixing a Stetson atop his mostly bald head as he stood. Tall and hefty, with a strong chin and ruddy cheeks, he identified himself as Sheriff Matthew Vaughan. "I was wondering if I might have a word with you."

Hoke stood and laid his pipe in a metal ashtray that he'd nailed to the corner of his porch rail. "Come on up."

Vaughan stepped onto the porch, his eyes flicking back and forth between Hoke and me. "Can we..." He gave a nod toward me. "Talk in private?"

"Of course," Hoke said. "Boady, don't you have to go clean Schenicker's warehouses today?"

"Uh...yeah," I said. I didn't want to leave, but I backed off the porch, taking one last look at the sheriff's face, searching for the slightest clue as to the nature of the visit. For his part, Sheriff Vaughan watched me through a stone mask.

CHAPTER

3

I JOGGED HOME, PAUSING AT THE KITCHEN DOOR JUST LONG enough to let Grover in from the carport, and then I raced to my bedroom, and to my window, where I pressed my ear against the screen to listen.

We didn't have air-conditioning back then. Instead, Mom had an old window fan in her room that faced out and pulled air in through all the other windows of the house. The breeze felt good on my skin, but the noise of the fan in the other room—as slight as it was—stepped on the voices coming from Hoke's porch. I ran to Mom's bedroom, shut the fan off, and returned to my window.

My room faced the road, and sitting at that window put me as near as I could get to Hoke's porch without being outside. I caught a word here and there, but most of the conversation evaporated before it got to me. I held my breath, hoping it might help—but got nothing. I'd waited fifteen years to see a sheriff's car on Frog Hollow, so I'd be damned if I was going to sit in my room and miss out on the happenings next door.

Having grown up hooked on reruns of Fess Parker playing Daniel Boone on TV, I often thought of myself as a kindred spirit to that legendary man—Daniel Boone, that is, not Fess Parker. I spent countless hours tracking animals through the woods, tiptoeing noiselessly through dead leaves, even getting down on my hands and toes in a kind of spider crawl. I once got within spitting distance of a wild turkey before it noticed me and took off. But I had never practiced my skills on a human before and figured that the time had come to give it a try.

I ran back out to the carport, slipped over the railing, and snuck around the back side of my house. At the corner, I paused to take a peek and make sure that neither Hoke nor Sheriff Vaughan was looking my way. Hoke leaned against the porch rail facing the sheriff, who remained out of my line of sight. Perfect.

Our propane tank stood at the edge of the property line, only thirty feet or so from Hoke's front door, and if I could get behind it, I would be within earshot of his porch, give or take. I got down on my hands and knees and eased my way through the gap of yard where I could be easily seen if Hoke happened to turn around. The voices coming from the porch grew clearer and more distinct with every inch.

There were dead leaves clustered around the base of the propane tank, so I laid my body out over them like I was in the top of a push-up; then I carefully, slowly lowered myself down, the crunch of dried leaves—to my ears—seeming to rise up louder than the hurried ripping of Christmas wrapping paper. When I came to rest on flat earth, I tilted my head to aim an ear at Hoke's porch. It took a second or two to calm my breathing before I could hear the two men talking, plain and clear.

"So when Lida Poe worked for you, what'd she do?"

"Books, receptionist, filing, nothing too complicated. Her late father and I went to high school together. I gave her her first job out of college—kind of a favor to him. She did a good job, though."

"You went to high school here in Jessup?"

"Jessup High, yeah."

"I understand it was just the two of you in that office—you and Lida Poe. Your wife was okay with that?"

Hoke didn't answer.

"Wasn't but a few months later that you lost your wife in that, uh...*accident*."

Vaughan heaped enough inflection on that last word that I could hear the accusation all the way out at my hiding spot behind the propane tank.

"I would advise you to be careful with your insinuations, Sheriff."

"I ain't insinuatin' nothin', just statin' a fact. I gotta tell ya, though, surprised the hell out of me you didn't wind up in prison over that deal. Got a friend up in Columbia who was on the force back then. He admits they dropped the ball. Shoulda followed up after they took ya to the hospital."

"That's on them, not me," Hoke said.

"Didn't get charged with a damned thing."

"I didn't ask for any favors."

"Yeah, sure enough, but my buddy also told me some scuttlebutt—stuff he'd heard about you and Miss Poe. She's pretty easy on the eyes for a colored gal."

Again, Hoke didn't answer.

"You know what I'm talkin' about?" Vaughan continued. "A couple lonely folks workin' late at night. Things happen. Now, I'm not sayin' nothin' one way or t'other. I'm just tellin' ya what I heard."

"Given my former profession, does it surprise you that cops back then made up stories about me? But that's all they were—stories—and you'd be wise not to put stock in it."

"Oh, I don't give it no nevermind, but it makes a man curious. If it's all the same to you, I'd like to hear it from the horse's mouth. Were you and Lida Poe ever romantically involved?"

"She was half my age."

"That argues for my point, not yours."

"Lida worked for me—that's all."

"It just seems a bit coincidental—she starts workin' for you up there in Columbia. Not long after that, the rumors about you and Lida get going, and then…well…there's that business when your wife died—what was that…May of 'sixty-six."

"You're wearing out your welcome, Sheriff."

"I'm not sayin' anything nefarious happened. I'm just tryin' to understand what I've been told. You got all crippled up and then—poof—Miss Poe goes and finds herself some new young stud. Up and married him—least, that's what I heard."

"I didn't pay attention to Ms. Poe's personal life."

"And that's about the same time you moved back here to Jessup. Is that why you came here? Got jilted?"

"I grew up over in Dry Creek."

"From what I hear, though, you had quite the life up there in Columbia. Makin' money hand over fist. You give all that up to move back to the woods and live like a hermit? All because ya grew up here?"

Hoke's tone dropped a few notes and came out slow and ugly. "Sheriff, why I moved to Jessup is none of your damn business."

The sheriff did his best to match. "This is a criminal investigation, Mr. Gardner. We're talkin' 'bout fraud on a major scale, and a missin' woman—someone from your past, who's run off with all that money. So, thank you kindly, but I'll be the judge of what is or ain't my business."

"You need to get off my porch now," Hoke said.

At that, Sheriff Vaughan seemed to stammer some, his voice taking on more honey than before. "Now, Hoke—can I call you Hoke? I'm just followin' the trail, that's all. You say there's no affair—well, fine, there's no affair. But there's a couple things that have me scratchin' my head. Like, for example, four years ago when Lida's husband ran off and left her, what does she do? She moves here to Jessup just like you did. How do you explain that? Her husband dumps her and—bang—here she is. And here you are."

"We were acquaintances—that's all."

"Is that why she came to Jessup?"

"You'll have to ask her."

"Uh-huh. And where might I find her?"

"I wouldn't have the foggiest."

"When's the last time you had contact with her?"

Hoke paused for a considerable amount of time before saying, "She called me when she first got to town. Said she wanted a fresh start. Had a friend who could get her a job at Ryke in the purchasing department, but she didn't think they'd hire her because of her skin color. She wanted a reference; that's it."

"A fetchin' gal like her...good with numbers but not with men...can't imagine she had too much trouble getting hired on at Ryke no matter what color she was."

"Again, Sheriff, I don't know about her personal life."

"What if I told you that she'd been seen out with an older man—a white man? Would that be you?"

"Are you accusing me of a crime, Sheriff?"

"No, nothin' like that."

"Am I under arrest?"

"No."

"Then I'll thank you to get off my porch...now."

"Look, Mr. Gardner—"

"I said, get off my porch!"

The men went silent for a bit, and then came the thump of heavy footsteps as Sheriff Vaughan made his way off the porch.

Peeking above the top of the tank, I could see the back of

Hoke's shirt as he remained leaning against the rail. I backtracked, still on my hands and knees, keeping an eye on Hoke's shirt to make sure that he didn't turn, and then I scurried around the back of the house, climbing over the rail of the carport to keep out of Hoke's sight.

Once back inside, I turned Mom's fan back on and went to my room to change out of my school clothes and into my work clothes—blue jeans, a white T-shirt, and my Converse sneakers with tears along the arches of both shoes. Ready for work, I sat back down at the foot of my bed, my elbows resting on the windowsill, and let the breeze cool the sweat on my neck and face. Sheriff Vaughan had gone, and Hoke sat in his rocking chair, his book open on his lap again. He had relit his pipe and had his feet resting on the wooden porch rail, as calm as could be.

Hoke knew Lida Poe. They had been in Columbia together. She'd worked for him back in…What'd the sheriff say? May of '66? Ten years ago.

I closed my eyes and tried to place myself inside Hoke's house, where I'd been hundreds of times over the years. I tried to remember what pictures he had on his walls, or if he had any trinkets on his mantel that held a clue as to where he'd come from. All I could see were a couple pictures of outdoor scenes, the kind of thing you'd find at any rummage sale. In my mind's eye, I found nothing that gave a hint of a life before here—not a single photo or keepsake that might tie him to his past, and it began to dawn on me that I knew very little about my neighbor.

Hoke moved in next door to us when I was five, the same year that my father died. I remember the funeral that year—or at least I remember wearing a little black tie and getting hugged by people I didn't know. I remember Christmas, and the wish that I made to the baby Jesus that made my mother cry. But I have no memory of being told that my father was dead or the first time that I met

Hoke Gardner. It's almost as if I woke up one morning to a world where my father was gone and Hoke was there—like he'd lived there all along.

Across the road, the construction crew started carrying tools out to their trucks—a sign that quitting time was drawing near. I needed to get to Schenicker's and clean his warehouses—one of my after-school jobs.

I threw my school clothes into the hamper and headed out into a world that held more shadows than it had only a couple hours earlier. Walking past Hoke as he sat on his porch smoking his pipe, I waved, and he gave a smile back. I'd seen that smile a thousand times, but never before had it looked like a disguise.

CHAPTER

4

FROG HOLLOW ROAD EMPTIED ONTO A GRAVEL COURTYARD, A turnaround surrounded by three warehouses and Wally Schenicker's farmhouse, all built on land his family had owned forever. The first warehouse, the one we called the shed, sat off to the left as you entered the courtyard—nine o'clock on a watch face. The shed, the oldest of the three warehouses, held Wally's forklift, a large pile of scaffolding bucks, and a muddle of truck parts, old tools, and construction knickknacks—crap that Wally deemed worth keeping because "you never know when you might need one."

Straight ahead at twelve o'clock was his house, two stories that had once held a family with three kids—Wally being the only one to survive to adulthood. He was one of those bachelor-farmer types, the third generation to live in that house and the first to admit that the ground around it was simply too damned rocky to make a go of being a farmer. Instead, he started up a drywall company, a respectable operation that had at its core seven full-time employees—and with summer coming on, there'd be more added, one of whom would be me.

That summer marked my second year working for Wally, doing just about anything that required a strong back and no particular skill. During the school year, I cleaned his warehouses, a task that required me to drive his one-ton truck full of discarded sheetrock scraps down a trail to his illegal landfill. I had become a master at driving that stick shift—if you ignore the fact that I never got above second gear on my short trips to the dump.

The previous summer, I worked for Wally at a near full-time basis, making as much as a hundred dollars a week, most of which I gave to Mom to help pay bills. The leftover money I socked away in my get-the-hell-out-of-Jessup fund, a wad of bills that I kept in a coffee can buried out in the woods. I had almost seven hundred bucks saved up so far.

The other two warehouses were big and yellow and stood at two o'clock and five o'clock on the dial. We called them the "big warehouse" and the "middle warehouse." My mother worked in the big warehouse, the one at two o'clock, which had an office that took up a quarter of the building. She did Schenicker's books and taxes and that kind of stuff, a job she started back when my dad worked for Wally as one of his Sheetrock hangers—the thing that brought our little family to that dead-end section of nowhere.

As I neared the courtyard, I saw Angus Halcomb sitting on the tailgate of his dad's pickup. Angus was Jarvis Halcomb's first cousin, related by blood but as different from Jarvis as a boy could be, which is why I got along with Angus but hated Jarvis. Angus was hitting a Zippo cigarette lighter against his leg, practicing a maneuver I'd seen his dad, Milo, do a thousand times—pop the lid on the downstroke and roll the flint on the upstroke. *Flick-flick*. Angus was having a tough go of it, though, the lid popping back shut on every attempt. *Flick-flick*.

I sat on the tailgate beside him. "Whatcha doin'?" I asked.

This being Friday—payday—the men had knocked off a little early to gather in the big warehouse, have a few beers, and wait for their paychecks, which my mother scrambled to finish. Even though Angus wasn't old enough to drink—legally—the rule at

Schenicker's had always been that if you were old enough to work you were old enough to have a beer at the end of the week.

"Dad's in a bad mood." *Flick-flick.*

I wanted to say "What a surprise," his dad being the kind of guy who reveled in pointing out how life screws him over. But I filtered my thoughts and said, "What's the matter?"

"Mom left again." *Flick-flick.*

I thought back and counted; this was the third escape I knew of for Angus's mom. "Don't worry," I said. "She'll come back."

"Naw, not this time," Angus said, his chin dropping an inch closer to his chest. He stopped flicking the lighter. "She took her stuff—I mean everything. I heard her yellin' at Dad about me...sayin' that I'm eighteen now, and I'm not her problem."

My breath caught in my chest a little at the coldness of those words. While it was true that Angus was legally an adult, he'd taken a tumble a few years back that left him a bubble or two off-center. The story I'd heard was that when he was fifteen, Angus fell out of the back of a pickup because the driver had popped the clutch as a joke. He'd hit his head on a rock and the resulting damage led the Halcomb clan to agree that Angus should drop out of school and go to work hanging Sheetrock with his dad.

Jarvis and Angus were the same age and more like brothers than cousins, but it was Jarvis who popped the clutch on that truck. They'd taken Cecil Halcomb's old Chevy out to a fishing hole on the family farm, and when Angus jumped in the back to collect the rods and tackle, Jarvis thought it would be funny to lurch the truck forward and surprise his cousin. Now, Jarvis walked like king shit through the halls of St. Ignatius, while Angus lacked the wits to join him there—or so decreed the Halcombs.

Don't get me wrong, Angus didn't yammer and drool like some village idiot, but he rarely talked, preferring to answer questions with a shrug or a light chuckle. And honestly, if you didn't know about the thump to his head you might just think that Angus was shy and not slow at all. I could tell that he tried to act older around the other guys or when his dad was watching, but away from them, I could see the kid on the other side of that fall. I can't say that Angus and I were friends, but when no one else was around, we got along just fine.

Flick-flick.

Across the courtyard, the side door of the big warehouse stood open, and from where we sat, I could hear Milo Halcomb telling jokes, his bellowing voice carrying the spiteful punch lines up to us—mostly stuff about how terrible women can be. And he followed each punch line with his own booming laughter.

Flick-flick.

Angus seemed to hit the Zippo against his thigh a little harder when Milo's voice came at its loudest—the insults against his mother at their harshest. I had never seen that Zippo before, gold and shiny, and since Angus didn't smoke, it struck me as odd that he'd have a lighter at all.

"New lighter?" I asked.

"It's Dad's," he said.

Flick-flick.

Angus hitting his dad's new lighter against his leg like that was an unmistakable act of defiance. Milo had a thing about people touching his stuff, a lesson I'd learned the hard way the previous summer. Around the Fourth of July, Angus bought a gross of bottle rockets, and we divided them up for a bottle rocket fight out in the courtyard, taking up positions on opposite sides of the turnaround and firing at each other from a distance of about twenty yards.

He had a punk—one of those sticks that look like incense—to light his bottle rockets. I dug around in the trucks and found a lighter in the ashtray of the flatbed. It was worn and silver and had what looked like a woman swimming through stars on its face. I took a closer look at the silhouetted woman and came to the conclusion that she was probably naked, although it was hard to tell with all the wear. I broke my bottle rockets out of their wrappers and laid them out on the ground in front of me where they'd be easy to grab. Then I flipped open the lighter, set the flame going, and started shooting bottle rockets at Angus.

It was fun until Milo showed up. Angus skipped a shot past me at the exact moment that his old man rounded the corner of the warehouse. The bottle rocket bounced off Milo's leg and exploded on the ground, but that was more than enough to send him into a frenzy.

He stormed toward Angus at first, but when he saw the lighter in my hand, he came to me, his face all twisted and red. He yanked the lighter out of my hand and yelled, "Is this your lighter?"

"No," I said, barely able to get the word out.

"That's right, it ain't. It's mine. Did I say you could use it?"

"No."

"I don't go to *your* house and take *your* stuff, do I?"

"No," I said again, not mentioning that I found the lighter in the flatbed, which wasn't his truck. I expected him to lay into me a lot more—him not being the kind of guy to let a thing go once he had the upper hand—but at that point Milo walked over to Angus and slapped him upside his head, knocking his son to the gravel.

"What the hell's wrong with you? I swear you're as dumb as a fence post sometimes."

Milo grabbed Angus by the shirt collar, lifted him off the ground, and kicked him in the seat of his britches. "Get in the truck and stay there till I'm ready to leave—and no playin' the radio."

Flick-flick.

As Milo spouted more jokes about Angus's mom running off, Angus hit that Zippo against his leg harder and harder, his swipes growing so violent that I thought he might break the lid off his father's new lighter, a move that would, no doubt, lead to a beating once Milo found out. I wanted to calm Angus down, distract him from Milo's put-downs, so I said, "I'm sorry about your mom."

Angus shrugged and stopped playing with the lighter for a second. "I figured it was comin'," he said. "In a way, I'm glad she's gone. Dad can be a hard 'un to live with. She's better off this way."

I didn't want to agree too loudly, so I just nodded. "You gonna be okay?" I asked.

"Dad drank the last of his whiskey last night," Angus said. "So it shouldn't be too bad. But just in case, I'll pro'bly camp out in the woods this weekend."

Another bad joke from Milo and another roar of undeserved laughter drew my attention back to the warehouse and my mother, who would be sitting in the office, separated from Milo by a single wall. I could only imagine how tight her shoulders had to be from listening to that blowhard. I said goodbye to Angus and made my way to the office, which had a door that opened to the courtyard and another that took you from the office into the warehouse. With the warehouse's big sliding door being open, I held little hope of slipping past the men unnoticed. And of course, Milo saw me.

"Boady!" came the booming voice. "Get your ass in here."

I paused—just a few feet shy of the office and safety—then turned and entered the warehouse. There were four men sitting on buckets laid out in a semicircle. I counted five empty beer bottles at Milo's feet.

"Never get married, Boady," Milo said with a liquid slur in his voice.

I didn't respond.

"They say they'll stick around, but do they? Hell no. I just lost a hunnert and fifty pounds. Best damned diet in the world, I'll tell ya that." He gave a barreling laugh, and as he did, he looked at the other men in the semicircle to make sure they were joining in, which they were.

Wally Schenicker, a short man with more stomach than he needed, came out of the office to join the group. He hoisted his roly-poly body onto a four-foot-tall stack of Sheetrock, and did a butt walk backwards until his haunch set securely on the pile, his belly protruding out over a large belt buckle of a cowboy riding a bucking bronco. Milo took advantage of the new audience to tell another joke.

"Wally, what do ya call a woman who can't make a decent sandwich?"

Wally shrugged.

"Divorced!" Again Milo laughed the loudest.

"I s'pose," Schenicker mumbled through a fake laugh. Then he looked at me and said, "Boady, you want to go give your mother a hand?"

Wally was doing me a favor by getting me away from Milo, and I appreciated it. I always liked that about Wally. If you didn't know him better you might think that he stayed out of arguments, standing on the sidelines like some distracted referee. But those of us who paid attention knew what he was doing.

I saw this side of Wally the most when it came to the way he treated my mother, prohibiting cuss words in her presence and coming down hard on anyone who dared to speak ill of her behind her back. He was seven years her senior, and they spent almost every day together sitting on opposite ends of that small office, but he never made a pass at her. I saw something protective in the way he regarded her—a brother looking out for a younger sister.

I turned to go into the office, but Milo called my name one more time. "Wait, Boady. Ya didn't hear this one. What's worse than findin' out that your wife has cancer?"

I didn't even bother to shrug, because I could see Milo itching to say the punch line.

"Findin' out it's curable."

I stretched my lips into a grin and nodded, pretending to laugh, but something in Milo's eyes told me that he saw through me.

I headed into the office, where I found my mother, as I always found her on Fridays, bent over her desk, punching numbers into her calculator and scribbling digits into her ledgers. My mother was a small woman, made even smaller by the way she pulled her shoulders in when she worked at her desk. And even though Schenicker had no dress code, my mom chose to wear collared shirts—every day—buttoned high to the throat.

"Hey, Mom."

"Hey." She didn't look up from her work. "Yours ain't ready yet."

"That's okay," I said, sitting down at Schenicker's desk. She always did my check last, which made sense, because unlike the other guys, I had no place to go on a Friday night.

I opened the drawer where Wally kept a pile of magazines and dug through his selection: *Field and Stream, Sports Illustrated,* even a couple *Guns and Ammos*—although I don't think Wally ever hunted or cared all that much about sports. Under those magazines, I found a copy of *People,* which appeared to be the only magazine in the drawer showing any sign of having been opened.

I pulled it out, just to have something to look at, and settled into Wally's chair to keep silent company with my mother until all the checks had been cut. Then I delivered the paychecks to the men in the warehouse—each man looking at the amount of his check and squinting slightly as if cyphering the numbers in his head.

When I gave Milo his check, he looked at the number, curled his lip into a sneer, and then in a voice so low that only I could hear it, said, "Ya know, pretty soon here, life's gonna stop kickin' me in the nuts. Mark my words, boy."

CHAPTER

5

I N THE SAME WAY THAT DEER WILL CREATE A PATH IN THE WOODS, always going left around a tree when going right would be just as easy, my mother and I had fallen into our own routines. For example, on weekdays we ate breakfast together, although I can't say we actually shared a meal. It could better be described as fifteen minutes of common proximity before heading out to our respective worlds. We sat at the same table and ate from the same box of sugarless cereal. In the winter we might have oatmeal—she'd cook it, and I mixed the powdered milk, although I preferred to mix the milk the night before, because I liked my fake milk cold.

On weekends, however, we ate on our own. Mom sipped coffee and nibbled toast on our back porch, while I downed something quick and easy on my way to the big oak tree down at Dixon's pond—fishing gear in hand. That Saturday, though, I didn't do my usual grab-and-go. Instead, I pulled a pack of graham crackers from the lazy Susan, poured a glass of instant milk from the fridge, and went outside to sit on the back porch with Mom.

Our backyard wasn't much to look at, sloping gently away from the house for about ten paces, where it butted up against what we called the south woods, a thick patch of trees that rolled out as far as the eye could see—somebody else's land, not ours. The porch, barely big enough to hold two lawn chairs, never struck me as a place to relax, probably because, while my mother took in the chirping of birds or the darting of squirrels, all I saw were the things that needed fixing: the rickety porch rail, floorboards rotting away for want of paint. But that day, because I had questions that poked at me, I joined my mother there.

I took a seat next to her without either of us passing a morning greeting—she was quiet that way—and she didn't look up either, preferring to keep her gaze on a male cardinal preening himself out in a tree. I never saw the silences between Mom and me as being awkward; they were so frequent and enduring that a lack of silence would have been the weird thing. I opened my graham crackers, the crackle of the waxy paper cutting into my mother's well-tended tranquility.

We had talked briefly, the night before, about the goings-on over at Tilly Dixon's old house, comparing notes and finding that she had learned from Wally Schenicker what I had gotten from Hoke—that the house had sold, and they were fixing it up for the new neighbors—and that was it. I considered telling her about Sheriff Vaughan's visit to Hoke's place, but held off because Mom was a nervous person on a good day, and the last thing she needed was one more broken stitch to fret about. Besides, if I told her what I heard, I would have had to fess up as to how I heard it, and spying on Hoke would have gotten me grounded from the woods and from Dixon's pond.

Still, it ate at me how little we knew about Hoke Gardner. The stuff Hoke and Sheriff Vaughan talked about had kept me up deep into the night. Hoke had been married, yet nothing he and I had ever talked about hinted at a wife—much less a dead one. And what kind of job did he have up in Columbia that had cops holding a grudge against him? Why hadn't Hoke ever mentioned that he knew Lida Poe when her name had been in the newspaper?

And then there was that *accident* Sheriff Vaughan mentioned—is that how Hoke crippled his arm?

It had to have been past midnight before I surrendered to the notion that I needed to broach the subject with my mother—carefully. And that was why I joined her on the back porch that morning.

I'd once asked my mom about Hoke's arm and the burn scars, to which she replied that she didn't know what happened. I found her answer unsatisfying and told her that I planned to ask him myself. She laid into me and said that under no circumstances would I do such a thing. So I never did.

That morning, though, I decided to come at it from a different angle. I had eaten half of my crackers before I started down the clumsy path I'd been working on.

"Milo sure was in a mood yesterday," I said.

Mom shuddered a bit and said, "I thought he'd never stop tearin' into that poor wife of his."

"I think Angus is takin' it pretty hard too."

"My heart goes out to that boy."

"D'you think that's what happened to Hoke?"

My gawky pivot caused Mom to blink and look at me like I'd just called her by the wrong name. "What on earth are you talkin' 'bout?"

"I ain't never seen him datin' or nothin'. You think he had a wife once and...I don't know...things went bad?"

"I think that if Hoke wanted us to know about his personal life, he'd tell us."

"I guess so, but we really don't know all that much about him."

I thought my statement would be enough to get the ball rolling, but my mother must have seen it as rhetorical, because she simply shrugged and tried to find her cardinal again.

I gave it another go. "I mean, he's lived next to us for,

what...almost ten years now? Has he ever told you anything about what he did before he got here?"

She thought about that one for a moment, her cardinal no longer there to hold her attention. "I remember him sayin' once that he used to live in Columbia, but I don't think he ever said what he did there."

"Don't that strike you as odd?" I said. "We've known him all these years and he ain't never once said what he used to do? Or what happened to him?"

"People have a right to their privacy, Boady. Hoke's a nice man. Don't you be botherin' him, okay?"

She didn't sound upset or angry—more like she was taking Hoke's side in a debate that Hoke and I weren't even having. And because I was getting nowhere, I finished my graham crackers, excused myself, and headed for my tree, grabbing my fishing pole off the wall of the carport on the way.

My path to Dixon's pond started across the road from Hoke's place, cutting up the hill and twisting around rock formations, buckthorn, and scrub until it crested. At the top, the woods gave way to a grazing pasture that hadn't seen a cow in years. The path straightened as it shot down through the field, ending at the base of the leaning tree.

With a trunk as big around as a tractor tire, the leaning tree stood at the edge of Tilly Dixon's cow pond and had grown at such a low pitch that with a good run, I could scale it without using my hands. It split about ten feet up, half of the tree turning skyward, the other half leaning out over the pond as if as a sapling it couldn't decide whether to seek the sky or the water. The part of the tree that reached out over the pond had this one branch as big around as a five-gallon bucket, which stretched out parallel to the surface of the water. I spent much of my childhood on that branch.

Over the years that tree had been many things to me. In my younger imagination, it had been a castle where I fought against infidels and a pirate ship standing against the Spanish Armada. It was a jungle gym, a swing, and a trapeze all in one. As I grew older it became a sanctuary—my church. In the tree's embrace, I stitched together the patchwork memory of my father, talking to him on occasion, his reply nothing more than the rustle of leaves in the breeze. I spent hour after hour cradled in the branches of that tree, sitting and thinking and waiting—for what, I didn't know.

The sun took its time climbing up the edge of the sky, with me doing little more than watching my bobber dip in the ripples. By high noon, I'd only caught three tiny bluegill, and so I changed my plans. It had been unseasonably warm that spring, and when the breeze failed to keep me cool, I stripped down to my underwear and jumped in the water.

Dixon's pond wasn't much bigger around than Schenicker's courtyard, and just deep enough that I could touch my toes to the bottom and still have a bit of sunlight on my outstretched fingertips. But the water was cool and clear—until my squirming muddied things up—and there wasn't any better way to kill a slow Saturday morning.

When I got tired of swimming, I went and lay up against the tree trunk to dry off, taking the spot where Grover used to nap and wait for me, back when he was more my dog than my mom's.

Truth be told, Grover was never meant to be my dog. Hoke brought him home one day—a clumsy pup with big paws and a short attention span—with the idea of having a companion to sit beside him on the porch. With me being a six-year-old kid back then, I had no choice but to play with the dog. After a while, Hoke couldn't bear to keep us apart, and he gave Grover to me. When Mom told me that Grover would be my dog, I bawled and threw my arms around his neck, sobbing repreated thank-yous to my mother. The thing is though, I don't remember ever saying thank you to Hoke.

Lying up against the tree that day, my thoughts, as they so often did, gravitated to my plan to leave Jessup. I'd heard that a sixteen-year-old can't sign a lease, so I would have to lie about my age to get a place to live; if that didn't work, I'd just find a patch of woods and set up a tent, live there until I could rook my way into a small apartment. I was willing to bet that there were landlords out there who would gladly turn a blind eye to my age if I showed them my money.

Soon, however, my daydream switched tracks, and I began thinking about Lida Poe. I wondered if she made the same type of plans as I did, trusting in the combination of human greed and cash to get by. I pictured her holed up in some crappy ghetto, pretending to be just another struggling rat in the race, all the while having that embezzled money hidden in her sock drawer.

I didn't like that version of the dream, so I put her on a beach, living in a foreign land where a dollar could buy a week's worth of groceries. She would become a painter or maybe make turquoise jewelry, and she'd have a guard dog named Roscoe to warn her if danger was near. I liked that image of Lida Poe much better, so I stayed in that daydream—leaning up against the tree—until the sun dried me off.

When I finally went home, I emerged from the woods to find Hoke sitting on his porch, writing in a large black book with a red spine. There had to be more than one of those books, black with the red spine, because in my earliest memories of Hoke, he held that book on his lap, a pencil sticking up from the fingers of his good hand as he scribbled his thoughts.

I had asked him a few times what he was writing, and he

replied with vague comments like he was exorcising ghosts or answering questions that no one yet knew to ask. He would say things like that, and as a little kid I felt like I should know what he was talking about but didn't, so I never pushed the issue. As I got older, though, I understood that his answers were meant to divert the conversation away from his books. He wanted to keep his secrets, and so I let him.

I waved my hello and he tossed his chin the way he did whenever he had something occupying his good hand. As I crossed the road, I saw a truck with ALISTAIR FLOORING written on the side, backed up to the front door of the Dixon place. I also noticed a big red car parked in the driveway, the car looking too fancy to be something a carpet layer might drive. Curious, I set my fishing gear down on the side of the road and walked up onto Hoke's porch, taking my seat in the second rocking chair as usual.

"Catch anything?" he asked.

Hoke had been the one who taught me to fish, instructing me in the art of casting and patiently working with me until I had figured out how to let loose the thumb stop at the top of my arc, not too early and not too late. He made me spend a week practicing in my front yard before he took me to Dixon's pond to try out my skills. I remember the first fish I ever caught, a thirteen-inch catfish that Hoke said probably set a record for that pond. I was so happy with myself that I named the fish Gus. We let it go, of course. I think Hoke knew that I would have lost my mind had he suggested we eat the thing. I still used the same Zebco 202 that he gave me for my birthday that year, and I never again caught a fish from that pond as big as Gus.

"Just some little ones," I said.

On the floor of Hoke's porch were three newspapers, the *Kansas City Star*, the *Jessup Journal*, and the *Columbia Missourian*, that last one having a new significance after hearing Hoke talking to Sheriff

Vaughan about his past. Hoke closed his book and set it aside, the way he always did when I came by. Then he picked up the *Journal,* opened it to a half-finished crossword puzzle on the back page, and started mulling a clue—as if that flashy red car in Tilly Dixon's driveway didn't demand any attention at all. I rolled my eyes at his stubborn calmness and asked what I came to ask.

"Whose car's that over there?"

Hoke answered without looking up. "That belongs to a guy named Donald Rigby. He's the realtor that sold the place. Came by to check on the progress of the work."

"You talked to him?"

"Yeah. Nice guy."

"Did he tell you anything about the new neighbors?"

"A little bit."

"And?"

Hoke put his thighs together for a makeshift table. Then, using his bad arm as kind of a paperweight, he folded the paper and handed it to me. "You might be interested in the top story today."

I read the headline on the front page: "RYKE PLANT GETS NEW MANAGER." The change in management at a manufacturing plant probably didn't make for headlines in most towns, but Ryke was the biggest employer in Jessup by a good stretch. In fact, if Ryke were to dry up, I'm not quite sure how much of the town would have remained.

I began reading and learned that Cecil Halcomb—Jarvis's dad, and the man who'd run the plant for the last fifteen years—had been demoted by the bosses up in Minneapolis after evidence of embezzlement was discovered. Those words triggered my memory of Sheriff Vaughan talking to Hoke, saying something about Lida Poe and fraud.

"That embezzlement... is that about Lida Poe?"

I saw something sad in Hoke's eyes when he answered. "That's not the part of the article I was referring to, but yes, that's about Lida Poe. They think she stole money from Ryke and took off."

"You think she did it?"

Hoke looked at me as if he were trying to see through me, and I could tell by his squint that my attempt to get him to admit he knew Lida Poe had failed. He leaned back in his chair. "Just read the article."

Farther down, I read about a man named Charles Elgin who would soon arrive from Minneapolis to take over operations at Ryke. I kept reading to the end of the article and saw no other names.

"Charles Elgin? That's our new neighbor?"

"That's him."

I thought back to the conversation I'd overheard in the lunchroom and asked, "Is he a black guy?"

"I don't know. Why do you ask?"

"I heard some talk at school."

"Does it matter to you—what color he is?"

"No. I mean, I ain't prejudice or nothin'."

Hoke lifted his pipe from his shirt pocket, set it in the crease of his lap where his thighs met, pulled out a pouch of tobacco, and began packing his pipe. Once he filled the bowl, he returned the tobacco pouch to his pocket and lit the pipe, taking a couple good puffs of smoke before he spoke again.

"You're not?" he said.

"I'm not what?"

"Prejudiced."

"Shoot, no," I said. "It's wrong to make folks drink out of different fountains just cuz of their skin color. They can't help bein' the way they are."

"And what way is that?"

I thought for a moment, trying to come up with the best way

to explain it to Hoke. "I mean, there's a reason there ain't no black quarterbacks playing pro football. They can run fast and block and stuff, but they ain't as smart as whites. That don't make 'em bad people. They're just different."

Hoke puffed on his pipe, his eyes fixed on the smoke as it rolled away and disappeared, as if he were barely paying attention to my prattle.

"Well, it's a good thing that you're not prejudiced," he said.

"Heck, no. I think that if a black man sets his mind to it, he can be just as good as a white man."

"Just as good, huh?" Hoke looked at me, his left eyebrow raised.

"Sure. Look at Bob Gibson. A great pitcher even though he's black. Just goes to show ya, they can get there if they try."

"I see."

Hoke picked up another newspaper, opened it, and set to reading it like I wasn't even there. That was just his way. He never seemed to find urgency in the happenings of the world around him. If Jessup wanted to go to hell in a handbasket, it would need to wait for Hoke Gardner to finish reading his damned newspaper before it could grab that man's attention.

I propped my feet up on the rail and watched the Dixon house as a man in a light blue leisure suit stepped out, waved to Hoke, and then got into the red car and drove away.

"Oh, by the way," Hoke said. "When I was talking to Mr. Rigby earlier, he happened to mention that Charles Elgin is bringing his family with him from Minnesota, a wife and a son."

"A son?"

"Name of Thomas, I think. Same age as you."

"My age?"

"According to Rigby."

A thousand thoughts clanged and flailed inside of my head at that moment, but all I said was "Hmm."

CHAPTER

6

MONDAY PROMISED TO BE A CRAPPY DAY. THE WEATHER CAME in low over the hills, the rain misty but wet enough that it forced me to take my mother's umbrella—red with yellow polka-dots—to the top of the road to wait for the bus. My stop was the bus's farthest delivery, making me first one on in the morning and the last one off at the end of the day. I took my usual seat in the very back, turned sideways, and plopped my feet onto the seat to keep it all to myself. No one ever tried to sit beside me, but with my feet there my solitude seemed a choice.

Most of the kids who rode my bus attended the Catholic elementary school in Jessup. In fact, the only other kids on the bus who went to St. Ignatius were a pair of twins, sophomore girls, who chose to have nothing to do with me. I was fine with that—or so I told myself. When I first started riding the bus to St. Ignatius, I made a point to sit near them, a seat ahead or behind, just in case they decided to include me in their conversation. It made sense that they'd eventually give in and seek input from the only other high school–aged person on the bus. When it never happened, I took to sitting in the last row, hogging the seat and occupying my time with more important things like counting the number of telephone poles along the route.

With all the distractions that came at me that weekend, I had pretty much forgotten about the pudding incident until about bedtime on Sunday. That's when the thought of Jarvis and the Boob Brothers knotted up in my chest so much that I could feel my heart thumping against my ribs.

I'd been watching as the bus neared the school, making sure that Jarvis and his boys weren't lying in wait at the bus drop-off. Satisfied that it was safe, I stepped off the bus, umbrella in one hand, gym bag in the other, and jogged the half block to school, pausing one last time at the door to be certain that no ambush awaited me.

Inside, the halls teemed with students, some half-asleep, others zipping around like horseflies. I didn't see Jarvis anywhere, so I headed in and down the steps to my locker, hopeful that they might have forgotten the whole pudding thing.

I walked behind some tall kid I didn't know, using him for cover as I made my way to my locker. Every few steps, he would stop to say hi to someone or slap hands with a friend, and I would turn sideways and pick at the zipper of my gym bag, as if I'd been standing there all along. When he moved again, I followed. I made it to my locker without being seen, did a quick transfer of books, and hung Mom's umbrella on the coat hook. When I turned to go to my homeroom, I saw Bob about twenty yards away, his eyes on me, his lips pulled up in this *gotcha* kind of grin.

I took off in the other direction, bouncing through the crowd, making my way to the stairs, my homeroom being one floor up. When I turned at the landing, I saw Bob weaving past bodies, closing in on me. I took the next flight three steps at a time.

Twisting and spinning around students, I tried to get to my homeroom at the far end of the hall, but midway there, I stopped cold. Jarvis and Beef were standing on either side of the door like sentries, waiting for me. I looked behind me and saw Bob crest the top of the stairs. He whistled a loud shriek that brought Jarvis's head snapping my way. We locked eyes.

I dropped to a squat—legs bumping up against me, the faces of irritated students mouthing silent curses as they parted to go around me. I needed to get into a classroom and invoke sanctuary from whatever teacher I might find inside. I pulled the nearest door open and stumbled into silence—no lights, no teacher, only rows of desks with typewriters on them. I had broken into one of the few rooms that did not host a homeroom in the morning.

Son of a bitch!

I ran to the window, contemplating a jump—two stories down to a concrete sidewalk. Would that mess me up more than Jarvis would? I opened the window, hoping they would think that I jumped out, and then ran to the teacher's desk at the head of the classroom, sliding under it, curling my knees up to my chest.

No sooner had I tucked into my hiding spot than I heard the creak of the door opening and voices.

"He had to come in here," Bob said. "I was watchin', and he didn't double back."

The shuffle of leather shoes followed a path to the opened window.

"He didn't jump, did he?" Beef said.

"Holy crap," Bob said with a half laugh.

"No," Jarvis said. "I don't think so."

I could hear whispers and then the scuffing of grit on the wooden floor as they walked toward my position. I cupped my hands over my mouth to muffle the sound of my breathing, and when I saw a pair of legs step in front of the desk, I stopped breathing altogether. I tried to come up with a plan, but started going dizzy from holding my breath. Then suddenly, the desk lifted off the floor and moved backwards, one of the Boob Brothers on either end, leaving me in a ball staring up at Jarvis.

I scrambled to my feet, my haste knocking me off-balance and causing me to fall back into the teacher's desk. Bob stood to my left, blocking the door, Beef to my right, blocking the window. Jarvis stood ahead of me, his thumbs tucked into his front pockets.

"Your name's Boady, right?" He said it as both a question and a statement.

I nodded and looked around at the fix I was in. If I jumped over the desk behind me, I could yell and knock over some typewriters and raise a commotion, but I doubted that I could make enough noise to compete with the din of the students in the hallway. I searched for a plan B but saw none.

As I calculated my escape, Jarvis took a step toward me and I flinched.

"Calm down. I ain't gonna hurt you," he said.

"Sure you ain't," I said, raising my fists. "But it's gonna take all three of ya. I swear to God it will."

"Seriously," he said. "If I was gonna beat your ass, you wouldn't be standin' there. I woulda just kicked the crap out of ya while you were under that desk."

I looked at Beef and Bob, who made no attempt to close in on me. "What do ya want?" I asked.

Jarvis stepped backwards and leaned against the chalkboard. "Ya know, that was pretty funny...what ya did to Bob last week."

Beef let a small laugh slip, but Bob kept his expression cold, probably not seeing the humor in the tumble he'd taken.

"It was either really stupid or really brave. We're split on that one. Personally, I think it took a lot of guts, but Bob here thinks ya have a death wish. What do you think, Beef?"

Beef considered the question as though his vote would determine my fate. Then he said, "Guts."

"Exactly," Jarvis said. "I mean, look at him—fists up like he's ready to take on all three of us. Most kids would've wet themselves by now. You might wanna put those down." He pointed at my hands, still balled up and ready. "We don't want 'em goin' off by accident."

I slowly lowered my hands to my waist, but kept the fists.

"You may not believe this, Boady, but I admire what ya did."

Bob gave an audible snort, and Jarvis shot him a sharp glance, his face turning angry for that split second before returning to me with a smile.

"In fact, I think you should sit with us at lunch today. We could use a guy like you."

I had come to accept the thought of fighting Jarvis. I knew that I would lose—badly—but at least I understood that version of reality. This nice Jarvis had me itching all over.

"What d' ya want?" I asked.

"Hey, you don't wanna sit with us? That's fine. I just thought I'd make the offer. You seem like a tough little dude, that's all."

"You wanna hang out with me...because I tripped him?" I thumb-pointed at Bob. "So, if I punch him in the face—what then? I get invited to your next kegger?"

Jarvis and Beef both laughed, but Bob did not.

"See?" Jarvis said. "I told ya he had guts."

Feeling more and more comfortable about my survival, I asked, "If you're not here to beat me up, then why'd ya chase me?"

"Got a proposition for ya."

"A proposition?"

"Ya ever heard of the CORPS?"

A spike of ice ran down my spine. Everyone had heard of the CORPS—Crusaders Of Racial Purity and Strength—but only in whispers and rumors, tales full of shadows and guns and crosses. The look on Jarvis's face told me that our conversation was about to go well beyond rumors.

"You've heard of 'em, right?" Jarvis repeated.

"Yeah."

"Well, let's just say the CORPS wants ya to help 'em out with something—maybe they want ya to become a member. What do ya think of that?"

"Why would the CORPS give a rat's ass about me?" I said, trying to deflect the conversation away from where I saw it heading. "I'm nobody."

The first bell rang to signal the herd of students to their home-rooms. Jarvis looked at the clock. "Let's cut to the chase here. You have some new neighbors movin' in."

"New neighbors?"

"Folks by the name of Elgin?"

I couldn't hide my surprise at the unsettling turn in our conversation.

"Yeah, we know all about 'em," Jarvis said.

I don't know if Jarvis caught his slip, but the CORPS *they* had become the CORPS *we*.

"And you happen to be in a position to be helpful," he said.

"They ain't moved in yet," I said, as if that mattered.

"They will, and that's where you come in. You'll be like a scout—keep your eyes and ears open."

"You want me to spy on 'em?" I asked.

"Not spy, just...ya know, keep tabs on when they're home and not home, that kinda thing. If ya hear anything about my dad, Cecil, or 'bout the Ryke plant—let us know." Then Jarvis stepped close enough to put his hand on my shoulder. "My cousin Angus says you're a stand-up guy, the kinda guy a fella can count on. Is he right about that?"

I shrugged. "I s'pose."

"Me and my friends—we're always lookin' for stand-up guys like you. And if Angus is right—if ya come through for us—well, you couldn't ask for a better group of buddies."

Then Bob spoke up. "You also need to keep in mind that ya get to keep your ass in this deal. If it was up to me—"

Jarvis shot him another look, and Bob stopped talking.

"There's a lot ridin' on this, Boady. A lot of folks are watchin'—folks you don't wanna piss off, if ya get my drift. We gotta send that black sonofabitch back to Minnesota before he screws things up so bad they shut down the plant altogether. This town needs that plant, and my dad's the only one that can keep it up and runnin'."

The door latch popped behind Bob, scaring the hell out of me and causing everyone to turn. Sister Tarsilla, probably the oldest of the nuns at St. Ignatius, entered the classroom with a stack of papers in her hands, paused, and then licked her lips to speak.

"You boys shouldn't be in here," she said, her voice barely audible even though she did her best to yell. "Didn't you hear the first bell? And who moved my desk?"

I picked my books up off the floor and scrambled past Bob, who had turned his back on me to face Sister Tarsilla. Nodding to the sister as I passed, I ran into the hallway and to my homeroom, getting to my seat just as the second bell rang.

CHAPTER

7

I DIDN'T SIT WITH JARVIS AT LUNCH. INSTEAD, I RACED TO THE cafeteria early so that he and the Boobs were still in the back of the line as I paid for my hot dogs. Then I pretended not to see them and headed to the outdoor courtyard. I expected my defiance to, at the very least, earn me a punch to the arm the next time Jarvis and I passed in the hall. But later, when I saw him on my way to sixth hour, he gave me this creepy wink, like we shared some sort of conspiratorial bond. That's when it hit me that he thought we had reached an agreement in the typing room. I didn't see any harm in letting him linger under that misunderstanding.

The sky had cleared up around midday, and by the time I stepped off the bus that afternoon, the humidity had grown so thick that it reached up from the ground to slather my neck and back and chest with sweat. I unbuttoned my shirt all the way down and propped my mom's umbrella over my shoulder like a hobo's stick, my gym bag hooked on the handle.

As I neared the bend in the road, the outline of something large and white began trickling through the patch of cedar trees up ahead. I rounded the bend to find a truck parked in Tilly's driveway, white with big red letters on the side spelling out FARRIS MOVING AND STORAGE COMPANY.

The new neighbors had arrived.

A ramp sloped out of the back of the truck, and a few of the larger pieces of furniture and some boxes had been set neatly around the yard in small piles. Near the shed, the one Tilly used as a garage back when she could still drive, the movers had parked a golf cart on a trailer; it had three sets of golf clubs strapped to the back. Next to the golf cart stood a barbecue grill, one of those gas ones that turned on with the push of a button. By the road, only a few feet away from me, three shiny bicycles leaned on kickstands next to a riding lawnmower.

I walked to the edge of the property and squatted to get a better look at the bikes—ten-speeds, sleek and bright with not a speck of dust on them. My bike, a single-speed green Schwinn with a flat tire, hung on a hook at the front of our carport. With its high handlebars, banana seat, and two-foot-tall sissy bar, it was a kid's bike that Mom bought at a rummage sale for my eighth birthday.

As I stood there slack-jawed, counting the sprockets on the back wheel of one of the ten-speeds, a large black man stepped out of the house and walked to the ramp of the moving van, his face soft with high cheekbones and sleepy eyes resting behind thin eyeglasses. He had massive hands that rubbed his Buddha belly when he stopped to look up into the back of the truck. At first glance he appeared to be in his mid-thirties, but patches of gray hair over his temples moved him north of forty.

He wore dress shorts and a thin black leather belt—not proper attire for moving furniture—and I knew then that I was looking at my new neighbor, Charles Elgin. I have to admit that something about him moving his stuff into that big ol' Victorian house seemed off to me, like a guitar being played out of tune. Don't get me wrong—Jessup had its share of black folk, but most of them lived up on Goat Hill, a collection of slab houses clustered in the older, northern side of town.

Mr. Elgin walked up the ramp and then came back down carrying a leather office chair. He paused on the porch to rest, and about that time, two younger white guys wearing red T-shirts with the Farris logo on them came out of the house and skipped up the ramp into the truck. Elgin was about to pick up his chair again when he saw me. He stood, arched his back as if to untangle a knot, and gave me a wave. I waved back, feeling suddenly odd for standing on the edge of this man's lawn coveting his bicycles.

I walked backwards toward my driveway, my eyes scanning the windows of the Dixon house for any sign of the boy that Hoke had mentioned but seeing nothing beyond the reflection of the sun. When I reached my side of the road, I felt Grover's nose against my leg, and I knelt down to give him a proper petting, pressing his ears back and kissing the top of his head—all the while watching my new neighbor wrestle his chair through the door.

As I often did when I had questions, I looked to Hoke's place and saw him sitting on his porch, paying no mind to me or the moving van, his attention fixed on the book in his lap. I gave Grover a few more scratches to his head and walked him to his blanket deep in the shade of the carport before heading over to Hoke's.

Hoke was writing in one of those books again, the black ones with the red spines, and when he saw me coming he finished his thought and put the book aside. I took my seat on the chair beside him. "Today's the big day," I said, nodding in the direction of the moving van.

"Appears so."

"You go talk to 'em yet?"

"Stopped by earlier and offered to give him a hand." Hoke only had the one good arm, which made me think he might be making a joke, but I could never tell with him.

Elgin walked out of his house, paused at the back of the truck, and wiped his face with a white handkerchief. He pointed and gave instructions to one of the movers, but I couldn't make out what he said.

"Did ya meet his family?" I asked.

"They're not here yet. The boy's finishing his school year, so the missus stayed with him up in Minnesota."

I heard a vehicle coming down the road, and I set my gaze on the bend, thinking it might be the sheriff again. When it turned out to be Milo Halcomb in his pickup truck, I felt a tinge of disappointment. As he neared the Dixon house, he slowed to a crawl and stared intently at the movers, his attention so fixed on them that he didn't even notice me and Hoke sitting on the porch. Angus on the other hand gave me a wave.

Seeing Milo brought to my mind the conversation I'd had with Jarvis, when he'd asked me about the CORPS. They were supposed to be a super-secret group, but I knew about them from Angus. I don't think he was supposed to be talking about them, and he didn't tell me too much, but he let it slip once that he'd been to one of their meetings where they drank beer, shot guns, and talked about some big battle they saw coming.

It was that last part, the talk about the battle, that made the whole undertaking seem a mite sinister to me. Angus didn't talk about the battle as something that might happen. To him it seemed a sure thing. "As sure as the apocalypse," he said. "It's just a matter of time."

"Hoke, you ever heard of the CORPS?" I asked.

My question, probably a bit out of the blue, got Hoke's attention, and he turned in his seat to face me, a ponderous expression on his face. "What do *you* know about the CORPS?" he asked. Hoke had a habit of answering a lot of my questions with another question. He could be downright irritating that way. I said, "I heard some kids at school talkin' about 'em. That's all."

"You just steer clear of the CORPS," Hoke said.

"But who are they? What do they do?"

"They're nothing more than a gang of yahoos too damned stupid to—" He stopped and settled back into his chair, his gaze fixed on the men hauling furniture into the Dixon house. I wasn't sure if he had said all that he had to say on the subject, so I waited, just in case he needed to collect his thoughts. Then he said, "People like to break things down into us and them—you ever notice that, Boady?"

I don't think Hoke could have been more vague if he tried, so I just nodded my head.

"Whether it's a group of friends or a family or something big like the Olympics, people like to belong to a group. You see what I'm getting at?"

"I think so," I said, although I was lost.

"It's almost human nature to divide folks into us and them."

"But what's that got to do with the CORPS?"

"What could be easier than dividing people up by color? Us and them. We're white, they're black, and that makes them different from us. And not only are they different, but we're the ones who make the rules, so we make ourselves better than them. Because of that, the most worthless white man can ride high in the saddle, knowing that on any given day, he's better than a black man."

"So...about the CORPS?"

"Boady, the CORPS is a bunch of ignorant Ku Klux Klan wannabes, a gaggle of dolts who need to feel superior, so they find a group they can pick on, and set to causing trouble. And because there's strength in numbers, they make it a club. You put enough like-minded idiots in a room, and pretty soon their backward way of thinking starts to take on an air of legitimacy. If I were you, I'd stay away from anyone you hear talking about the CORPS."

A rumble of an engine pulled my attention away from Hoke,

as Milo's truck barreled its way up the road—Angus now behind the wheel with Milo in the passenger seat, his elbow resting out the open window, a can of beer in his hand. As they passed us, Milo looked at me—no smile, no wave, not even a nod of the head—just a cold stare like someone had done something to piss him off.

When they passed the Dixon place, Milo hurled the beer can, hitting one of the ten-speed bikes at the edge of the yard.

CHAPTER

8

HOKE HAD SAID THAT THE REST OF THE ELGIN FAMILY WOULD be coming later, but I never asked *when* later, and if he knew, Hoke hadn't offered. So every day for a week, I came home from school and poked around my front yard, hoping to see someone other than Mr. Elgin moving in and out of the house. By Saturday, I had all but given up.

Schenicker asked me to level off the dump that Saturday, a task I had done enough times that the novelty had long worn off. The dump was set back in the woods far enough that you couldn't see it from the road. A trail, barely more than two tire tracks worn into the chert, bounced and twisted its way to the mouth of a small ravine where we dropped Sheetrock scraps. About once a month, Wally had me push the piles over the edge using the bucket on his old Ford tractor. Over the years, we had dumped enough Sheetrock into that ravine to fill and level out a section about the size of a baseball infield.

Sheetrock, as Schenicker argued, was made from rocks, so he shouldn't need government approval to put the leftover gypsum back into the ground. Still, he had a rule that we keep the landfill a secret, so that trespassers didn't take advantage. The only other person who Schenicker allowed to discard trash there was his friend George Bauer, a guy who owned a few apartments up on

Goat Hill and who dumped the crap that his renters left behind: furniture, clothing, old mattresses, and the like.

I'd met George a handful of times down at the dump, when he and I both showed up to empty out a truckload. We'd chatted the way guys do, and he came across as a paler version of Wally, if that was possible, but nice all the same. And where Wally was *aw, shucks,* George was *yee-haw,* one of those glad-handers who kept a smile on his face and a cap on his head. It occurred to me that George Bauer might be Wally Schenicker's only friend—other than my mom, that is.

That particular Saturday dawned warm and cloudless, and the way I saw it, I had plenty of time to do a little fishing before heading down to the dump. So I threw on some jeans, slipped my bare feet into my tennis shoes, and stuffed a T-shirt partially into my back pocket. Grabbing my fishing pole, a small tackle box, and an apple for breakfast, I set out for the pond.

As was my habit, I charged down through the pasture on the back side of the hayfield, picking up speed so I could dash up the sloping trunk of the leaning tree. I knew the exact speed that I needed to reach in order to make it up the trunk without having to use my hands, and then I'd let inertia take me out onto my fishing limb.

I hit the tree at a half sprint, scaling the trunk in three steps and shooting out onto the branch. It was then, in that moment when everything in my world seemed so tidy, that I saw the stranger dressed in dark clothing, eyes wide, feet firmly planted in my path. The Elgin kid.

I tried to stop—it didn't work. The tread on the bottom of my worn-out sneakers had no more stopping power than an overripe tomato. I went into a slide, my arms jutting forward, my legs frozen in midstride, my toe catching a knot and launching me headfirst into the kid's chest.

"Oof!"

My face smashed against his sternum, smooshing my nose and sending a starburst of pain into my skull. My rod and tackle and apple sailed out of my hands, heading for open water. The kid and I twisted together, becoming airborne, me flailing my arms out, him grabbing for my shoulders. I felt a sprig of oak cross my palm and grabbed it with all my strength, the bark grinding into my skin as we swung down.

Had it just been me falling, I think I might have stayed out of the water, but he had clamped onto my back, and with his added weight we didn't stand a chance. We swung down like a human pendulum until the pain forced me to let go, and we plunged into the water.

The kid's arms and legs pushed and kicked as he clambered to get to the surface. I, on the other hand, simply held my breath and relaxed, letting my body find its way up, part of me wanting to stay hidden in the water for as long as I could. By the time I surfaced and wiped the water out of my eyes, he had pulled himself into the shallows at the edge of the pond.

He wore blue-jean shorts and a black T-shirt, which clung to his brown skin. Strands of moss hung from his shoulders, and his red sneakers were covered with mud. He rolled onto his backside and dragged himself into the weeds.

I swam out a few feet to where my tackle box floated and gave it a shove toward shore. Then I dove down to the muddy bottom beneath the fishing limb to retrieve my pole, finding it on my third attempt. Side-stroking until I could touch, I gathered my tackle box and my apple, which bobbed in the shallows, and pulled myself onto shore.

He was skinny, like me, and maybe an inch taller, if that. Tiny water droplets caught the sunlight and sparkled against his dark skin, and his close-cropped hair remained unaffected by the water, where my straggly brown mop had become matted to my head. He looked at me with a mixture of irritation and curiosity painted on his face.

I grabbed the T-shirt out of my back pocket, wrung the pond water out of it, and used it to wipe off my apple, ignoring his stare. I took a bite.

"Are we going to pretend like you didn't just tackle me out of that tree?" he said finally.

"I'm kinda leanin' that way," I said. "Hungry?" I held the apple out toward him, acting like this was just another day in Jessup.

"No thanks, I already had breakfast...that wasn't dipped in pond water."

I shrugged and took another bite.

He picked a string of moss out of his hair and flung it away. "You're the kid who lives in that little house across the road, right?"

I had never heard my house referred to as little before, but it was true—two bedrooms and only a partial basement. Still, you don't call someone's house little, even if it is. I didn't answer.

"What's your name?" he asked.

"Boady Sanden."

"Boady?" The kid wrinkled his brow. "I never met a Boady before."

"Actually, it's John."

"John?"

"Well, it's kinda both."

"Let's try this again." He spoke slowly and deliberately. "Hi, I'm Thomas Elgin. And you are?"

"My name is John Boady Sanden, but people call me Boady."

"You don't like John?"

"John's my dad's name too. When I was a baby, folks took to callin' me Junior, so Mom put a stop to it by havin' everyone call me by my middle name, Boady. Just kinda stuck, I guess."

"I don't suppose your dad works at the Ryke plant."

It made some sense that he might ask that, seeing as half the county seemed to work there. I shook my head and said, "My dad's dead."

I hated when people accidentally fell into a discussion of death by asking about my father. They would bring up the topic in small talk, with no more thought than asking about the weather. But then their faces would change once I told them that my dad was dead. They would look away and stammer toward some new topic of conversation, as if I might not notice that they brought it up in the first place.

In truth, I never knew how to talk about my dad. If I spoke casually about his death, it seemed disrespectful. I was, after all, the man's son and should be sad no matter how much time had passed. But if I answered with melancholy, I felt dishonest. I loved the memory of my father, but most of what I knew of him came from a box of old pictures I'd found in my mom's closet—that and the stories that she and Schenicker told to me. I filled in the missing parts by daydreaming about him.

But Thomas didn't seem fazed by me saying that my father was dead, and asked how he died.

"He was workin' on a church ceiling and fell off some scaffolding. It happened a long time ago."

"Sounds rough."

I shrugged again. "I don't really remember." Then, to get us off the topic, I said, "I hear you're from Minneapolis."

"Edina. My dad got transferred here to take over at the Ryke factory."

"But you've been to Minneapolis?"

"Sure. Lots of times."

"What's it like...livin' in a city? Is there a lotta crime in your neighborhood?"

"I live in Edina."

"So..."

"No. There's not a lot of crime."

"Are there gangs?"

"Gangs?"

"Like in New York."

"It's a suburb."

"But at least there's lots to do, I bet."

"Tons: concerts, ball games—I was supposed to go to this new amusement park called Valley Fair next week. They just opened it up. I was going to take my girl, but that didn't happen because...well, I'm here."

"You have a girlfriend?"

"*Had* a girlfriend. She dumped me when I told her I had to move to Missouri. So here I am—no girlfriend, no Valley Fair, no nothing...except...you, I guess."

The way he said it made me sound like one of those door prizes that you'd just as soon leave without. "Well, welcome to Jessup?" I said, not trying to hide my snide tone. "You managed to land yourself in the armpit of the world. Congratulations."

"Believe me, this wasn't my idea; they made me come. If I had any choice in the matter...I mean, I had a girl. I had friends. I could just walk down the street and in ten minutes have a game of baseball going. What's there to do here? Nothing."

Even though getting out of Jessup had been a major preoccupation of mine, I felt a need to defend my home. "We got the woods," I said, as if that needed no further explanation. When he didn't unwrinkle his forehead, I added, "There's creeks and campin', and ya got the pond here. I don't s'pose you fish, do ya, Tom?"

"Thomas."

"Huh?"

"I prefer Thomas."

I was trying to be neighborly with this guy, but damn, he made it hard. "Do you fish... *Thomas?*"

"I don't have my fishing pole unpacked yet."

"That's okay," I said. "I can nigger-rig ya a pole easy enough."

He sat up straight and looked at me like I'd just thrown a handful of mud at him. "You can nigger-rig me a pole?"

"Sure. I got extra line in my tackle box. All we need is a cedar switch."

"You can *nigger*-rig me a pole?"

Finally I saw why he was having such a hard time. "It's just an expression," I said.

"Jesus Christ. What kind of backwoods, redneck..." He rolled onto his feet and stood up.

"Don't get huffy. It don't mean nothin'. We say stuff like that all the time."

"Drag me to this Podunk...jerkwater..." He turned and headed up the bank, shaking his head. "This is messed up. I left Minnesota for this?" He didn't look back, and the sound of his grumbling grew smaller and smaller until it disappeared over the hill.

After he'd gone, I went about getting my fishing line ready, turning over a stump to find a worm, baiting my hook, and casting out my line. If he came back, I wanted him to see that I didn't care that he left. The fish ignored me, but then, I ignored them as well, my attention pulled to the crest of the hill, waiting for Thomas to come back. A couple times I thought I heard the swish of weeds against pant legs, but it turned out to be an errant breeze rustling the leaves.

After an hour of sitting there, watching the empty hay field, I decided that it wasn't a good day for fishing after all, and I headed home.

CHAPTER

9

I DIDN'T LEVEL THE DUMP UNTIL EVENING HAD SETTLED IN, AND by the time I got all the scraps pushed back, the sun had slipped behind the trees. The moonless dusk fell thick around me as I walked back up the trail to Frog Hollow, the night filled with the pleasing chords of whippoorwills, crickets, and katydids. Small critters rustled the dead leaves as they scurried away, frightened by the sound of my footsteps in the gravel.

The road between Schenicker's and Hoke's places took me up a stretch of road covered by a thick canopy of oak branches, under which I stepped lightly as I listened to the night. When I neared my house, a hint of music floated on the breeze, coming from the Dixon place. Light shining through the uncovered windows opened the old house up like a picture book, and I could see the Elgins moving around inside.

Tilly had rarely kept more than one light on at a time, and the upstairs had been all but abandoned. She had outlived her husband by ten years, and in those years her world shrank to the point that she never had to leave the main floor of her house, cordoning off a living area made up of the kitchen, dining room, family room, and the cook's bedroom and bath, which she occupied as her own. The fireplace in the family room remained unlit, its chimney clogged with swallow's nests. The rich maple banister, which curved elegantly in a perfect slide between the first and second floor, collected dust, waiting for the day when a child might once again race down its back. The beds upstairs went untouched, sacred relics stored in silent tabernacles. The house, built in the hope that generations of Dixons would warm its floors, had been reduced to a handful of rooms graced by a single pair of tiny feet in worn gray slippers.

One time, just a year or so before she died, I saw Tilly moving through the upstairs, wandering the silent hall, pausing to stare into the vacant spaces, her tiny frame dwarfed by the archways and bold wooden trim of the bedrooms. She stared into the rooms as if the images in her mind took form and moved through the house with her, bringing life to the emptiness. I somehow assumed that when she died the house would die with her, but now the old place sparkled with life and light, and something about that struck me as being all wrong.

Across the road, at my house, a pale blue light flickered through the living room window, where I would find my mom sitting on our faded brown couch, the rest of the house cloaked in darkness, her sadness kept at bay by the glow of the television.

The sadness—my term for it—had come to our house when my father died. As a child I had no better way to describe why my mother never smiled, why she sometimes shut herself in her room after supper or stared at the blue hum of a television until she fell asleep on the couch, why she never asked me where I was going when I charged out of the house in the mornings or where I had been when I came home late. For my mother, speaking seemed a thing that took effort, as if a heavy weight pressed her into efficiency and each word came with a price.

The sadness had come suddenly, a misplaced step on a scaffolding plank, and now it clung to her like a cold wet robe. As a child, I used to say prayers while kneeling next to my bed, my mother at my side. I prayed to God for my father's soul, and I prayed that God would keep us safe and healthy. But then, after Mom left, I would slide out of bed and ask God to make her happy. I watched and I waited, and waited some more. Eventually I quit praying.

When I was ten, I found a box of postcards that my mother kept on a shelf in her closet, cards that she'd gotten from my father when he served a peacetime deployment in Germany. Mom had been his sweetheart since high school, and he wrote such loving things to her, ending each missive with "Missing my Songbird." I thought that to be a lovely sentiment, although for the life of me, I couldn't figure out where the nickname came from. My mother never sang. Once, I thought about asking her, but that would have exposed my crime of snooping through her things.

In that same box I found a bunch of pictures taken of our little family before my father's death; my favorite shots were of the three of us having a picnic. We were happy, my mom and dad smiling like little children. I looked to be about two years old in those pictures, sitting on my father's broad shoulders, pulling at his hair. My mother sparkled with a happiness reserved for someone just starting a marvelous new adventure, her eyes young and alive with laughter as she pushed me on a swing.

I made quite a few secret trips to my mom's closet back then, and I fell in love with the people in those pictures. I wanted so badly to remember that part of my life. I would close my eyes and try to recall any day I might have had with my father. I tried to remember my mother happy like that, but I couldn't.

Looking back and forth between my house and the Elgins', I couldn't bring myself to go home—to sit in silence next to my mother and mark the passing of time with the television. I wanted to run into the woods, and be someplace where being alone made sense.

As I stood there shrouded by the night, a small flame flared on Hoke's porch, and I turned to see him sitting in the darkness, watching me watch the Elgins.

"Hey, Hoke," I said, walking up and taking a seat in the chair beside him. "Place looks a lot different, don't it?"

"That's the truth." he said. "You met the boy yet?"

I shrugged.

"Is that a yes or a no?"

"I met him. Can't say I'm all that impressed."

"Oh, really? I thought you two might hit it off."

"It's hard to hit it off with someone who has a stick up his butt."

Even in the darkness I could tell that Hoke cracked a smile, but he took a pull on his pipe to hide the slip. "What makes you say he's got a stick up his butt?"

"I ran into him down at the pond. Invited him to go fishin', but he just insulted me and walked off."

"He insulted you?"

"Yeah, he said that I live in a little house."

"I see." Hoke took a few more puffs on the pipe before he spoke again. "I suppose calling your house *little* might be a bit unwarranted. Do you think he meant it as an insult? Maybe that's just an adjective that popped into his head?"

"He didn't need no adjective. He coulda just said, 'Do ya live across the road?' Tha'da done just fine."

"I guess you're right about that, but you might want to give him a break on that one."

"You can give him a break if ya wanna. Not me."

"And he didn't want to fish with you?"

"I offered to rig him up a pole and he got all mad about it."

Hoke let his pipe hand rest on his stomach, the way he did when he pondered stuff, and I could just picture his forehead creasing up with thoughts. "Is that all you did? Because that doesn't sound like enough to make a guy mad."

"Well...what I said was...'I could nigger-rig a pole for ya,' but that's not bad. Everyone says stuff like that."

"I see."

"It's just an expression, and he gets all pissy 'bout it."

"When you say that everyone says stuff like that...have you ever heard me say something like that?"

I thought hard but couldn't think of a time that I'd heard those words come out of Hoke's mouth. "No," I said.

"And your mother, has she ever said it?"

"Well, no, but—"

"So not *everyone* says stuff like that."

"But plenty of folks do. I've even heard black folks say it."

"I suppose, but who's to say they don't have that prerogative?"

"So they can say it but I can't?"

"Boady, there are some words that carry the weight of history, and that's one of them. It's a word we came up with so that we could make that whole race of people something less than *we* are. Us and them, remember?"

"I was only asking if he wanted to go fishin'."

"Is that really *all* you were saying."

"I never said *he* was one."

"No. You offered to *nigger-rig* a fishing pole—slap something together that is less than a real fishing pole."

Hoke didn't get it. "But he's the one who acted like he was all better'n me," I said. "He wants me to call him Thomas and not Tom—like he's royalty or somethin'. I *tried* to get along with him—I did."

"I know you did, Boady. You're a good kid with a good heart. But sometimes when you look down at the surface of a pond, all you can see is your own reflection, not the depth of what's on the other side."

I was getting nowhere with Hoke, and I was growing tired of

trying to explain such a simple thing to a man who should know as much. The Elgins had stopped playing their music, and lights were shutting off across the road. When I saw Mom's television go off, I used that as an excuse to take my leave, probably angrier about what happened at the pond than I was before I sat down with Hoke.

CHAPTER

10

THE NEXT WEEK MOVED ABOUT AS SLOW AS A WEEK COULD GO, in part because it was the last week of school, not counting finals week—and clocks never seem to tick at the right speed when summer vacation loomed so close—and in part because of the way things stood between Thomas and me.

I ate my lunches in the courtyard to avoid Jarvis, but I soon figured out that he didn't seem to care all that much about my not being around, which brought me to the conclusion that they never really wanted me to sit with them. They must have thought that their offer of friendship was the kind of low-hanging fruit I'd be unable to resist. Granted, it would have been nice to have a friend or two at St. Ignatius, but Jarvis Halcomb? I had no doubt I'd have been dubbed the third Boob Brother. Of course, from their perspective, why bring me in if they didn't need to? If they could seal my cooperation—which they seemed to think they had—without having to suffer the indignity of sitting with a scurvy freshman like me, well, all the better.

But coming home at the end of the day was what really made the week plod along, like a funeral dirge. I'd gotten used to being invisible at school, but I never thought that problem would follow me to Frog Hollow Road. Every afternoon when I got off the bus, I'd walk my long walk down the road, hoping that Thomas might be out in his yard doing this or that, and I might wave to him or nod—give him an opening to carry over an olive branch. I mean, there were just the two of us out there, so it stood to reason that he'd get tired of being bullheaded. But he stayed inside. Busy with unpacking, I told myself.

On that Monday, I cleaned off our carport—something that Mom wanted me to do anyway—while keeping an eye out for any movement across the road. If Thomas happened to come out of his house, I would just happen to be outside as well. On Tuesday, I changed the oil in Mom's car, a chore that Hoke had taught me back when I was eleven. On Wednesday, I mowed the grass, taking extraordinary care when I trimmed with my hedge clippers, making the task last twice as long as normal.

By Thursday I still hadn't seen Thomas, and I was running out of chores, so I decided to clean the leaves out of the gutters, something I'd never done before. I took a small trowel up onto the roof with me to scrape away years of sediment that had packed into the gutters as thick as plaster. It was then, as I knelt at the edge of my roof, that I finally saw Thomas again.

I heard him first. I had taken a break from gutter-scraping to wipe sweat from my face when the faint sound of a raised voice clacked its way across the road. I settled onto my butt and focused my attention on the front door of the Dixon house, perking my ears. The argument came in muffled clumps at first, but I could tell that there were two voices, Thomas and his dad, bashing back and forth and sometimes stomping on top of each other.

Then Thomas stepped onto the porch, turned, and yelled at his father. "I didn't ask you to bring me here, did I? Why couldn't you just leave me in Minnesota?"

He jumped off the porch before his dad could answer, although it didn't strike me as the kind of question that wanted to be answered. Thomas ran to the shed, jumped onto one of the ten-speeds, and took off up the road, taking no notice of me sitting on my roof. Thomas's father stepped to the edge of the porch, his chest inflated the way a chest does when the coming holler is going to be a big one. But then he saw me sitting there and the exhale came out of Mr. Elgin with no sound. He kept his eyes on me for a second or two and then turned to watch Thomas disappear around the bend.

When Friday came, I didn't look for an excuse to linger around the house before heading down to Schenicker's, in part because I had warehouses to clean, and in part because watching their fight the day before gave me a queasy feeling in my gut. I had no business prying the way I had, yet I was starting to see what Hoke meant when he said that thing about seeing the depth of the pond.

The big warehouse had a pallet full of quick-setting joint cement parked inside the door, dropped off by one of Wally's suppliers. Over a hundred bags, twenty pounds each, needed to be carried to the back corner of the warehouse, and I had a pretty good guess who would get that job. I went into the office to ask Schenicker about it, but he wasn't there yet, just Mom sitting at her desk, figuring out the paychecks.

Without looking up, she said, "I saw the mom today."

Neither of us had yet seen Thomas's mother, although I had heard her singing once, the sound, low and husky, coming from one of the open windows on the second floor.

"She was plantin' flowers along the porch when I went home for lunch," Mom said. "She waved at me, and I waved back."

"Did you go talk to her?"

Mom stared at her books and didn't answer, which was itself an answer. Mom's shyness would have blocked her from walking over to make the acquaintance of our new neighbor, but like a dunce, I asked the question anyway.

I was trying to find a way to move past my stupid question

when Wally came in and asked if I could help him stack the bags of quick-set. I was happy to oblige, carrying two bags at a time to his one. We were barely getting started when Milo and Angus pulled into the courtyard, Milo parking his pickup up by the shed so Angus could unload some scaffolding bucks. Milo walked down to the office, waving at us as he passed and went inside. I figured he needed to make an adjustment to the footage he'd worked that week, something that happened regularly on Fridays.

I continued hauling bags back to the dark corner of the warehouse, but kept an eye on the office door, expecting to see Milo come out, but he remained inside. After my third trip back, I took a peek into the office and saw Milo leaning on Mom's desk, his hand raised as if brushing the back of his knuckle against Mom's cheek. Mom tucked her shoulders up and turned her face away from his hand.

I pushed the door open, slamming it into the wall, and yelled, "Milo!" so loudly that he nearly jumped out of his skin. I had no plan for what to do after that. I had no words prepared, no action readied. I wanted him to stop touching my mom, and my charge had accomplished that.

Milo looked like he was going to haul off and hit me, something that would have left a sizable bruise. He stood a good six feet tall, with arms as hard as knotted rope, and when he clenched his right hand into a fist, I thought that was it. But then Wally came in and Milo relaxed, rolling his cheeks up into a liar's smile.

"What's goin' on?" Wally asked.

"The kid here just scared the crap out of me," Milo said.

"He was touchin' my mom."

"She had a smudge of dust on her cheek. I was just wipin' it off."

It's hard to escape dust when you work at a drywall company, but my mother had managed to do it for over a decade. Milo was a goddamned liar.

"I got some beer on ice out here," Wally said, waving Milo out of the office.

He followed Wally, and as Milo passed me, he whispered, "Son, ya best be careful not to bite off more than you can chew." He didn't shove me or throw an elbow, like I half expected, but gave me a smile that could have meant any number of things. I took it to mean that this wasn't over.

"You okay, Mom?"

"I'm fine." I could hear a quaver in her voice.

"What'd he say to you?"

"I'm fine," she said again. "Why don't you go finish up with those bags? I gotta get these checks done."

I hesitated but gave in and went back to work, carrying the bags past Milo, who sat on a stack of Sheetrock, drinking beer with Wally.

"I'm tellin' ya, Wally, you should be worried about that new neighbor of yours. He's a sneaky bastard. You know what Cecil says? He says Elgin's tryin' to lay the groundwork to have him fired. Ain't enough they demoted Cecil to give that bastard a job. Now they want to frame him for all that money that got stoled. Hell, everybody knows Poe took the money."

As he talked, Milo rubbed at a faded tattoo on his right shoulder, a sword pointing down his arm, a flaming halo rising above the handle of the sword. I asked him once about the tattoo, and he told me to mind my own business. Later Angus told me that the sword was the mark of the CORPS. When I asked Angus what it meant to have such a tattoo, he looked nervous and shook his head. We never spoke of it again.

Schenicker breathed in, grunted a sigh, and shook his head. He had an odd habit of breathing in deep and then sighing, as if moved by some profound thought, but it was just his way of letting you know he was paying attention.

"I mean, this shit's gettin' serious," Milo said. "I heard tell Elgin wants to get Cecil out the way so he can shutter the plant. Close it up lock, stock, and barrel. Those bastards up in Minneapolis or wherever, they know Cecil won't cotton to layin' off half the town, so they gotta get rid of him. That's why they're makin' up this cock-and-bull story. But if they think they can get away with somethin' like that, they don't know my brother."

Angus came into the warehouse, and instead of grabbing a beer, he helped me carry the bags of quick-set, neither of us saying a word as we worked.

"We'll just have to wait and see, I s'pose," Wally said.

"Wait and see, my ass. You mark my words, if this ain't nipped in the bud, it'll be all she wrote. And you should be more worried than anyone," Milo said, pointing at Schenicker. "They're in your neighborhood. First one of 'em moves in, then all his kin are right behind. Pretty soon this road'll be nothin' but another goddamned Goat Hill."

"I don't know about that," Wally said, almost to himself.

"You mark my words," Milo said. "What we need is a little nigger-knockin', that's what we need. Go back to the old ways of keepin' things squared up."

I had never heard the term "nigger-knocking" until I started school at St. Ignatius. Stories floated like ghosts through the corridors of that school, bragging tales of white men packed tightly together in nondescript cars, driving down the streets of Goat Hill looking for blacks walking along the sidewalk. The car would then speed by, and someone in the car would throw a soda bottle, or reach out with a broomstick and hit the black person in the back. One time, they found a young woman unconscious on a sidewalk after some good ol' boys went nigger-knocking on Goat Hill. They never caught the ones who did it.

Angus and I had carried the last of the bags back, and I

dragged the pallet to the side of the warehouse and leaned it against the wall.

"Angus, grab a beer," Milo said. "And get one for Boady here while you're at it."

"That's okay," I said. "I still gotta clean the warehouses."

"Nonsense," Milo said. "One beer ain't gonna hurt ya."

Mom wasn't a fan of my drinking beer with the guys, but she didn't put the kibosh on it, either. Angus handed me a beer, and I played with the pop top but didn't open it.

"Boady, you know why coons can't hang Sheetrock?" Milo said. "It's cuz their heads are too soft. That's a biological fact. They have thinner skulls than us whites, and when you go to hold the sheet on the ceiling, they can't do it."

I seemed to recall Milo once telling me that blacks weren't as smart as whites on account of their skulls being thicker than ours, giving them less room for a brain. I thought better than to point out his inconsistency.

Then Milo said, "I hear you and my nephew Jarvis are friends now."

His question caught me off-guard, and I didn't answer.

"You can learn a lot from a kid like Jarvis. He's good people—the right kind of people, if ya know what I mean."

"Not like those porch monkeys up the road," Angus said.

Angus rarely piped up like that around his old man, probably so as not to accidentally say something that might piss Milo off. But on this new subject of the Elgins, Angus seemed to walk on safe and well-trodden ground, and his comment made his father laugh.

Milo scratched at the CORPS tattoo on his arm. Then he smiled at his son—something I'd only seen a couple times in my memory—and said, "That's right, boy. Not like those monkeys up the road."

CHAPTER

11

THE NEXT MORNING, SATURDAY, I AWOKE TO THE SOUND OF lightly crunching gravel on the road in front of my house. Pulling myself up to the window, I saw Thomas Elgin riding his bike toward Schenicker's. As I dug around the floor of my closet for a pair of blue jeans and a reasonably clean T-shirt, I heard it again, this time heading up the road. I went to the kitchen, poured a bowl of cereal and carried it out to the carport, taking a seat on the rail to eat in the warm morning breeze. From there, I watched him ride by three more times—the kind of thing I used to do to scratch the itch of boredom.

I took my bowl to the sink, rinsed it, and returned to the carport to find Thomas's bike parked alongside the road, down near my path to the pond. I had cut that trail back when Tilly was alive, so I wouldn't have to walk past her house every time I wanted to go fishing.

Ambling like a guy with no place in particular to go, I made my way to where Thomas's bike leaned on its kickstand. There I waited and listened to see if he might be in the woods nearby. When I didn't hear anything, I slipped into the trees and up the hill, being careful to avoid stepping on leaves or sticks or anything that might announce my presence.

Where the woods ended and the hayfield began, I paused

again. I didn't hear anyone, but I noticed a shoe print in the dirt—Thomas's shoe print. Squatting down like some cavalry scout in a movie, I traced a finger around the outline. In all the years that I'd been running through those woods, I had never seen the shoe print of another kid—ever. This was my path. I had cut it with a machete and worn it down with my many trips to the pond. No one else had ever used it, not even Hoke, who preferred the cow trail that ran back from Tilly's barn when he took me fishing.

Staring at that shoe print got me all gummed up inside, because it occurred to me that at the end of that trail sat a guy who—even though he and I were the only kids around—wanted nothing to do with me.

It's not like I'd never had a friend before. In third grade, I took up with a kid named Michael Peck, latching on to him like a chigger that whole school year; but then his dad moved the family to Nebraska. In fifth grade I had a friend named Axel Smith, who called me Buddy—the only time I'd ever had a nickname. I even did a sleepover at his house once. But in sixth grade, when *Thou shalt be popular* became a commandment, he found new friends, boys who had passed some test that I had apparently failed. By eighth grade, the only kids left were the ones who snuck away from school during recess to smoke cigarettes under the train trestle, and hanging out with them got me sent to St. Ignatius.

I walked through the hayfield, the overgrown shoots swishing against my jeans. At the bottom of the hill, Thomas sat on the fishing limb, his back to me, one leg hanging down and the other folded into his chest. At the base of the tree I stopped, feeling for the first time ever that I needed some kind of permission to climb up my tree—*my tree*. It was then that I realized that my tree grew on his dad's property.

"Hey," I said.

Thomas turned to look at me, not seeming at all surprised by my being there, and said, "Hi."

I waited, and when he didn't ask me to come up, I said, "Mind if I join ya?"

"You're not going to push me in again, are you?"

"I'll do my best not to."

He gave me a half smile, which I took to mean that I could climb up. The fishing limb could fit two people easily enough, although it had never done so before. Thomas turned sideways, and I took a seat beside him facing the same direction, our feet dangling above the pond.

I figured that I should be the one to start things off, so I said, "I didn't mean anything by what I said the other day, saying that thing about...you know."

"Is that really the way people talk around here?"

What I wanted to say was that people around here say a lot worse things than that. Hell, what I said was nothing compared to some of the phrases folks tossed back and forth, but I thought I'd leave that discussion for another day. Instead, I simply said, "Yeah."

"This was only supposed to be temporary," Thomas said. "They were going to send Dad down here to straighten things up. But then without even asking me, he says that we're moving to Missouri—for good. I had friends back home. I was on the golf team. Now it's like I have to start over with everything."

"If it's any consolation, I hear Jessup High has a really good golf team."

"They're putting me in some Catholic school, Saint something-or-other."

"St. Ignatius?"

"Yeah."

"You're goin' *there*? That's my school."

I couldn't help sounding like I thought the idea was crazy—

probably because that's exactly what I *did think*. His mom was putting him in a school where upperclassmen threw pudding on you just because of your skin color. He had no idea what lay ahead, but that too would be a discussion for another day.

"Mom says it's the one to go to if you want to go to college."

"I wouldn't know about that. I ain't goin' to college."

"You're . . . just a freshman, right?"

"Yeah."

"And you've already made up your mind?"

"It's not that I made up my mind; I just ain't college material."

He looked me up and down as if something about the way I sat on that tree branch might disprove my point. "You're not?"

"No, and goin' to St. Ignatius ain't gonna help me none. I only go there cuz Mom makes me. I got this scholarship, so I go for free."

"You got a scholarship? I thought you said—"

"It ain't no academic scholarship. They're tryin' to bring country kids into the city, and I got snared in the net."

"I think my dad had me set for college before I was even born. He wants me to go to business school like him, but I don't know . . . I really like—"

He stopped talking as though he'd gone a step too far.

"What?"

"You'll think it's stupid."

"No, I won't. Try me."

He pursed his lips to one side and squinted at me as he considered whether or not to tell me his secret. Now I had to know.

"I won't tell anyone," I said.

"Promise?"

"I promise."

"I was in the school play and . . . man, I had fun. We did *West Side Story* and I played one of the Sharks. I don't know . . . maybe

I want to be an actor or something. You can't tell my parents, though. Dad would royally freak."

Thomas's revelation fell woefully short of the blood-oath bombshell I expected—but he trusted me with his secret, and the way I saw it, that was a hell of a thing. I even considered telling him my big secret, my plan to leave Jessup in a year, leave Mom and Grover and everyone. But I bit my tongue. I figured there'd be time later on to turn over some of those heavier stones.

CHAPTER

12

We stayed in that tree all morning, Thomas asking me about living in Jessup, and me asking him about life in the big city. I told him about my trails, and my campsites, and about copperheads and scorpions. He told me about skylines and malls and about canyons of glass and steel.

Around lunchtime, we reached the subject of music. I put it out there that I loved Aerosmith and Lynyrd Skynyrd. He came back with Earth Wind and Fire, and Marvin Gaye. After a great deal of negotiating, we agreed that we both liked the Doobie Brothers, and when he asked me if I had any of their cassettes, I simply said no rather than explain that Mom and I hadn't yet moved from eight-track to cassettes.

"I have two of them," he said, and with that we left the tree and headed up to his house.

I hadn't been in the Dixon house since before Tilly died. We used to buy eggs from her in those last years when the house seemed gray and cold. But that day, as Thomas and I approached the house, it seemed to radiate in a way it must have long ago when the Dixons first built it. The Elgins had raked away years of twigs and leaves and mowed down the weeds that had overtaken the lawn. Charles Elgin had rented a power sprayer and hosed down the outside of the house, blasting at the dust and dinge until it shined with a luster I'd never seen. And the flowers—Mrs. Elgin had lined the porch and one whole side of the house with pansies and marigolds, tucked inside a ribbon of red cedar mulch.

The inside of the house also wore new clothes: soft pastel walls replacing the faded wallpaper, hardwood floors where there had been linoleum, carpeting that still held the smell of chemical freshness, new appliances, new countertops. As I stood there taking in all the changes, it occurred to me that this was no longer the Dixon house; it was the Elgin house.

While Thomas went upstairs to get his boom box, I wandered around the front room looking at the furniture, leather pieces that matched the way they do in display rooms. It made me think about our couch at home, the one with the brown blanket throw on it to cover up holes in the armrests.

A bowl of fruit sat in the middle of a large oak coffee table: apples, oranges, and peaches. I touched one of the peaches expecting plastic or wax, and the thing dimpled under my finger. Real fruit, ripe, sitting right there in the middle of the living room. It made me realize that I hadn't yet eaten any lunch. My mouth watered as the aroma of that peach reached up to me. I looked around; I was alone. Would they notice if I ate one? Should I? No, that would be rude, but man, that peach smelled delicious.

As I debated my next move, Mr. Elgin's deep-throated voice spilled out of what used to be Tilly's bedroom—and before that, the maid's quarters—a decent-size space just off the front room. I moved a step or two closer and heard only Mr. Elgin talking, the absence of a second voice suggesting that he was on the phone. Good manners dictated that I not listen, but then I heard him say "Lida Poe" and I couldn't help myself.

I went to the staircase and sat on the bottom step, as if waiting there for Thomas, which put me just outside the door to the maid's quarters. Through a gap in the doorway, I saw that they had turned the room into a study for Mr. Elgin, his desk stacked high with binders and papers. He sat out of my line of sight, except that I could see one of his legs crossed over the other, the suspended foot tapping against the air.

"My running total is just shy of a hundred and sixty grand," he said. "Every one of those invoices had Halcomb's name on it, but it's not his signature. It's close, but not the same."

Pause.

"I thought of that too. If he messes up his own signature, he can say they're all forged. Blame it on Poe."

Pause.

"I agree."

Pause.

"I don't see how Cecil could *not* have known about it. A hundred and sixty grand missing and you don't notice it? It doesn't smell right to me."

Pause.

"Yeah, but if we fire him, all hell's going to break loose down here. The guy's related to half the county and he's already planting the idea that I'm here to close the factory. He may act like a hayseed, but he's smart. He's playing a long game and giving himself cover every step of the way."

Pause.

"Yeah, that's my thought exactly. If I can get something a little more concrete, something we can point to and say 'Cecil Halcomb screwed you guys over.' We can let him go then, and it won't be so bad."

Pause.

"I'll keep at it. I have a line on a handwriting expert up at the University of Missouri. Maybe he can figure out who signed those invoices. It had to be either Cecil or Lida Poe."

The sound of footsteps on the front porch made me jump. I

moved away from Mr. Elgin's office and leaned against the back of a couch just as Mrs. Elgin came in. She had lighter skin than both her husband and Thomas, and she had freckles; I didn't know that black folk could get freckles. I remember thinking that she was pretty for a black woman.

She stopped, and regarded me with a raised eyebrow as she tugged off her gardening gloves. I could see that my presence in her house had her confused, so I stepped forward to introduce myself.

"Hi, I'm Boady Sanden. I live across the road." I raised my hand for a shake.

"You're the boy who threw my Thomas into the pond the other day?"

My hand sagged. "Um..."

Then her face broke into a grin and she took my hand and shook it. "He came home looking like a half-drowned cat." Her grin grew bigger.

"Yeah...that was...funny," I said. When she didn't throw me out of her house, I judged that Thomas hadn't told her about what I'd said to him. I remember thinking at the time that it was pretty white of him to keep that a secret.

She introduced herself as Jenna, and right about then her husband came out of his office and she introduced him as Charles. We shook, and his hand nearly swallowed mine. He nodded his hello and moved to the dining room table, where he had a bunch of papers spread out.

"Mom! Where are the batteries?" Thomas yelled from the upstairs.

"What size you need?" she called back.

"D-cells."

"They're in the linen closet on the bottom shelf."

"And...where's the linen closet?"

"It's that narrow door next to the bathroom."

Jenna paused to listen for the creak of the closet door being opened, then closed.

"Thanks!" he yelled.

She turned her attention to me again. "I believe I saw your mother walking up the road earlier this week."

"Yeah, she works at the drywall company down there." I pointed in the general direction of Schenicker's. "She's the bookkeeper."

"I'd love to meet her. When do you think would be a good time to invite her over?"

"My mom's...well, she's shy—I mean really shy. She gets nervous meetin' new people, and sometimes she can't get her words out right. I'd be happy to ask her, though. Just don't take it personal...ya know...if she doesn't..."

"I see," Jenna said. "What's her name?"

"Emma."

"That's a pretty name."

"I got it!" Thomas called from the top of the stairs, a boom box, big and shiny and beautiful, in his hand. "It needed batteries."

"Did you boys have lunch?" Jenna asked.

"No," Thomas said as he leapt over the final three steps of the staircase.

Jenna wrapped an arm around him before he slipped past her, the grab as much of an embrace as a catch. Thomas pretended to be annoyed by the move, but his smile gave him away. It may have been just another moment for them, as common as salt, but I remember feeling a strange sort of envy as I watched Jenna playfully hug her son.

"Why don't you grab a piece of fruit or something," she said.

Thomas slipped out of his mother's arms and detoured to the coffee table. "What do you want, Boady? Apple, orange, or—"

"Peach, please," I said.

He tossed me the top peach, the one with my finger mark already on it, and we headed out the door.

We took up positions on the front porch, him leaning against the house and me against the rail, and listened to his Doobie Brothers cassette. He talked about his ex-girlfriend, how they snuck out of a basketball game to have their first kiss. But in the next breath, he complained of having to come up with fresh compliments every day because if he repeated the same one too many times she would accuse him of not trying hard enough. I'd managed to make it through my freshman year without having that problem.

When we got to that song "Black Water," Thomas stopped the tape and rewound it over and over again as we tried to master the a cappella section near the end. During one of those attempts, I noticed Jenna standing at the front door, her gaze fixed on my house across the road.

Thomas and I went through the song again, getting the ending pretty close, but not good enough for him.

Behind me a car came down the road — the mailman, who was actually a mail-woman named Helen. She shoved some letters into the Elgins' mailbox and headed down to Schenicker's.

When Helen came back up the road, Jenna leaned in to her screen door, causing it to squeak open an inch. Thomas didn't notice. Helen stopped at our mailbox, paused to deposit some bills, and then drove off. A few seconds later, Jenna pushed through the screen door and shuffled off the porch, taking quick steps at first but then easing into a more natural gait. I looked over my shoulder and saw Mom making her trip out to get our mail as well.

Jenna arrived at her mailbox the same time as my mom, Jenna flashing a warm smile and saying something that I couldn't hear. Then she crossed the road and shook hands with Mom, who kept her eyes cast down as though fascinated by the mail in her hand. Jenna did all the talking at first, but then Mom said something that made Jenna laugh, and they both looked over at Thomas and me.

Did my mom just crack a joke?

Thomas remained oblivious as he practiced singing the high notes of that a cappella part. Our moms talked for a little while longer and then Jenna returned with her mail. As she climbed the steps, she said, "Your mom's coming over for tea later, and I forgot to ask how she likes it."

"Tea?" I said, surprised at the turn of events. My mom was coming over for tea—with a woman she'd just met. "She likes it sweet."

"I've never made sweet tea before. How much sugar should I add?"

"We do a cup per pitcher."

"A whole cup?" Jenna winced slightly as she said that, but then her smile returned, and she went inside.

CHAPTER

13

Finals week arrived on that Monday, and man, did it suck. I hadn't paid attention all semester, which forced me to pull a couple all-nighters to cram a hodgepodge of knowledge into my short-term memory—hopefully enough to walk away with Ds. I didn't shoot for great grades—or even mediocre grades. I planned to drop out in less than a year, so why strain myself. But I needed to get at least Ds to avoid summer school.

Jarvis Halcomb hadn't made a big deal about my not sitting with him in the cafeteria, and for a while there, I thought I might have slipped through the cracks. But that all changed on that last day of finals.

I'd taken to eating my lunch within earshot of Brothers Evan and Bart as they gabbed about the most boring stuff on the planet. That last day, I had just finished my first hot dog when the chairs to both my left and right pulled away from the table and the Boob Brothers sat down next to me like a couple of sweaty bookends.

"Hey, Boady," Bob said. He had a smile on his face, but a malicious twinkle in his eyes. "How's the hot dog?"

Beef let his gaze float around the room, past Brothers Evan and Bart, who paid less attention than normal to the lunch crowd.

"Jarvis wants to have a chat," Bob said.

"What's he want?" I asked.

"You'll just have to come outside and find out."

"And if I don't?"

Bob reached under the table, grabbed my thigh, just above the knee, and squeezed. He had strong hands, and the pinch of nerves and muscle caused me to nearly collapse to the table.

Beef leaned over and whispered to Bob, "Let go of him." Bob hesitated but then loosened his grip. I hadn't realized it, but I'd been holding my breath to keep from screaming out. Then Beef looked at me and said, "He just wants to talk, that's all. Don't make things worse than they are."

Worse than they are?

Beef stood up first and went to the brothers to distract them, asking them if they had big plans for the summer. Bob lifted me out of my chair by my collar, leaving his hand on my shoulder to lead me past the brothers, who chuckled as they told Beef about their summer missionary work.

Jarvis waited for us out in the courtyard, at the far end of a brick retaining wall where trees and hedges gave the feel of seclusion. He held a brown paper bag on his lap, his hands wrapped around it as though it carried more than just his lunch. Bob plopped me down beside Jarvis and then squeezed up next to me.

"You've been avoidin' me," Jarvis said. "I offer to be your friend, and you act like you're better'n me." He put his arm across my shoulders and gave a tug. "You don't think you're better'n me, do ya, Boady?"

"No," I said, although the words barely came out.

"That's good. I was startin' to think ya didn't take our little talk serious—like ya had some idea that this is all a game. Let me tell ya—it ain't no game. We're watchin' ya. And just because this is the last day of school, don't be thinkin' you're gettin' out of this. It don't work that way."

It was as if he could read my mind. From the moment Bob

pulled me out of my chair, I had been calculating the number of minutes until the final bell. After that, I would be free of Jarvis forever. I just had to get through three more class periods.

Jarvis handed me the paper bag as Bob looked around for teachers. There were none to be seen. "Open it," Jarvis said.

I rolled the top of the bag open and peeked inside. I didn't get it at first. I looked at Jarvis and then back into the bag. It appeared to be a spray can.

"This Saturday you're gonna stay up past your bedtime, and when everyone's asleep, you're gonna sneak across the road and paint a message on the side of that nigger's house."

My heart thumped hard in my chest at those words. I looked in the bag again and saw that it was red spray paint. "Why?" It was the only thing I could think to say, but I already knew the answer.

"Because that sonofabitch has been spreadin' shit about my ol' man." I think Jarvis's words came out louder than he'd intended, and he brought his tone back down to a low growl. "He's screwin' with the wrong people and tryin' to make my dad a scapegoat. Elgin's gotta go, that's all there is to it, and that's where you come in."

"We just wanna scare him," Bob added. "It's not like we're askin' you to go beat someone up. All ya gotta do is paint NIGGER GO HOME on the side of his house."

"And add this." Jarvis looked around again to make sure no teacher could see him. Then he pulled his shirtsleeve up to show a tattoo on his shoulder—a sword pointing down with a halo of fire rising above the handle. The same tattoo that I'd seen on Milo's shoulder. Tattoos were forbidden at St. Ignatius, and the sword on Jarvis's shoulder gleamed with fresh red ink. "Draw this sword on the house," he said. "Right next to the words."

"I can't draw," I said, as if that were my biggest concern.

"You don't need to be Rembrandt," Bob said, drawing in the air with his finger. "It's just a long line down for the blade, a short line across at the hilt, and then a half circle over that."

I don't know what surprised me more, that Bob had so easily detailed the spray-paint version of Jarvis's tattoo, or that he properly used the word *hilt* in a sentence.

"Why can't one of you do it?" I said. "Why bring me into this?"

"Ya live right there. You can just walk across the road, do it, and go back to bed. No fuss, no muss. And like I said before, you're bein' watched, and the guys watchin' you... well, they ain't the kind of guys you wanna piss off. But get this right and you'll be in fine company. My friends don't forget it when ya do 'em a favor."

"What if I get caught?"

"Ya won't get caught," Jarvis said.

"And if ya do," Bob said, "you keep your mouth shut."

Jarvis put his arm around my neck, more of a headlock than a hug. "Boady knows better'n to talk. Besides, he's got a mother to protect. Her name's Emma, right? A shy little thing, from what I hear. Be a shame if something bad happened to her."

A shiver ran down my back.

"Just you and your mom livin' out there—all alone. Sounds like the kinda situation where you could use some friends like us."

"You leave my mom out of this," I said. "You wanna push me around, fine, but you leave her—"

Jarvis gripped the back of my neck and squeezed like he wanted to crush my spine. My shoulders bolted up to my ears, and my hands flew up, grabbing his fingers, the bag with the spray paint falling to the concrete sidewalk below us.

"Do you have any idea who you're messin' with?" Jarvis hissed into my ear. "You don't make demands. You don't bargain. You do what you're told and shut the hell up."

Bob cleared his throat in a loud, obvious way, causing Jarvis to ease up on my neck. Brother Bart had come outside to check on the outdoor crowd and noticed our little trio. He was walking our way.

Jarvis whispered, "Say a word and I'll rip your face off." Then he relaxed his hand, but left his fingers on my collarbone, like we were buddies having a friendly conversation.

"What are you boys doing over here?" Brother Bart asked.

"Just eating lunch," Bob said, although none of us had any food in our hands.

"Whose is that?" Bart pointed at the bag on the ground.

Jarvis looked at Bob and Bob at Jarvis, neither wanting to speak.

I slid off the wall and grabbed the bag. "It's mine," I said. "I was just about to throw it away."

I walked off before anyone could say a word, dropping the bag into the first garbage can I came to. I didn't turn around until I made it safely inside the building. When I did, Jarvis glared at me, pissed as all get-out.

CHAPTER

14

I STILL HAD THOSE THREE CLASS PERIODS TO SURVIVE—A STUDY hall, my history exam, and the last class of the year, an empty hour when everyone would be bouncing and fidgeting as they waited for that final bell to ring, the sling that would launch us all into summer vacation. Why the school didn't just let us go after our last exam, I didn't know, but if nothing else, St. Ignatius loved its rules.

I managed to get to study hall without getting beat up and made use of my time there reading three chapters about the Great Depression and World War II, chapters that I was supposed to have read a month ago. With three minutes of study hall left, I asked for permission to go to the restroom, figuring that I could get to my locker, empty it out, and be at the door to my history final by the time the bell rang. If I planned it right, I could be in my seat before Jarvis and the boys left sixth period.

I hurried through the empty corridor toward my locker, which took me down to the first floor. When I got to the bottom of the steps, I stopped in my tracks, confused by what I saw. My locker door stood open, and all its contents—books, papers, pens—lay scattered on the floor. Approaching carefully, a deer ready to run at the first snap of a twig, I found the pages of my books torn from their covers and tossed into a semicircle that fanned out from my locker door, my pens and pencils snapped in half, my three-ring binder crushed.

I tiptoed over my things to peer into the locker to see if they left anything untouched, finding only a can of red spray paint. On the back of the locker they had sprayed the sign of the CORPS—a long vertical line for the blade, a short line for the crossguard, and a half circle over the hilt, just like Bob had described it. I knelt down and began sliding my papers together, not sure why I felt that I had an obligation to clean up the mess. Under my binder I found my calculator, something I'd paid for out of my own pocket; they had smashed that, too, knocking most of the buttons off. I picked up a couple of calculator buttons and started pushing them back into their sockets, where they wiggled like loose teeth.

At some point, the bell must have rung because I became aware of students walking by, politely stepping over and around my things. As I reached for the plus button from my calculator, a size-twelve clodhopper stepped next to my hand. I didn't have to look up to know the shoe belonged to Jarvis. I froze, not knowing what to expect. Then I slowly reached out and picked up the calculator button.

"Had to be stupid, didn't ya?" Jarvis spoke quietly, but with a rasp in his throat like he had been gargling sand. I took his question as rhetorical and didn't answer. "Maybe you're too thickheaded to understand. So, do ya get the message now?" When I didn't answer a second time, he kicked my binder down the hall.

Students gathered in the periphery of our squabble, I suppose waiting for a fight to break out. I kept my eyes cast down at my calculator as I fit the plus sign into its hole and then reached out for the equals sign. I could hear the whistle of air spinning through Jarvis's flared nostrils as my silence grew louder.

When my fingers pinched the tiny calculator button, Jarvis lifted his foot and stepped on my hand, the tread from his boots grinding into my knuckles, my pinky twisting crooked under his weight, pain rocketing up my arm and filling my chest cavity.

I dropped to my elbows and screamed, "Get off!" But Jarvis put more weight on my hand, leaning down so that his face nearly touched my ear. "You messed up, Puke."

He said more than that, but the searing pain blocked out the sound of his voice. I started cussing. But I couldn't even hear my own words through the ringing in my ears. My fingers throbbed, my arm shook. He was crushing my hand.

I'd once stepped on a feral cat while exploring the hayloft in Tilly Dixon's cow barn. The poor thing had been hiding under a piece of burlap, and when I stepped on that cat's tail, she tore into my leg like some calico demon—no thought, no plan, just single-minded fury. That cat scratched the crap out of me before I knew what had happened. As Jarvis bounced his weight down on my hand, I understood that cat. I became that cat.

I drew my left foot under me, clutched Jarvis's ankle with my free hand, and drove my shoulder into his knee with more power than I thought I could muster. I caught his leg with all of my weight, freeing my crushed hand and sending the blood pulsing through it once more. The attack caught Jarvis, the star wrestler, by surprise, throwing him sprawling to the floor.

I didn't wait for a countermove. I continued in the direction of my momentum, springing to my feet and charging over Jarvis's body. He reached up and caught the pocket of my shirt, which tore free, taking a patch of shirt with it. Something slammed into my knee, and I went tumbling forward, twisting onto my back. I expected to see Jarvis pouncing at me, but instead he rolled around on the floor holding his face—where my knee hit him.

I stood and ran.

My history exam was on the second floor, and when I turned the corner on the staircase, no one was chasing me. Jarvis still lay on his side, one hand on his knee and the other on the left side of his face. Half of the kids in the hall were looking at him in disbelief, and the other half looked at me, the sentiment—*you poor bastard*—obvious in their expressions.

I paused to take a breath at the top of the steps and saw Bob standing near the door to my history classroom—I suppose as a backup plan in case I hadn't gone to my locker. He didn't see me, so I ducked into the boys' restroom, headed to the farthest stall, climbed up onto the toilet seat, and locked the stall door.

One by one, boys left the restroom, the scratch of shoes on the hard tile floor marking the fall of their numbers until the room fell silent. I waited, squatting in my stall until the second bell rang. I would be late for my history exam, but I'd get there in one piece.

I peeked under the stall divider and saw no feet in the restroom, so I eased down off the toilet, opened the door, and stepped out—and there sat Beef, his butt planted on the vanity, back against the wall, feet propped up on the edge of one of the sinks, his arms resting comfortably on his knees. For a big guy, he folded up tighter than I expected. When he saw me, he smiled.

The exit lay around the corner beyond his left shoulder. He must have seen my eyes dart toward the door because he said, "You'll never make it."

I knew that to be true, so I raised my fists up in front of my face in my best Muhammad Ali stance. I had no way out except through Beef, and if he planned on beating me up, he'd have to work for it.

"Put your dukes down, pal, you're gonna hurt yourself," Beef said with a slight chuckle.

I glanced around for Jarvis and Bob, but we were alone.

"Can't Jarvis fight his own battles?" I asked.

"Fight? What fight?"

"Ain't you here to beat me up?"

"I s'pose I could if you want me to, but no, that ain't why I'm here."

"What do ya want, then?" I said, lowering my hands.

He slid off of the vanity and held out the piece of cloth that had once been my shirt pocket. "I just wanted to give ya this." He kept enough distance between us to show his appreciation for my mistrust. I didn't take the cloth so he laid it on the vanity.

Neither of us moved.

"Look, I know what y'all say about me—that I'm one of Jarvis's Boob Brothers. Y'all think I'm just some dumb jock, a thug, but it ain't like that."

"So you didn't distract the brothers at lunch today so Jarvis could corner me alone?"

"Well...yeah, I s'pose ya got me there." Beef shrugged and looked down at his feet as if he were embarrassed. "Here's the thing, Boady. Jarvis and I have been best friends since kindergarten. He's like a brother to me. He ain't as bad as he makes out, and there's more to what's goin' on here than what ya know."

Beef looked at me as if wanting me to chime in, maybe say that I understood, but I didn't.

"Ya see, he's got a dad who...Well, let's just say it's tough livin' with Cecil Halcomb on a good day, but lately, with this thing at the factory and stuff...Jarvis is takin' the brunt of Cecil's bad news. I know Jarvis can be a jerk sometimes, but—"

"You want me to feel sorry for Jarvis Halcomb?"

Beef smiled his understanding. "I guess not. I just thought you should know that Jarvis is in the middle of his own problems, and when he does stuff like what he did today...well, just keep in mind that he's doin' it for his ol' man more'n anything else."

"I gotta get to my history final," I said. "I'm late."

Beef tipped his head toward the door. "Go ahead."

I walked cautiously past him; Beef never moved. But as I pulled the door open, he said, "Just one more thing. You ride the number four bus home after school." He said it as a statement, not a question.

"How'd you know that?" I asked.

"Jarvis knows a lot about you. For example, he knows that the number four comes up from the grade school, and you have to wait for it...way out there at the end of the block...away from teachers. He also knows that the only other kids who'll be at that bus stop with you are two girls who happen to be his cousins."

"What's he gonna do?"

"What do ya think he's gonna do?"

"Why are you tellin' me this?"

"I'm not gonna carry water just cuz Jarvis tells me to. I'm not like Bob. I don't agree with what's going on, so I'm givin' you a friendly warning. That's all."

"You'll warn me, but you won't stop him?"

Beef let out a heavy sigh. "It's complicated."

"That's the thing, Beef," I said. "I really don't think it is."

CHAPTER

15

I WALKED INTO MY HISTORY FINAL TEN MINUTES LATE. COACH Thayer gave me a dirty look as he handed me the exam.

We didn't have assigned seats in that class, but I always sat at the same desk, as did everyone else, once the pecking order had been established. On the first day of class, I claimed a seat in the row of desks that lined the windows—my preferred location for daydreaming—but before I could get settled in, Brock Nance had walked up and told me that I was sitting in his seat. It being the first day of class, I knew that was a lie, so I pretended to search the desktop and then announced that I could not find his name on it. He looked around to make sure there was no teacher in the room yet and then punched me in the chest.

I slid one seat over, not wanting to move more spaces than I had to—as though that were some kind of victory. Then a friend of Brock's told me that I was sitting in *his* seat. By the time I found a desk I could stay in, all the good ones had been taken, and I ended up sitting along a wall with no windows.

It was stuff like that—a lot of stuff like that—that made my freshman year at St. Ignatius such a crucible. Conversations pinged around me every day, talk of movies, parties, dates, plans, all of it born in a world I'd never seen, a world that apparently couldn't see me either—at least not until I sat in the wrong seat. And so I spent most of my time in class focusing on my rock band doodles and my daydreams, wrapped in the chill of my invisibility.

As I took a look at the first page of my history exam, I came to regret not reading more chapters than I had—and not paying attention in class. I'm sorry, but no matter how interesting a particular war might be, Coach Thayer's lectures never got more exciting than the hum of a car tire on pavement. One time I had fallen asleep, my elbows on my desk, my fists propped up against my cheeks to hold my head up. I had gotten pretty good at pretending to read while snoozing. But this time Coach Thayer caught me and threw a chalkboard eraser at me, hitting the top of my head. I woke up in a cloud of dust.

The rest of the class had a pretty high time with that one, everyone laughing at me—everyone, that is, except for Diana, the black girl Bob wanted to dump pudding on. She sat to the left of me in history, and I seem to recall that she alone stood out as having a hint of pity in her eyes. I had come to detest St. Ignatius by then, but after that eraser incident—well, my desire to get the hell out of Jessup hit a hard boil.

As I pored over the multiple choice questions on the exam, I recognized a few of the answers from the chapters I had just read in study hall. I filled those in first. Other questions struck a vague chord in my memory, so I half guessed at those. After my first pass through the test, I had as many answers still blank as what I'd filled in. I tried to dig in deeper, find the corners of my brain where Thayer's lectures might have accidentally stuck to the wall, but my mind kept drifting to Beef's warning about Jarvis. He would be waiting for me at my bus stop.

I could skip out of my last hour, again ask to use the restroom as a way of taking off early—but to what purpose? Walk all the way home? That would take hours and have Mom calling the highway patrol.

I shook those thoughts away and refocused on my test. I hadn't yet answered enough questions to get my D, and Thayer included a section of questions that went all the way back to the beginning of the semester. I hated it when teachers did that. I closed my eyes and searched through the fog for any terms I could remember from the Industrial Revolution.

Bob would be with Jarvis at the bus stop, but would Beef? Would he step in and stop it? He had never stopped Jarvis before. He hadn't stopped them when Bob set out to dump pudding on Diana. If Beef had put his foot down back then, I wouldn't have needed to trip Bob, and all this wouldn't be happening to me.

Focus! I looked at the clock—only fifteen minutes to go, and still so many empty spaces on my test. *Laissez-faire? What the hell is laissez-faire?* If I flunked history, I'd have to go to summer school. That would screw up all my plans. I needed to work for Schenicker and earn as much money as possible so I could get out of town at sixteen. That test suddenly held my fate, and I had reached the point where I would have to start filling ovals in at random.

Through the windows, I could almost see my bus stop at the corner of the property, obscured by a small cluster of cedar trees so that my beating would remain out of the sight of the teachers. I could hide in the trees until the bus came and then dart onto it at the last minute. Jarvis wouldn't follow me onto the bus, would he? No, but he would follow me home, catch me alone at the top of Frog Hollow. Somehow I needed to make him think that I never got on the bus at all.

"Ten minutes," Coach Thayer called out.

Dammit!

As I pulled my focus away from the window and back to my test, I saw a small movement that grabbed my attention. Diana had turned her test sideways with all of her ovals filled in. Was she doing that on purpose? I had never so much as said boo to her. I told myself that I was imagining it, but then, without looking at me, she tapped her finger to her paper.

I put my head down and stretched my eyeballs to the left as far as they could go, just enough to get a look at the pattern of her dots. I began filling that same pattern on my page.

Thayer called the test just before the bell rang, and I handed in my answers—the known, the borrowed, and the guessed—fairly confident that I'd done well enough to pass. I wanted to thank Diana, but to do so meant drawing attention to our conspiracy. She looked at me and gave me the smallest of smiles, and I returned it.

When the bell rang, I stayed in my seat. Beef said that Jarvis didn't plan on getting me until after school, but I didn't want to run into him in the hallway and change his mind on that score. Thayer didn't look up from the book he was reading as one group of kids left and another—mostly sophomores—came in. No one paid me much attention. When the second bell rang, Thayer looked up and started talking about this being the last hour of the school year, and how we should try to keep it down because there could be some other classes still taking tests.

Then he noticed me, cocked his head like a curious dog, and said, "Mr. Sanden, are you lost?"

I stood up and walked out the door, giving him a forced smile as I passed, but not an answer to his question. Outside, in the empty corridor, I walked casually to my last class.

That last hour passed with the speed of falling dominoes. The other kids congregated in small clusters, gabbing as they waited for that final bell, but I sat in my seat, staring out the windows, my mind flipping through ideas, none of which seemed to get me out of my predicament. Then I noticed that our teacher, Brother Marcus, was doing a crossword puzzle and not paying the least bit of attention to us students. Like the rest of the teachers, he'd already checked out. I could use this.

With fifteen minutes left before the bell, I went to Brother Marcus and requested permission to use the restroom. He looked up at the clock and then at me.

"Make sure you're back before the bell rings," he said.

"No problem," I answered, knowing that he'd never notice if I didn't return—not with the lure of his crossword puzzle pulling at him.

I walked down to a part of the school that had already been put up for summer—the cafeteria and gymnasium—all of it as quiet as a crypt. I slipped into the empty courtyard and made my way to the back side of the gym, walking like I had every right in the world to be doing what I was doing, just in case some random teacher happened to look out a window.

From there I ran full-bore to the south, off school property, heading in the opposite direction of my bus stop. Once I got beyond the sight of anyone in the school, I circled back, staying hidden as I worked my way up a side street toward the front of school.

My bus picked us up on the west side of the block, but I climbed up into a cedar tree on the east side, only a few feet away from a stop sign. I settled in and waited for school to let out.

I couldn't hear the bell ring from my perch, but the flood of kids gushing out told me that the school year had ended. Soon, Jarvis Halcomb drove his red four-wheel-drive out of the parking lot, with Bob riding shotgun. He headed past my bus stop, and for a second I thought that Beef had pulled my leg. But then I saw the nose of the truck slide up and park in an alley, one that gave him a perfect view of my bus stop.

Bob got out and jogged along the tree line across the street from St. Ignatius, taking up a position behind a hedge only a few feet from where I would have been standing as I waited for the bus.

Cars full of noisy kids peeled out of the parking lot and past my tree, their horns blaring and their stereos cranked, the occupants whooping and hollering at being set free for the summer. No one saw me in my hiding spot—but then again, they never really saw me when I wasn't hiding either.

As the flow of cars reduced to a trickle, my bus turned the corner at the far end of the block, stopping to pick up the two girls. It waited for a couple minutes, I assume to give me a chance to come running up from the school. Bob left his hiding spot and circled around to get a better view, in case I had somehow slipped past him. Jarvis then appeared on the opposite side of the bus, also swiveling his head to find me.

When the bus pulled away, they watched it head in my direction, shrugging their shoulders and talking with animated gestures. Then they walked back toward Jarvis's truck.

When the bus stopped at the stop sign beside my tree, I jumped down and ran to stand in front of it. The driver, a man I knew only as Augie, waved at me to move out of his way. He knew who I was, and he knew that I belonged on the bus, but Augie had a rule: If you're not at the bus stop at your pickup time, you don't get a ride.

"Get out the way," he hollered out his window.

"I gotta get on the bus," I hollered back.

"You know the rules. Now get out the way."

"I ain't movin'. I'll stand here till the Rapture if I need to, so ya might as well open the door."

I could hear the loud roar of Jarvis's dual exhaust coming up the street behind the bus, but Jarvis couldn't see me where I stood.

Augie cursed me under his breath—I could tell by reading his lips—but he gave up rather quickly, opening the door and swinging a hand to gesture me in.

"If ya shut that door on me, I'll be right back out here," I said.
"Get in!" he yelled.

I hugged tightly to the side of the bus as I made my way to the door, and I could see the side mirror of Jarvis's truck sticking out of the row of cars waiting behind the bus. Augie grumbled at me as I climbed on, but he kept his voice low enough that the littler kids didn't hear the curse words. I ducked into the first open seat I came to, sinking into the bench to hide.

After the bus pulled away, I peeked over the back of the seat and watched as Jarvis turned off. He hadn't seen me.

That's when I began to grasp it: I had survived my freshman year at St. Ignatius Catholic High School. I should have been jubilant. I wanted to be whooping and pumping my fist in the air like those kids who drove past me as I hid in that tree, but I didn't feel jubilant. I had a feeling that this thing with Jarvis Halcomb wasn't over—not by a long shot.

CHAPTER

16

As soon as I stepped off the bus, I got busy putting that awful year at St. Ignatius behind me. It helped that life on Frog Hollow Road had more moving parts than ever before—the biggest one, of course, being Thomas.

It didn't take long to figure out that Thomas was a talker—I mean a real jabber jaw—going on and on about the sports he'd played and the girls he'd kissed. I countered with the fact that I had a job and could drive a stick shift. The way he yakked, though, you'd like to think he was twenty years old instead of just fifteen. Yet the day I took him to a ravine, deep and steep and covered knee-high in dead leaves, he rolled down the hill, hooting and thrashing like a six year-old. And the time we swung on vines dangling down from an enormous hickory tree, it was Mr. I've-Already-Kissed-a-Girl who screamed the Tarzan yell first.

Then one day I let it slip that I planned to run away from Jessup.

We had walked deep into the woods, heading toward a section of land I had explored many times before. Our trip took us to a gully just off County Road 51, where people had taken to dumping their junk—big things like appliances, tires, and old televisions, stuff they didn't want to pay to throw into the Caulfield County landfill. I'd discovered that ravine a few years back when I was exploring with Grover, and over the years I pulled a couple hundred bucks' worth of soda bottles and copper wire out of there, money I tucked away for my escape from Jessup.

That day, we arrived at the junk pile to find that someone had rolled an old AMC Gremlin to the bottom of the hill. When I saw it, I was as excited as a kid at Christmas. The old car, green and rusted, lay upside down, smashed nearly flat from the roll, but I could get at the engine from the underside.

"They didn't scrap it out," I said with a big grin on my face. "There's got to be twenty-five bucks' worth of copper in there."

"It's a Gremlin," Thomas said. "There's not twenty-five bucks' worth of anything in there."

"I'll need wrenches. We can come back later and pull the starter and alternator and stuff."

"You're serious?"

"Of course I'm serious. More money for my get-out-of-Jessup fund." I heard the words slip out before I could stop them.

"What get-out-of-Jessup fund?"

I leaned on one of the tires and contemplated how much to tell Thomas, deciding in the end to tell him everything. "When I turn sixteen, I'm gone. I've been saving up money. Got near enough to buy an old pickup truck. But you can't tell my mom. Promise me."

"That's crazy. What will you do for money?"

"Drywall. I already know how to do a bunch of it. I've been watchin' and learnin'."

"You're going to drop out of school to do drywall? That's stupid."

Something turned sharp inside me, and I aimed my words like a blade. "Drywall was plenty good enough for my dad," I said. "Not everyone needs to live in a big house like yours."

I walked away from Thomas with tears welling up in my eyes, I was so mad. I kept walking until I got to the creek, where I sat down on a rock the shape of a tortoise.

I heard Thomas approach, stopping and starting a couple different times like he was unsure what to do. I dried my eyes before he got there, and when he sat next to me, he said, "I'm sorry. I shouldn't have said that."

"Don't worry about it."

"No, I'm an ass, and I'm really sorry."

"It's okay—just keep it between us."

"I won't tell. I promise. But..."

"But what?"

"Doesn't mean that I won't try to talk you out of leaving. Just giving you fair warning."

"You go right on and talk," I said, letting a smile slip. "It's what you do."

We got home late for supper, as happened a lot despite our best intentions. Our mothers were both in the Elgins' kitchen making rhubarb crisp, which brings me to another moving part from that summer—the way my mother took to Jenna Elgin.

It's not that I thought they shouldn't have gotten on the way they did. It's just that Mom had built up some pretty thick walls after Dad died, and there were only a few of us allowed in. Jenna, however, seemed to skip right through some hidden gate.

It began with tea that first day, and a couple days later, tea again. Then I awoke one Saturday morning to find Mom sitting on the Elgins' porch with Jenna, sipping coffee, nibbling on cinnamon rolls, and talking. And just like that, Mom had replaced her Saturday-morning ritual of sitting alone on our back porch with a new one.

The rhubarb crisp came as a surprise to me because Mom made it from scratch, and Mom rarely cooked anything from scratch. Also, I couldn't remember her ever making rhubarb crisp before. She picked the rhubarb from a row of stalks that grew on the edge of our property. Mom once told me that Dad had planted the rhubarb there because it was his favorite dessert. Being just a kid, and not understanding that rhubarb needed a ton of sugar to make it edible, I'd once taken a bite of a raw stalk, the sour taste pulling my face into a twisted wad. I couldn't imagine anyone wanting *that* for a dessert. But the rhubarb crisp she made that night tasted better than anything I'd ever eaten—and I'm not just saying that because she was my mom. It was incredible, especially with the dollop of ice cream that Jenna brought to the table. I honestly didn't know that my mother had that in her.

That summer, at least those first few weeks after school let out, gave me some of the best memories of my life. It seemed like we packed a whole season into a handful of days. But then things got busy at Schenicker's, adding another cog to the machinery of my world. And the biggest shift happened on a Friday. I remember because that's the day I figured out that Milo Halcomb hadn't been around for a while.

I had three jobs in the summertime: I cleaned the warehouses, as I did year-round; I scrapped out houses, hauling the leftover drywall scraps out so that the mudders could do their thing; and I sanded walls. Of the three, sanding was my favorite. After the mudders finished covering all the cracks and nails with joint cement, I came in and made it all smooth, prepping the walls for painting. I loved sanding because it paid a cent a foot. Everything else I did for Schenicker paid a buck and a quarter per hour. Working by the foot—piecework, we called it—meant that the harder I worked, the more I got paid. Sanding was how I made the big bucks.

Schenicker taught me how to sand walls the previous year, and by the end of that summer I had pretty much mastered the task. There was one week in August when I spent every day sanding the walls of a twelve-unit apartment building. I earned a hundred and thirty-five dollars—almost as much as Milo and Angus made. I figured that when the time came to leave Jessup, I'd have at least one skill that could get me hired on somewhere. From there, I would work my way up and become a hanger like my dad.

I had been sanding a split foyer that Friday, and when Wally picked me up, I was covered in white dust from head to toe like someone had dumped a bag of flour on me. I tossed my gear and water jug into the back of his truck and gave my clothes one last dust-off before climbing into the cab. On the drive back to the warehouse, Wally detoured to another jobsite where Milo and Angus were hanging rock.

"Stay here," Wally said, reaching into the glove box. "I just need to run their checks in."

That's the moment when it occurred to me that I hadn't seen Milo at the shop since that day he touched Mom's cheek. Pieces of a puzzle started falling into place; conversations and actions had been going on around me that had flown over my head, things like Wally hauling boxes of nails out to the jobsite or Angus coming by to pick up scaffolding without Milo in the truck.

Schenicker delivering Milo's paycheck was the missing piece. Wally was keeping Milo away from the shop, away from my mother, a scolding that must have galled Milo something awful. Wally never let on that he'd given Milo a talking-to. When Wally came back to the truck, we headed for home, and if he noticed the stupid grin on my face, he didn't mention it.

On the way home, we passed a hill with the start of six new apartment buildings. Wally pointed and said, "Did your mom tell you that we got the bid on those?"

"You did?" I said, excited at the prospect of earning some more big paychecks.

"We'll stock the first one in a couple weeks. Gonna be busy this summer."

"That's fine with me," I said.

"Truth is, I need to bring on some more help, and I'm thinkin' about givin' you a partner, someone to help with the scrappin' and sandin'. Your mom thinks I should hire your friend Thomas. What do you think?"

I have to admit, my first thought was over-the-top selfish. Hiring Thomas meant sharing my footage pay with him. I would have to train him, which would slow me down and dig further into my bottom line. On the other hand, it would be nice to have someone to talk to as the days dragged on—better than nice, actually. Those were my first thoughts.

My second thought was about Milo Halcomb. "What's Milo gonna say about it?" I asked.

Wally looked at me and something in the arch of his brow told me that he'd covered that ground already, either to himself or with my mother. "I didn't know Milo got a vote," he said.

"I'm not sayin' he gets a vote, but... you know how he is."

"Yeah, I know how he is, but I'm still the boss around here." I don't know if Wally said that to convince me or himself of that point, but he came across as less than confident.

I tried to picture Milo sitting on a jobsite somewhere, and in walks Thomas, the kid whose dad took over Cecil Halcomb's job—whose house I was supposed to vandalize. I wanted to have faith that Wally knew what he was doing; I mean, Milo had worked for Schenicker for a long time, but something rancid churned in my gut when I imagined Milo and Thomas anywhere near each other.

"So, what d'ya think?" Wally said. "Could ya use a partner?"

My thoughts returned to Thomas and me working together, eating lunches side by side, coming home covered in a layer of joint-cement dust, and those thoughts made me smile. "Yeah," I said. "I think a partner would be great."

CHAPTER

17

THE TASK OF ASKING THOMAS IF HE WANTED TO WORK FOR Wally fell to me, and I couldn't wait to tell him. Wally dropped me off at my house, so that I could take a quick shower and wash all that dust away. Then, clean as a whistle and wearing my usual jeans and a T-shirt, I headed over to tell Thomas the news. That's when I saw the sheriff's car parked across the road at the Elgins' house. Up on the porch, Charles Elgin and Sheriff Vaughan were face-to-face, talking. Mr. Elgin held a stack of papers, pointing at them, and the sheriff looked half interested at best, his arms folded across his chest.

For a split second, I thought maybe Jarvis had managed to relay his threat to the Elgins without my help, but the way Charles kept tapping his stack of papers with his index finger told me that it was something else.

Out back, Mom and Jenna pulled rocks and weeds out of Tilly's old garden, another project they took on that summer. I angled toward the garden so as not to interrupt Mr. Elgin and the sheriff, but I stayed far enough away that Mom didn't put me to work. When I asked Jenna if Thomas was around, she hollered back that I should check his room.

Vaughan and Mr. Elgin put their squabble on hold as I bounded up the porch steps and through the door, nodding to each as I passed. Once I was inside, they took up their discussion again, low and whispery, and I heard Charles say the name Lida Poe just as the door closed behind me. I fought against the urge to eavesdrop again, surrendering to my better angels and heading up the steps.

I found Thomas in his room inspecting his gear for our camping trip that weekend. We'd been planning the excursion for a couple weeks, and Thomas seemed barely able to contain his excitement. His sleeping bag and tent were both nylon and shiny, and probably weighed less together than my old sleeping bag alone, a bulky thing with a broken zipper that Mom bought at a rummage sale. Thomas also had a backpack—I mean a real hiker's backpack, with a frame made out of aluminum tubing and straps to tie on his tent and sleeping bag. I would be carrying my stuff in my dad's old army duffel bag.

"I got my Cub Scout mess kit," he said, pointing at the compact assemblage of pans and plates near his pillow. "And a canteen...and look, I have a knife with a compass in the handle—it's Dad's."

"We won't need a compass," I said, trying not to sound too jealous. "I never get lost in the woods."

"Well, I'm bringing it anyway, because if you get eaten by a bear or something, I'll need to find my way home."

"You don't need to worry 'bout bears down here," I said. "Mountain lions, on the other hand, they'll kill ya just for the fun of it."

Thomas looked at me with questioning eyes, a look that gave me a great deal of satisfaction.

With Thomas so excited about the camping trip, I'd almost forgotten why I came over. "Whatcha doing Monday?" I asked.

He rolled his eyes. "Probably digging rocks out of that stupid garden."

"You wanna come work with me?"

He cocked his head and narrowed his eyes as if looking for a prank. "Doing what?"

"Buildin' houses…you know, that drywall stuff I've been tellin' ya about. Schenicker and me were talkin' today; he wants to bring ya on."

"No kidding? Doing that sanding stuff?"

"Yeah. You'll pro'bly make between eighty and a hundred dollars a week."

"Hell yeah. I'll have to ask Mom, but yeah, that sounds perfect."

I suspected that Jenna knew all about my mother's plan to get Thomas hired at Schenicker's; hell, Jenna probably knew about it before Wally did.

"You're sure about this?" Thomas said. "You're not joking?"

"Swear to God."

"I'll go ask her."

Thomas charged out of his room and down the stairs, taking them two at a time. I had only made it halfway down the steps by the time he hit the back door. I had every intention to follow him out, but again I heard those voices coming from the porch, louder now and tinged with anger. From the steps, I could hear them well enough that it didn't feel sneaky—it wasn't my fault if their voices carried.

"I can't arrest someone on what *might've* happened. I need evidence," Vaughan said.

"But Cecil Halcomb was right there. He had to—"

"Again, you're veerin' into speculation. That's not how investigations work. I have to deal in facts—cold, hard facts. All that money found its way into Lida Poe's bank account, not Cecil Halcomb's."

"So you won't even question Cecil?"

"Mr. Elgin, we're done here." Sheriff Vaughan stepped into

view on the other side of the door, fixed his hat on his head, and made his way down the porch steps. "I'll be in touch if anything important pops up."

With that, Vaughan left. I scrambled back upstairs before Mr. Elgin came inside, ducking out of sight in time to hear him stomp through the front room and into his study, where he slammed the door shut.

CHAPTER

18

WITH THE NEXT MORNING CAME OUR CAMPING TRIP. THOMAS and I had laid everything out on his front porch, organizing it to be packed. We decided that he should carry the tent, his sleeping bag, and both canteens of water.

I stuffed my sleeping bag into Dad's duffel. On top of that, I carried our food—half a chicken for supper, and bacon and eggs for breakfast. I stuffed the food into plastic bags and put it in a water jug full of ice, which worked better than a cooler because it fit neatly into my duffel. I carried the mess kit. He carried the flashlight.

After we went through our checklist one last time, Thomas took a seat on the edge of the porch while I helped adjust his backpack. Then I slung the strap of my duffel bag over my shoulder and lifted it, bouncing it around until I got the balance just right. We were about to head across the road—the campsite I had chosen for our first excursion lay about five miles in the woods behind my house—when a pickup truck rounded the bend. It was Milo's truck, and I could see Angus behind the wheel, and Jarvis Halcomb riding shotgun.

The truck slowed and my chest went all hot and queasy. I wanted to warn Thomas, or run, or yell for Charles, but I did nothing; I just stood there in that flush of panic. Jarvis looked at me, and grinned. Then he reached his hand out the opened window, folded his fingers into the shape of a gun, and jerked his hand up twice—as if firing a bullet at each of us.

Angus picked up speed once they passed, and they drove down the road to Schenicker's.

"Drop your stuff," I said as my duffel fell to the grass.

"What was that about?"

I unbuckled Thomas's backpack and nearly shoved it off his shoulders. "I'll tell you later. Just come on."

Free of our gear, we ran down the side of the road, staying to the right where the curve kept us out of view of anyone down at Schenicker's. When the nose of Milo's truck came into view, we took to the woods, quietly slipping through the trees, tiptoeing until we could see them.

Angus had the pickup backed up to the shed, and he and Jarvis were loading scaffolding bucks into the bed.

"Who is that?" Thomas whispered.

"Jarvis Halcomb," I whispered back. "Cecil Halcomb's boy."

"Jarvis? My dad was just talking about him. Said Cecil had him on the payroll, but the kid never came to work. Been getting paid forty hours a week for almost a year without ever showing up."

"He didn't show up because he was in high school all year."

"Well, Dad fired him. Cecil got mad as hell and threatened to have everybody walk out and shut down the plant if Dad didn't hire him back." Then Thomas paused and asked, "Does he work for Schenicker now?"

"Naw, I don't think so. Milo does side jobs on weekends. Jarvis is pro'bly helpin' him out so he can make some money now that he's not gettin' that check from Ryke."

"So that pretend gun—I know why he aimed it at me. My dad fired him. But why you?"

"Well, I kinda kicked him in the side of the face on the last day of school."

"*You* kicked *him*?"

I didn't tell Thomas the full story. I couldn't without admitting my cowardice. When Jarvis ordered me to paint a sword on the side of Thomas's house, I ran away. I didn't say no. I didn't tell anyone. I just ran.

"It was as much an accident as anything," I said. "But I s'pect he's holdin' a grudge."

Angus and Jarvis had stopped loading the scaffolding and were leaning against the side of the truck talking. I strained to hear them, but they were too far away. I couldn't help but think that they'd seen us holding our camping gear. They would know we were headed to the woods. My imagination had a habit of running off, and try as I might, I couldn't help but picture them stalking through the woods trying to find us. It was a ridiculous notion given the miles of woods surrounding us in every direction, but that didn't stop me from thinking it.

A minute or two later they climbed back in the truck, with Jarvis at the wheel this time, and headed up the road. Thomas and I ducked behind the bushes as they passed us and then slipped out to the edge of the road to watch. As the pickup neared Thomas's house, it slowed, almost coming to a full stop in front of my duffel and Thomas's backpack. Jarvis looked around before hitting the gas and throwing up a cloud of dust.

We emerged from the woods and walked back to our gear, our footsteps a bit heavier than they had been before Milo's truck came around that bend. I couldn't shake the bad feeling I had, so before we loaded back up, I ran to my room, and grabbed my dad's old pocketknife. It wasn't as big as Thomas's knife, and it didn't have a compass in the handle—in fact it only had two blades—but it had once been my father's, and I kept the blade good and sharp.

Mom used to tell me that you could count on Dad having three things on him at all times: his wallet, his Timex watch, and his pocketknife. The wallet now lay in the bottom of a jewelry box on Mom's dresser, where it—his driver's license, pictures, insurance card, and even the twenty-three dollars that had been there on the day he fell—remained untouched. Dad's watch graced the nightstand next to his side of the bed. Mom kept it wound and set, its soft tick lulling her to sleep at night.

The knife, well, Mom gave that to me. She said Dad would have wanted me to have it. I kept it in my sock drawer, taking it out once in a while to sharpen it with a whetstone, something Hoke taught me. Of all the possessions Dad left behind when he fell, that knife meant more to me than all the others combined. I didn't carry it around on a daily basis, but if Thomas was bringing a knife on a camping trip, so was I.

CHAPTER

19

FOR OUR FIRST CAMPING TRIP, I WANTED TO TAKE THOMAS TO an old moonshiner's hideout that I'd stumbled upon when I was out exploring with Grover some years back. The camp had been cut into a patch of cedars so dense, you almost had to be a rabbit to get back there. The only reason I found it at all was because Grover caught the scent of a wild turkey on the other side of a thicket. He took off, and I followed him through a wall of thorns, cedars, and buck brush that opened into a patch of grass about the size of a double-wide mobile home, encircled by the wall of trees.

In the middle of the clearing stood an old rusted boiling vessel from a moonshiner's still, one that had been out of use for decades, with bullet holes shot through it. A giant oak tree rose up on the edge of the clearing, stretching high above the cedars, and I imagined a scene where one man brewed the moonshine while another sat in the branches of the oak tree, watching for trespassers or revenuers.

The hike to the moonshiner's camp took half the morning because we spent time sloshing through the creeks or looking for critters to chase. Grover didn't go into the woods with me nearly as much as he did when he was younger, but I liked to take him on my campouts, and I think Mom preferred that as well. He did a pretty good job of keeping up, despite the ease with which an errant scent could pull him off course.

Thomas seemed appropriately impressed when we entered the campsite, making a beeline for the old still, just as I had done when I first saw it.

"Wow! This is cool," he said. "Is it real?"

"It don't work or nothin', but it's real. Ain't you never seen a still before?" I acted like I'd been around bootleggers all my life, even though this was the one and only still I'd ever seen. "There's bullet holes in it. Probably had a gunfight with revenuers, or other moonshiners."

Thomas slipped off his backpack and poked a finger through the bullet holes. "You think anyone got killed?"

"Stands to reason."

"Maybe we'll see some old moonshiner's ghost tonight." Thomas had a hopeful grin on his face, so I grinned back, though in truth I wanted to kick him in the shin for putting that thought into my head.

Dropping my duffel, I sidled over to a hammock at the edge of the circle, a makeshift tangle of twine string that I'd constructed a year earlier. I eased myself gently into the creaking twine, unsure whether being out in the elements might have corrupted my work. It held. Then I lay back, put my hands behind my head, and waited for Thomas to notice me.

"Oh, cool!" he said, running over.

"No, no, no!" I waved my arms to no avail. He jumped on top of me, snapping the ties and sending us both tumbling to the ground, rolling in the direction of his momentum. Grover took this as a signal for playtime and jumped on top of us. I laughed so hard, I thought I was going to pee myself.

In time, we settled down and got to work setting up camp, pitching the tent, gathering firewood, and such. At one point,

Thomas rolled his sleeping bag out in the weeds and lay down on it, his fingers laced behind his head, his gaze fixed on the clouds. It looked so relaxing that I did the same thing.

"You know, brother," Thomas said, "this is the life."

Hearing Thomas call me *brother* warmed me up inside in a way that made me want to stay in that moment for a while. I know he probably didn't mean it the way I heard it, but still, it felt good.

We lay there in silence—a thing that didn't happen all that often with Thomas—and I remembered something that Hoke once said when we were sitting on his porch: You know you're truly comfortable with someone when you can sit with them in pure silence and not feel weird about it. Those weren't his exact words, but that was the gist of it.

Clouds floated above us, thin and wispy, no different from clouds I'd seen a thousand times before, but it felt different that day because I wasn't alone. Thomas saw those same clouds. He could hear the squeak of the squirrels in the trees behind us and the rustle of leaves as Grover sniffed around at the edge of the circle. The sights and sounds and smells had always been there, but something about having Thomas with me made everything seem better.

After a while, Thomas broke the silence by asking, "So, what's the deal with that Hoke guy?"

"What do ya mean?"

"Well...like, what happened to his arm?"

"He had some accident. I heard Sheriff Vaughan ask him 'bout it once."

"What kind of accident?"

"Don't know. Sheriff didn't say. He just asked Hoke 'bout an accident back in May of 'sixty-six. He also asked about a woman named Lida Poe."

"I know her," Thomas said with a tinge of excitement in his voice. "Dad's trying to find her so they can arrest her. Why would the sheriff ask Hoke about *her*?"

"She used to work for him, back when he lived up in Columbia."

"What'd he do there?"

"I don't know. He's never said."

"Doesn't that make you curious? I mean, he's got that bad arm...and Lida Poe used to work for him, and now she's on the run."

Thomas had no idea just how curious I was about Hoke, especially after that exchange he'd had with Sheriff Vaughan. I learned more in those few minutes than I'd known about Hoke Gardner after nearly a decade of living next door to him. But I was curious about Lida Poe, too.

"What exactly did Lida Poe do anyway?" I asked.

"She was stealing from Ryke, or at least she was in the middle of it. I don't know all the details, but I guess she made up a couple fake companies—had bank accounts for them and everything—then pretended to have Ryke buy stuff from those companies. Basically she was buying fake supplies from fake companies and pocketing the money. It's driving Dad crazy."

A rustle of leaves announced that Grover had decided to join us, coming out of the shade, his nose low to the ground. After circling around us a couple times, he stopped in front of Thomas, who sat up and gave Grover a good scratching on the top of his rump, something that caused Grover to wiggle back and forth with approval.

"You think dogs can see ghosts?" Thomas asked—and there we were, back on that subject again.

"What's the deal with you and ghosts?"

"I think it'd be cool to see one, that's all. Besides, a campsite like this would be better if it was haunted."

"You want ghosts? There's a haunted church not too far from here."

"Really? Where?"

I stood up. "Come on, I'll show ya."

An enormous cedar tree rose up at the edge of the circle, higher than the others, and it had a top that had been broken off when it was younger, giving it roughly the same outline as one of those Japanese pagodas. We scrambled up its spine, pulling ourselves onto the flat top where sturdy shoots fanned out like spokes on a wheel, giving it a nestlike feel.

"That's the Quaker church," I said, pointing to a steeple off in the distance. "They say it's haunted."

"You have Quakers down here?"

"I'm not sure if they were actual Quakers—they might be Mennonites or somethin' like that—but they had a small colony out there. A long time ago, a flood washed away the bridge that connected 'em with the rest of the world. They all just kinda moved on after that."

"And it's haunted?"

"People say there's an escaped convict died there. Others say that one of the Quakers killed another one, and the dead guy's ghost haunts the church."

"I thought Quakers were pacifists."

"We just call 'em Quakers. No one knows for sure what they were."

"Maybe they were a cult."

"Like I said—"

"We should go there."

"Um...I'm not sure. It's a long ways and—"

"You're not afraid of ghosts, are you?"

"No, but they have a fence around it and a ton of No Trespassing signs."

"Look, if you're scared, we don't have to go. It's okay."

"I ain't scared," I said, although my voice sounded unconvincing even to my own ears.

"Sure you're not."

I needed to turn the tables and that's when I thought of a way out. "I'll tell you what. I'll go there if you jump out of this tree."

Thomas looked at me like I was crazy.

"I'm serious. I've done it before. I call it tree jumping. You do that and I'll take you to that church come morning."

"Tree jumping? Is that anything like snipe hunting?"

"All you gotta do is stretch out flat on your backside and slide down the branches. The needles will slow you down."

"I'll tell you what. You do it first—just to prove that you aren't trying to get me killed."

I had tree jumped a few times in my life—the kind of thing you do when you're the only kid around and all you have is a tree to play with—but I'd never jumped from such a height. I leaned out to gauge my slide, and the tree suddenly seemed twice as tall as it did from the ground. Had I been alone, I would have chickened out.

"You going to jump? Or just sit there?" Thomas chided.

"You're welcome to give 'er a go if ya want."

"Just so you know, I can tie a tourniquet . . . in case you need one."

"You're not helpin'."

"Not trying to."

I gritted my teeth and rose up on shaky legs until I was near standing. *Three . . . two . . . one!* I stepped out, feetfirst, falling into the soft needles, the cedar branches bending under my weight. I came down with my arms and legs splayed out to the side, grabbing at the boughs with my hands as I slid. I kept my eyes mostly closed, relying on touch. The more I spread out my arms and legs, the slower I fell. I had this.

As I neared the bottom I could feel the limbs growing thicker and more rigid, so I put on the brakes, grabbing a decent-size bough and bringing my body to an elegant stop. When I opened my eyes I found myself six feet off the ground.

"Yeeeeha!" I whooped, sliding out of the tree. "That was...cool!"

Up at the top, Thomas wore an expression that I took to say: *I can't believe you actually did that.* So I smiled big and said, "Your turn."

He hesitated, pursed his lips, and gave a look down to the ground, the same way I had.

"All ya gotta do is keep your arms and legs out, and the tree will stop ya."

"So will the ground."

"I'm waitin'," I hollered up.

"Don't rush me."

"This'll be something you can tell your grandkids."

"If I live that long." Then more quietly, he said, "I can't believe I'm going to do this."

He slowly rose to a crouch on those top branches, swung his arms a few times in practice, and then leapt into the tree, the needles thrashing at his arms as he toppled down. And like me, within a few feet from the bottom, he stopped.

"Whoohoo!" he squealed. "That was intense!"

He slid out of the tree and turned to climb back up—with me on his heels. We took turns jumping out of that tree for a couple hours, until our stomachs called on us to start a fire and cook up some supper.

CHAPTER

20

I HAD A HARD TIME GETTING TO SLEEP THAT NIGHT, SOMETHING that had never happened out in the woods before. I had almost dozed off a few times when a crack of a twig or the rustle of leaves would pull me back to the world. It wasn't nothing more than critters moving around beyond the tree line, but in my head, I imagined Jarvis Halcomb tiptoeing through the woods, drawn to us by the smell of old campfire smoke. With each new sound, I popped my eyes open and perked up my ears — waited — then reassured myself that there was no way that Jarvis could find us. Still, with the next snap of a twig I would wake up again.

In the morning, we made a breakfast of bacon and eggs, the bacon cooked first, and the eggs fried in so much bacon grease that the yolks disappeared beneath the bubbling fat. Man, that tasted good.

We burned our trash and then used the melted ice from the water jug to douse the fire. Breaking camp, we stored our gear beneath that cedar tree that we'd jumped out of and headed off to the Quaker church.

The hike took us down through two valleys, and at the top of the second ridge, the woods opened up into what had probably once been an alfalfa field, now overrun with weeds and scrub. The field sloped gently down and then rose again, the church, with its swayback roof line, standing on a knoll on the opposite side.

Between us and the field stretched a shiny barbed-wire fence made of four lines of wire spaced about a foot apart. Unlike all the other fences that we had crossed on our journey, this one still wore its zinc coating, which meant that it wasn't all that old. If the Quakers left the area after a flood in the fifties, who put up that fence?

Along the fence hung signs that read: NO TRESPASSING and KEEP OUT. Don't get me wrong, I had no problems crossing fences, even ones with No Trespassing signs on them—hell, we crossed a couple of those on the walk to the moonshiner's camp   but something about this fence gave me the willies. I don't know if it was the newness of the wire, or the ghost stories, or both, but I had never crossed this particular fence before.

We paused near one of the Keep Out signs, and I assumed we were going to discuss the advisability of pressing on, but Thomas stepped back, took a run, and, using a fence post for leverage, jumped the fence clean, turning afterward with a grin and outstretched arms as though waiting for my applause. "High jump—chump!" he said.

"Wait a second," I said.

I called Grover and knelt down to pet his long ears. "You gotta stay here, boy. Don't try crawlin' through there. Understand?" Of course he didn't, but it made me feel better that we talked. Then I climbed the fence, one strand at a time, and crossed over.

Grover whined as Thomas and I made our way into the field, my head swiveling back a few times to make sure that he didn't try to slide through the barbed wire. He didn't. Instead, he put his nose to the ground and paced back and forth, trying to pick up a scent that might lead him to an opening.

The slope of the field made for an easy walk, and as we neared the bottom of the trough we came upon three wooden posts standing side by side about ten feet apart. As we got closer, I saw that the posts held cardboard targets, hung on nails; two of the targets showed the silhouette of a man's torso, and the third was a standard bull's-eye. Each of the targets had been riddled with bullet holes. A few yards up from the posts we found a plank propped up on a couple buckets, the ground beneath littered with broken bottles and beer cans shot through several times over.

"Target practice," I said, picking up one of the cans.

Thomas ran up the slope to a row of sandbags, where he paused for a moment before reaching down and raking up a handful of something at his feet. He held his hand out to me, opened his fingers, and let the small objects fall to the ground, clinking as they landed. "Bullet casings," he said. "Hundreds of them."

I joined him behind the row of sandbags where brass casings littered the ground. "We should pro'bly go," I said.

"Why?"

"I got a bad feelin' 'bout this."

"Let's just peek inside the church. We came all this way."

I gave a sharp listen for any sound of movement, but detected nothing. "Okay, but just for a second. Come on."

From up close, the church looked worse than it did from a distance, the paint mostly peeled away, the wood around its base rotted thin. Someone had nailed ragged plastic sheathing over the tall holes where stained-glass windows once hung.

Between the parking lot and the front door, someone had arranged three picnic tables in a semicircle around a fire pit, which smelled of animal fat and burnt oak. When I squatted next to it, I saw a thin trail of smoke, barely visible, curling from beneath one of the bigger logs. I turned it over to find a smoldering spark breathing at the center of the log—the final gasp of a fire that had burned there the night before.

"Someone was here last night," I said.

We both paused to listen, straining to hear any sound that might tell us that we weren't alone. Thomas kept his eyes on the front door of the church, but I looked down the long driveway toward the blacktop, expecting to hear a truck engine. Silence. No vehicles, no voices, no footsteps, not a sound—but damn it all if I didn't feel like someone was watching us. Maybe it was that Quaker ghost they all talked about, or maybe it was just my imagination.

"There's nobody here now, though," Thomas said, and I couldn't tell if he meant that as a statement or a question. After a few seconds of silence, he said, "Come on," and walked up to the door, carefully thumbing the latch and easing it open. He stepped inside, and I followed.

Right away, I saw a large Confederate flag hanging on the wall behind where the church's altar had once been. Thomas saw it too and looked at me but kept going.

The crunch of glass—broken beer bottles—echoed off the walls as we crept forward. Sunlight, poking down from a dozen holes in the roof, spiked through the air in crisp shafts that gave life to a swirl of dust motes. The place smelled of rotting wood and mold. Twelve rows of pews told the story of a small congregation. Sparse walls—no fancy molding like they had in the Catholic church—suggested that the worshippers who once prayed here had been in search of Jesus the shepherd, not Jesus the king.

Up in the front, a door to the right opened into a small vestry, the backstage area where the minister would have hung out before the start of the service. The room reminded me of the cloakroom in my grade school back in Dry Creek, long and narrow, barely wide enough for two people to pass without bumping shoulders. The roof inside the vestry seemed devoid of holes, and the room was packed with stuff—stored there to keep it dry, I supposed. On hooks sticking out of the wall, someone had hung a spare Confederate flag next to an American flag. On the floor below, a stack of those targets leaned against the wall.

Next to that, I saw a picture frame upside down on the floor. I picked it up and examined the photograph behind the glass: two rows of men, all wearing camouflage from head to toe, black bandanas covering their faces. The eleven men in the back row stood shoulder to shoulder, guns held across their chests, mostly rifles, but a couple shotguns. The men in the front knelt on one knee, their guns resting on their thighs. One man on the end sat cross-legged, his gun, a pistol, hanging lazily off his knee. He was the only one not facing the camera.

I scrutinized the men in the picture, looking for someone familiar—Jarvis or Milo—but the photo had been taken from such a distance, and was so out of focus, that they all looked alike. But then I came to the guy on the end, the one sitting cross-legged, something in the slump of his shoulders tripped a memory. Was that Angus?

Thomas picked up a stack of papers—flyers with a flaming sword in the middle, and *CORPS* written in bold letters across the top. It stopped my breath. On one side of the sword were the words *TAKE BACK YOUR COUNTRY!* On the other side it read: *YOUR BIRTHRIGHT! YOUR FIGHT!*

"We gotta get outta here," I whispered.

Then, a sound from the nave of the church sent my heart up into my throat. I put my hand on Thomas's chest to hold him still, and we listened. The sound came again, thin and muted like the scratch of glass underfoot. It came from a place between us and the only exit. We waited, and after a few moments of holding our breath, heard it a third time.

I put the picture down and Thomas laid the flyers on the

floor—staying absolutely silent. I listened, expecting the sound to come again, closer this time, but the nave remained quiet. I lifted a small flagpole from its resting place in the corner—eight feet long with a plastic point on the end—not much of a weapon, but better than nothing. Thomas picked up a chair. We waited—and listened—still nothing.

Whoever was out there either knew that we were hiding in the vestry and meant to sneak up on us, or he didn't know and was about to get the shock of his life. Our best course of action was to charge him, catch him off guard, gain the upper hand, and maybe make it to the front door.

I nodded toward the nave. Thomas seemed to understand my strategy, because he nodded back. Then I whispered, "Three, two, one."

We charged into the church, yelling like banshees, my pole held out in front of me, Thomas's chair high over his head. But when we entered the nave, no one was there. I breathed slowly, the air heavy in my throat.

Thomas noticed it first: a squirrel standing in the middle of the aisle, staring at us, its eyes as big as I've ever seen a squirrel's eyes get. The squirrel looked at us for a second and then scurried through a hole in the wall and disappeared.

With my heart once again in my chest where it belonged, we dropped our weapons and bolted out the door, not stopping until we got back to the fence.

"What is this place?" Thomas asked between inhales.

I put my hands on my knees and coughed and heaved, trying to catch my breath. "I think...it's the headquarters...of the CORPS."

"The CORPS?"

"Crusaders Of Racial Purity and Strength. It's a white supremacy group. This must be where they get together."

I climbed the fence, with Thomas right behind me. Once on the other side, we backed into the woods and sat down to rest.

"That's messed up," Thomas said. "And all those bullets, it's like they're practicing for a war or something."

"I'm sorry," I said.

"Why are you sorry?"

Truth be told, I wasn't sure why I said that; I just felt that it needed saying. "We should get goin'. Someone might come up the road any minute."

I looked up and down the fence line for Grover and didn't see him. "Grover!" I called out. Listened—but heard nothing. I called again, and a third time, and still nothing. So we tramped along the fence in the direction he'd been walking the last time I saw him—away from the church. Thomas kept looking over his shoulder at the posts that held those human-shaped targets peppered with bullet holes. After walking at least two hundred yards, I started to get worried. Grover had never been the most obedient dog, but he usually came after a while.

I stopped and held up my hand to signal Thomas to be quiet. I didn't hear anything at first, and was about to start walking again when a slight whine caught my ear—definitely Grover. We backtracked a little and stopped again, and heard it again. It came from deeper in the woods. I followed the sound to a clearing about a hundred feet away from the fence, where I found Grover with his nose down in the dirt.

I called him, but he ignored me—as he was apt to do when he'd locked onto a scent. He pawed at the ground, digging, even though he'd never been much of a digger. I walked to him, calling his name, my tone growing more irritated with each step. He continued to paw at the ground beneath a dead log.

I thought that maybe he'd trapped a small varmint under there, like a rabbit or a skunk, so I ran up to Grover and pulled him back by the collar. He had displaced about three gallons of dirt from underneath the log, and tugged against me to get back to his hole.

"Dammit, Grover, cut it out!" I pulled harder and this time got him away from the hole. I took my belt off and looped it through his collar, making a leash.

"Boady?" Thomas said, his voice coming across a tad shaky.

"I got him," I said.

"Boady!" he said again, insistent this time. I looked at Thomas, who stared down at the hole. Then he pointed. "Boady, look!"

Hugging Grover between my thighs to keep him still, I eased closer to get a look at what Thomas pointed at. When I got to the hole and saw it—the gnarled contour of a human hand.

CHAPTER

21

I HAD NEVER SEEN A DEAD HAND BEFORE. GRAY AND THIN, THE fingers curled, the skin drawn in tight around the bones as though all the fluid had been siphoned away. The sleeve of a pink sweater lay loose against the wrist. Stepping back to widen my view, the outline of the grave became obvious.

I dragged Grover to a nearby tree, wrapped my belt twice around a low branch, and secured it by poking a nub up through one of my buckle holes. When I let go of Grover, he gave a tug to try to get back to the hole but felt the belt and collar tighten and became still.

Thomas couldn't seem to take his eyes off the hand—a woman's hand, the bones being far too small to belong to a man. And the sweater was pink—also a woman's—and still somewhat intact, which meant that the body hadn't been there for all that long. It didn't take much thought to come up with an idea of who lay in that hole.

I turned my gaze to the path that Thomas and I had taken from the fence, wondering if I could see any signs of how she came to be in that clearing and in that grave. All those years of watching Daniel Boone on TV, and playing at it alone in the woods—now I had a chance to make it count. I scanned the scrub looking for signs that Lida Poe had been dragged into that clearing. I didn't see it at first—but then I did. It looked like any other sapling trying to make a go of it in that rocky terrain, but something about it called out to me.

"Look at that," I said, barely above a whisper.

I took careful steps up to the knee-high sapling and studied it as though it were an entire book waiting to be read. The top third had been broken over, with half-formed buds dry and dead above the break and leaves thriving below.

"They dragged her through here," I said, pointing at the dead leaf buds on top. "These leaves would've been bloomin' 'bout the time Lida Poe went missin'. They died cuz someone broke the stalk. See? These lower leaves bloomed, but the dead 'uns on top ain't much older'n a couple weeks."

I ran a finger along the broken stalk. "The break points at the grave. Chances are, it broke as they dragged her through."

"Wow," Thomas whispered.

I stood and walked slowly toward the fence, looking for more signs. I saw some broken twigs that may or may not have been disturbed by the gravedigger. But then, near the fence I saw a stone not much bigger than a persimmon, which had been kicked out of its hole. I pictured a man walking backwards from the fence, dragging a dead body. It might have been his heel or part of Lida Poe that dislodged that stone—I had no way of knowing, but it too shouted out to me, and I showed it to Thomas.

"How'd you see that?"

I shrugged to hide my pride. "This must be where he pulled her over the fence." Thomas ran his hand along the wire, inspecting it, his eyes up close, probably looking for strands of yarn caught in the barbs. I turned my attention to the field beyond.

If I hadn't been looking for them, I would never have seen the tire tracks—thin, barely visible weeds that had been broken under a set of tires and hadn't fully filled back in. They started at the fence and disappeared in the direction of the church. And about twenty yards down the path, I spotted a small section where the tracks grew more distinct.

Pieces of a puzzle were magically falling together in front of me. I should have felt somber, having just found a dead body, but I couldn't help getting excited. Also, Thomas seemed impressed, and that spurred me on.

I crossed over the fence with Thomas right behind me, and we walked to where the slope of the hill caused the vehicle to spin to get up to the fence. "Look at this!" I knelt down beside one of the tracks. The vehicle had passed through mud on its way back to the church, leaving a print of the tire's tread. We'd had a pretty dry spring, and what rain we'd gotten hadn't been enough to wash away the impression.

"I think it was a pickup," I said, pointing at the width of the tire. "Either that, or a car with snow tires, but I'm bettin' a pickup. And there's a chunk of tread missing." I touched a small section of the track where the tread pattern spread out to form a knob about four inches around. The pattern repeated a few feet down, which meant that it wasn't a fluke.

"We need to get the sheriff out here," Thomas said.

I was a little too caught up in playing Daniel Boone to agree right away, but Thomas was right. "I know a shortcut home," I said. "We'll leave our gear at the camp and come back for it later."

We walked back to Grover, being careful not to disturb the signs we'd seen, unhooked him, and started our run back to Frog Hollow.

Despite taking half a day to walk from home out to the moonshiner's camp, and another hour or so to get to the church, we made it back to Frog Hollow Road in a little over two hours, jogging most of the way and stopping only when we needed to catch our breath or call Grover. We crawled up out of the woods beat and breathless, our shirts dirty from sliding down hills and our jeans and shoes soaked from running in creeks.

We stopped at my house first, but Mom wasn't home. Across the road, we found her and Jenna in the garden and told them what we'd found, repeating it again for Charles who called the sheriff.

Vaughan said that he'd meet us on the blacktop out in front of the Quaker church and not to go down to the church itself. Then we all climbed into Charles's Chrysler Imperial and headed out, Mom riding up front to give directions.

Vaughan kept us waiting a good half hour, Thomas and I sitting on the trunk of the car while the adults stayed in the air-conditioning. What Vaughan had on his plate more pressing than a dead body—well, who could say. I thought maybe the sheriff took his time because the woman was already dead and wasn't going anywhere. I rethought that when Vaughan arrived and the first words out of his mouth were "By God, this had better not be a wild-goose chase."

That got under my skin, and I said, "It ain't no wild-goose chase. It's Lida Poe. She's buried up yonder."

Vaughan stopped in his tracks and wiped face sweat onto his sleeve. "Lida Poe? What makes ya think it's Lida Poe?"

"Who else could it be?" I said.

He looked at the five of us and then pointed at me. "You take me back there. The rest of y'all stay put."

I climbed into his squad car and we drove down the gravel drive to the church, parking nose-in by the fire pit. I took the sheriff around back and before walking through the field, I pointed at the thin remnant of broken weeds where the pickup had driven between the church and the fence.

"See those tracks?" I said. "They head up to the fence there. See it?"

Vaughan squinted. "I don't see no tracks."

"Look up the hill. See 'em?"

"Boy, just show me this body you think you found."

I marched into the weeds, keeping to the side of the tracks—the ones that Vaughan couldn't see—and as we neared the tread print, I pointed again. "See 'em now?"

"Well, there's somethin' there, I'll give you that."

"Look here." I stepped next to the tire print. "That's the truck that hauled her up here. There's a mark in the tread. And there's some signs in the woods that—"

"Son, are you gonna show me a body or not? I'm gettin' a mite tired of all this jabberin'."

His words knocked the wind from me. I'd done all that work, figuring stuff out, finding clues, and he didn't give a lick about it. I climbed over the fence in silence and headed back to the grave, not waiting on Sheriff Vaughan to get his lard ass over the barbed wire. He must have had a tough time of it, because I waited for quite a spell before I heard him call. "Where'd you go, boy?"

"I'm back here," I said. "With Lida Poe."

When he stumbled through that last patch of woods and into the clearing, I pointed at her grave and said nothing.

Vaughan knelt down, looked at the hand, and then said, "Okay, boy, I'll take it from here. Go on home now."

Go on home? No *Attaboy?* No *Good job?* We'd found Lida Poe; we'd worn ourselves ragged running home to get Sheriff Vaughan out here; we'd risked our lives at the Quaker church; and all we got for our troubles was *Go on home now?* I waited in some weird funk, thinking that there had to be more to it than that. When Vaughan saw me lingering he yelled, "Go on now—git!"

When I walked out of those woods, the anger in my chest was just a couple degrees shy of boiling.

CHAPTER

22

M OM AND THE ELGINS HAD PUT THEIR HEADS TOGETHER while I was with Sheriff Vaughan, and they decided that Thomas and I should go collect our camping gear from the woods and ride back to Frog Hollow with them. Although something about getting driven home from a camping trip seemed like surrender to me, under the circumstances, I welcomed the lift.

On the march to the moonshiner's camp, it occurred to me that Thomas and I were going to be famous. We'd found Lida Poe. People would be talking about us on the radio and in the newspaper. By the time school started in the fall, every kid in Caulfield County would know who Boady Sanden and Thomas Elgin were. I confess, I liked the idea of being more than just another shadow in the corner, even if that notoriety came at the expense of a dead woman.

We made good time so that our parents didn't have to wait too long, and when we emerged from the woods the sun clung to that corner of the sky where afternoon shifted to evening. A hundred yards down the fence line, near the burial site, the place buzzed with activity. Three squad cars lined the fence, and next to them was an old ambulance. The barbed wire had been cut and a couple deputies moved through the woods holding bags and staring at the ground; looking for clues, I reckoned.

Thomas and I crossed over into the field, but rather than head toward the church and the highway, I waved for Thomas to follow me toward the squad cars. We stopped at the spot where we'd seen the tire prints. They were gone. Every car parked on that hill must have taken the same path, obliterating the tread marks.

"That dumb sonofabitch," I muttered.

"They ran right over it," Thomas said.

I shook my head in disgust, dropped my duffel, and ran into the woods with at least one deputy shouting at me to stop. Thomas, with his bulky backpack strapped to his torso, stayed behind. When I came to the clearing, I had a mind to give Vaughan what-for, but Vaughan wasn't there. Two deputies knelt at the grave, and a man in a white shirt and black tie stood over the body as though supervising the exhumation.

Beneath the men laid what remained of Lida Poe's face: hollowed eyes, sunken cheeks, her gray skin stretched tight, pulling her mouth open, her teeth protruding from her jaw bone, no gums, no lips. And there, between her eyes, I saw a bullet hole, small and round and perfectly centered. It looked so clean and well placed that a person would have had to touch the muzzle of the gun to her skin before pulling the trigger. I looked away, but it was too late. I had already seen more than I wanted.

"Son, you shouldn't be here," one of them said.

With Vaughan not around, I couldn't have agreed more. I walked back out of the woods, the image of Lida Poe flashing on the back of my eyelids. I didn't tell Thomas what I saw, thinking that maybe the image might go away if I didn't dwell on it, but it kept me company as Thomas and I trudged back toward the highway. Every time I blinked, it seemed to burrow its way deeper into my brain. I tried to conjure up the picture of Lida Poe that I'd seen in the newspaper, pretty and smiling. That's the way I wanted to remember her, but memories aren't the kind of things that you can pick and choose for yourself.

We found Sheriff Vaughan out at the highway, talking to Mr. Elgin. A dozen yards beyond them, Mom and Jenna stood beside each other next to the car. The men looked to be in a heated conversation, so Thomas and I held up to listen.

"What do you mean, you don't have enough?" Charles said. "If Lida Poe's dead, that shoots your theory that you'll find her in Arkansas with the money. Someone had to help her—and that person probably killed her."

"Mr. Elgin, we're not even sure that is Lida Poe up there."

"How many missing women do you have to choose from?"

"I'm just saying, there's a proper way to do an investigation. You need to be patient."

I couldn't help but jump in. "So is it a proper investigation to let your deputies drive over the evidence? They destroyed the tire tracks."

Vaughan's cheeks turned red and he looked hard at me. "Boy, you ain't got no daddy to teach you any better, so I'll let that one slide. But if you ever talk to me like that again, I'll burn your britches."

"Sheriff!" Jenna snapped. "Who do you think—"

"And that goes for all y'all!" Vaughan hollered loud enough to shut Jenna down. "I want you off my crime scene—now—or I'll arrest ya for interferin' with an investigation." With that, Vaughan turned and stomped back down the gravel toward the church.

My mom came up to me and gave me a hug, hesitant and short-lived but a hug nonetheless. It was the last thing I'd expected.

In the midst of all the outrage that roiled in my gut, I found myself overwhelmed, not by having found a dead body or getting chewed out by the sheriff of Caulfield County, but by the feel of my mother's arms around me—even if only for a second or two.

I couldn't remember her ever hugging me before. I mean, there must have been a time, back before the sadness took her away, but still, I had no recollection of such a time. And despite the clumsiness of her effort—being out of practice as she was—the hug felt really nice.

"You okay?" she asked.

"Yeah . . . I'm fine."

We piled into the Imperial—Thomas, Mom, and me in the back seat, Thomas's parents up front, where Charles fumed over his conversation with Sheriff Vaughan.

"I don't know what I have to do to get that clown to question Cecil Halcomb," he said. "It's as if he's protecting the man."

Jenna said, "Maybe there're things going on behind the scenes that the sheriff can't talk about. It'll all come out in the wash."

"We're supposed to be coordinating our efforts. I've given him everything, but he treats me like a goddamned mushroom."

"There's only so much you can do," Jenna said.

"I'll tell you what I can do," Charles said. "I can fire Cecil Halcomb. Just demoting him wasn't enough. He's been undermining me at every turn. His spies keep tabs on everything I do. Well, I'm done with that crap. As soon as I get home, I'm calling him and firing his—" Mr. Elgin glanced at us through the rearview mirror as he reconsidered his word choice. "Cecil Halcomb is gone."

"Are you sure that's the way to go?" Jenna asked.

"I was hoping to wait until I talked to that handwriting expert, but to hell with that. Minneapolis said it's my call, and . . . well, I've made my decision."

CHAPTER

23

I DIDN'T HEAR MY NAME ON THE RADIO THE NEXT DAY LIKE I thought I would.

I remember there being a sense of unease in the air that next morning, something that a smarter kid might have understood, but not me—the forced smile on Jenna's face as she watched Thomas hop down the steps for his first day at work, the conversations between Mom and Wally that stopped when Thomas and I walked in. It was as if they could sense the first touches of a storm, despite the calm of a bright blue sky.

Thomas came to his first day of work carrying a canteen instead of a water jug and his lunch wrapped in a paper bag. I carried the beat-up black lunch box that used to belong to my dad, the kind that opened in half with my sandwiches in the bottom and a Thermos in the top. A man's lunch pail—although my Thermos still held Kool-Aid. After a quick run-through of what we'd be doing that day, we loaded our gear into Wally's pickup and set out for our first job.

There's a certain logistical juggle that goes with hiring people who don't have driver's licenses, and I always appreciated how Wally Schenicker went out of his way to move me around and keep me working. I'd like to believe all that running came out of the goodness of Wally's heart—and maybe it did—but part of me always suspected that guilt played a role in it. You see, Wally had been on that scaffolding with my father the day he fell.

They were repairing the ceiling at some church, and Dad, who was looking up, concentrating on his work, simply stepped into the air. The scaffolding had been four bucks high, which meant a drop of only twenty feet, a fall that should have been survivable had he not landed on a sawhorse. It was Wally who took him to the hospital. By all accounts, Wally had done nothing wrong, yet I sometimes got the feeling that he treated my mom and me as though he sought our forgiveness.

Our first job was a basement that needed to be sanded—nice and small, perfect for teaching Thomas the ropes. After that, we had a house to scrap out about two miles away, an easy trek on foot. At the second job we were to stack the scraps into piles and wait for Wally to drive out in the one-ton. He would drop off joint cement and then help load the scraps onto the truck.

On the drive out, Wally went over the plan with us a second time, as though something about the arrangement didn't sit well with him—and I think I knew what it was. Milo and Angus weren't quite finished hanging the house that we were going to be scrapping out that afternoon. But Wally assured us—repeatedly—that they'd be out of there by lunch.

When he'd finished drumming the instructions into our heads, I took advantage of the silence to turn on the radio. I normally preferred the FM rock stations, but that morning I tuned in to talk radio. Jessup had a station that put on a morning program called *Country Clatter*, where people called in to discuss any subject on their minds.

I was sure that news of us finding Lida Poe's body would be the hot topic of the day—but I was wrong. We caught the tail end of a news report that said a body, believed to be the missing Lida Poe, had been found by two hikers—*two hikers*, no names. After the news, the guy returned to his callers, who all wanted to talk about Cecil Halcomb getting fired.

"I've known Cecil Halcomb since grade school," one caller said. "That man's as honest as the day is long. Whatever they said he's done is a lie. I can guarantee you that."

The next caller, a woman with a middle-aged voice, took it a step further. "I'm tellin' you, I'm just sick about this. Cecil's done more for this town, bringin' jobs and all, it's a cryin' shame the way they're treatin' him."

The third caller, another guy, said, "I'll tell you what—there's a price to pay when ya come in from outta town and start steppin' on the local folks like they was trash. Them's our jobs they're messin' with. This is our town and—"

Wally clicked the radio off. "Idiots," he muttered. "Cecil's got half the town thinkin' he walks on water just cuz he signed their paychecks. Nothin' but a bunch of damned idiots. Don't pay 'em no mind."

The rest of the ride went by in silence until we passed a house under construction with Milo's pickup truck parked in the dirt yard. "That's the house that needs scrapping," Wally said, again making a point to mention that Milo and Angus would be gone before we got there.

He continued up the gravel road, heading north for a mile or so before crossing a rickety bridge made of wood ties on an iron frame. Once on the other side of the creek, we turned back south again, cresting a hill and pulling in to an old farmhouse—our first job.

The basement was smaller than I expected, a job I could have done by myself in half a day, yet somehow, even with Thomas's help, it took us all the way till noon. I had no idea how time-consuming it could be to train someone. It seemed like I spent more time watching Thomas and correcting his technique than I did sanding my own walls. I remembered how patient Wally had been when he taught me, and I did my best to be that way with Thomas. In the end, I think Thomas probably picked it up faster than I did.

We ate our lunches in that basement, leaning against the dusty walls that we had just made smooth. Thomas was back to his usual self, prattling on about who knows what all—and of course there had to be a girl in every story. When we finished, we left our tools at the remodel—to be picked up once Wally showed up with the truck—and set out on foot for our next job.

We had a good half mile to walk before we'd see the creek and another half mile to the bridge. The sky had turned dark while we were sanding that basement, and rain colored the horizon behind us a hazy shade of gray. Thomas suggested that we ford the creek when we got to it rather than walk the extra distance down to the bridge. I thought that sounded like a pretty good idea.

As we crested the hill—the creek visible just on the other side of an old bean field—I heard the low rumble of a vehicle groaning its way up the road behind us, the engine misfiring on one of its cylinders. In the distance, an old truck kicked up dust as it sputtered to gain speed.

We kept walking, Thomas in front of me, his eyes on the creek. The truck moved at a pretty good clip, the roar of its bad exhaust making it sound twice as big as it was. When the noise finally caught Thomas's attention, he turned to look, stopping in the road, his eyebrows raised in a question. Without saying anything, I reached out and nudged Thomas to the side of the road. The truck, only a hundred yards behind us, picked up speed.

Thomas stepped into the weeds, muttering something like "What the hell's his problem," although I couldn't really hear him over the noise. The driver had more than enough room to go around us but hugged our side of the road.

I joined Thomas in the weeds, turning to face the truck, my middle finger poised to let the asshole know that I didn't appreciate his recklessness. That's when I noticed something poking out of the passenger window—a stick. The truck swerved slightly in the loose gravel but regained its traction. The stick—a broom handle—emerged farther out the window, held tightly by a gloved hand.

My thoughts turned to sap. I knew what was about to happen, but I just stood there, my feet growing roots. The passenger moved up through the open window so that he sat in the opening, holding on to the roof of the truck with one hand and raising the broomstick high over his head with the other. On his face he wore a white Casper the Ghost mask.

The sight of that mask shot a cold surge of terror through me. I tried to yell, but I couldn't. The passenger began his downswing.

I felt Thomas grab my collar and yank me hard toward the ground.

I raised my left arm to block the broom handle. At that same moment, the truck caught the bump of gravel that lined the road, sending it lurching for the ditch. The passenger rocked in his tenuous perch, causing the broomstick to glance off my forearm with only a fraction of the intended force. A jolt of pain shot up my arm and through my body as I toppled backwards onto Thomas.

The driver, also wearing a Casper mask, his knuckles wrapped tightly around the steering wheel, fought to right the truck. It fishtailed and then straightened, tearing down the road toward the bridge.

"Son of a bitch!" I yelled. And just like that, my fear drained away. I jumped up and ran across the field toward the creek.

The truck rumbled toward the bridge, slowing as it crossed.

Not paying attention to my own feet, I tripped on a clod of dirt, falling headfirst into the field, skidding on my chest.

The truck bounced off the bridge, hitting a rut as it turned back south, heading in my direction. As I pushed myself up out of the dirt, a rock crossed my palm. White with glassy striations painting its surface, it looked kind of like a baseball and fit in my hand like one as well. I picked it up and began running again.

I felt no fear, no doubt, and no pain as I charged across the field, the furrows twisting and turning my ankles, but not slowing me down. I cradled the rock and ran.

Sixty yards to the creek and closing.

My heart pounded against my ribs.

Fifty yards.

My lungs heaved to take in more air.

Forty.

Blood hammered in my ears.

Thirty.

Gritted teeth. Thighs burning.

Twenty.

The passenger saw me.

Ten.

We were coming together like a wishbone, the truck barreling down the chalky road, separated from me by the creek. I launched into the air, my throwing arm cocked back behind my head. Below me, the water churned dark and calm in a big pool. As soon as I became airborne I heaved the stone with my last ounce of energy and watched it sail high, its trajectory guided by will and luck.

The passenger's face rose as he followed the arc of the rock, his eyes bulging behind the mask. He dove to the floor as it smashed through the windshield, the glass exploding into a million cracks and fissures.

I slammed into the creek bank, held on just long enough to see the rock smash the windshield, and then I fell backwards into the water.

I could still hear the truck, its engine revving, its gears grinding. I worked my way up to my feet to peer over the top of the bank. The truck was an older model, like from the fifties. It had gone off the road and climbed up an embankment, where it looked to be stuck on a stump or a rock, its tires clawing at the ground, smoke and dust rolling up in a thick cloud.

Something must have caught because it lunged backwards, skidding to a stop on the road. For a second I thought that the guys in the truck might come after me, especially the passenger, who stared at me through that mask, his fingers gripping the door like he wanted to rip through it, the hatred and rage burning so dark in his eyes that I could see it from my place in the creek.

I waited, not sure what to do. But then the passenger glanced past me to where Thomas raced through the field toward us, a rock in his hand. The passenger said something to the driver and the truck limped away, wounded.

I dropped back into the water and let my body float in the pool, my fingers trembling as my adrenaline drained away.

CHAPTER

24

THOMAS SLID UP TO THE EDGE OF THE CREEK LIKE A MAN stealing home plate, kicking a shoe full of dirt down into my face in the process.

"You okay, Boady?"

I pushed myself out of the water, finding a fallen log to sit on as Thomas climbed down into the creekbed with me. My arm hurt where the broomstick hit me, a walnut-size lump protruding just above my elbow. "I'm okay," I said, although I wasn't fully sure of that just yet.

"What the hell was that about? Who were those guys?"

I had to tell Thomas, but I couldn't meet his eye, and my gaze fell back to the water. "It's called...nigger knockin'," I said. "They were pro'bly goin' for you but got me instead."

After I got the words out I looked up. The expression on Thomas's face, horror, anger, and confusion all tied together in a single knot, made me ashamed. My side did this. We were the ones who wrote those rules.

Thomas didn't speak. He seemed to be wrestling with it all. Finally he said, "It happens so much you have a name for it?"

I didn't know what to say to that, so I just shrugged.

"Are you hurt?" he asked.

I held up my arm and showed him the lump. "It don't hurt all that much, unless I squeeze my fist."

"Can you climb out of here?"

"If ya give me a boost."

We sloshed through the thigh-deep water to the opposite shore, where Thomas laced his fingers together to make a stirrup, lifting me up the bank far enough that I could pull myself out. Then Thomas climbed out.

"You're a madman," he said, in a half chuckle. "The way you charged that truck like that."

"I broke his windshield," I said.

"They almost flipped over; I thought they would for sure."

We walked to the spot where the truck had gotten hung up on that stump. I could still smell the burned rubber from the driver smoking the tires to get untangled. I looked at the burn marks as Thomas scanned the ground at the edge of the road. He saw the tread print in the dirt before I did.

"That's the track!" he said.

I looked where he pointed and saw it too: in the soft limestone dust where the truck backed onto the road, a tire print identical to the one we'd seen in the field out at the Quaker church. A ripple of fear caused the bottom of my lungs to drop out.

"Holy crap," Thomas said.

For my part, I couldn't speak. The truck that carried the men in the Casper masks was the same truck that hauled a dead Lida Poe out to the woods. The possibilities spiraled in my head, tidy threads fusing together in a single question. Was the man in the Casper mask the same man who'd put a bullet in Lida Poe's head? If so, I had just locked eyes with a murderer.

Thomas stepped out to the middle of the road to look in the direction that the truck had been going when it limped away. We must have been thinking the same thing: What if the men in the truck changed their minds and turned around?

They knew we'd be on that road. They knew where we were

coming from, and so they had to know where we were going. Off
to the west, a thunderhead crawled over the hills, its chilly breeze
blowing against my wet T-shirt and jeans, sending a hard shiver
down my back—at least I think it was the breeze that made me
shiver. We still needed to get to that second jobsite, and we needed
to get there before the storm let loose.

The first heavy raindrops began to fall about the time we arrived
at the house, yet neither one of us wanted to go inside. It looked
empty enough. I checked the dirt at the edge of the road and saw
no sign that the truck with the bad tread had been there, but that
didn't stop us from picking up a couple rocks before going in.

The darkening sky cast shadows in corners where there shouldn't
have been shadows, but in the end, the house was empty. We had
barely finished our search of the place when the sky opened up
and dropped a wall of water outside.

It seemed incongruous to go to work after all that had just
happened, but what else could we do? We were miles from a
phone or any kind of help, and the house still needed to be
scrapped out, so I started showing Thomas the ins and outs
of scrapping—laying down the bigger pieces of Sheetrock and
stacking them full of the smaller ones to be carried out once Wally
arrived with the truck.

My left hand couldn't grip all that well, yet despite the injury,
we had cleared about half of the house before the sound of a
truck engine came in through the front door. We both ran to
look and saw Wally in the one-ton, spinning up through the mud
of the front yard, trying to get close to the door. The rain had
lightened up, but the mud made for a slippery walk as Wally came
trudging inside.

Our first order of business was to tell Wally about the pickup,
and the men in the ghost masks who attacked us. His eyes darted

back and forth between Thomas and me, as though he couldn't believe what he was hearing, his cheeks growing an ever-darker shade of crimson as the story progressed. And when I showed him the lump on my arm, I thought he might blow a gasket.

"Get in the truck," he said.

"But we—" I started, pointing at the piles of Sheetrock scraps we'd stacked.

"Just get in the truck." He turned and made for the cab. "We'll deal with that later."

Thomas and I jumped in, our shoes caked with mud, and Wally tore out of the yard, the one-ton spinning sideways until it found purchase on the gravel. Some of the buckets of joint cement fell onto their sides and rolled back and forth, banging into the sideboards as he drove, but Wally didn't slow down.

Our route veered through a subdivision where we'd done several houses over the past couple years. Wally made for a corner house under construction, sliding to a stop just short of the front door. He jumped out of the cab and stomped into the house.

I climbed into the back to secure those loose buckets, and could hear Wally yelling inside.

"Where's your ol' man?"

Then I heard Angus, his voice small and shaky. "He went to get cigarettes."

"When he gets back, you tell him that I want his ass at the shop. Pronto."

"He'll wanna finish the ceilings before—"

"Don't you do another goddamned thing. You tell him I wanna see him right now! Got it?"

"Yes, sir."

I finished tying off the buckets and climbed back into the cab as Wally hopped in. He fired the truck up and drove back to the warehouse, that last part of the trip far calmer than the first part—but none of us talked.

Back at the shop, Mom gave a look at my arm and I assured her that I was okay—just a bad bruise. Then Thomas and I found a job that needed doing, so we could hang around to watch the showdown between Milo and Wally. A supply company had dropped off four pallets of joint cement that needed to be stacked in the insulated room in the middle warehouse. So we went to stacking while Wally and Mom talked and paced in the office.

We were unloading our second pallet when Milo's truck came sliding into the courtyard with Milo behind the wheel, his face bent in anger, a cigarette pinched in his lips. He flicked the cigarette to the ground and stormed into the office, leaving Angus in the truck looking a little scared. Thomas and I ran to the big warehouse, slipped in through the big side door, and found Mom standing there. She must have known that things were about to blow. She put a finger to her lips to shush us as we came in.

"Who did it?" Wally yelled. "Who attacked those boys?"

"I don't know what you're talkin' 'bout," Milo said.

Mom had left the door to the office open enough that we could see the two men inside. Milo had his arms crossed and a smirk on his face, not the least bit scared of Wally. And why should he be? He stood five inches taller than Wally and had the stony features of a Marlboro man.

Wally, on the other hand, had a soft middle and arms that jiggled when he shook a fist. Yet it was Wally who stepped into Milo, teeth bared like a rabid badger and his face as red as Christmas ribbon.

"No one knew those boys were gonna be out there on that road," Wally snarled. "No one 'cept you and me. You set this up—so who did it?"

"Wally, you'd better step the hell back or we're gonna have us a problem."

"We already got a damned problem, Milo. What we're gonna have is a resolution. You got one chance to come clean."

"Or what?" Milo's smirk turned into a grin.

"Who did it, Milo?"

"I told ya—I don't know what you're talkin' 'bout."

Wally reached into his back pocket and pulled out a blue paycheck, shoving it into Milo's chest. Milo instinctively grabbed it.

"That's your last one," Wally said. "You're fired."

"You're...firing me?" Milo crunched the paycheck into a ball, and if he hadn't been mad before, he surely was now.

"Get out of my office," Wally said.

"You go straight to hell, ya goddamned little faggot!"

And just like that, something in the air shifted and all the fire left Wally's eyes.

"That's right, I know all about you and George Bauer. I've known for years. Hell, everybody knows. The boys wanted to bring the wrath of God down on ya, and who do ya think stopped 'em? Who do ya think's been keepin' the boys from burnin' your goddamned house down? I'm the one who put a stop to it—and you have the gall to fire *me*?"

Then Milo lowered his voice into some dark pit and said, "You just made the worst mistake of your miserable life." He shoved a shoulder into a stunned Wally Schenicker and walked out the door into the courtyard. He didn't notice us until after he got into his truck. When he saw us, he gunned the engine, peeling through a U-turn and shot gravel against the side of the warehouse. I stepped in front of Mom to shield her, but none of the rocks came near us.

As the growl of Milo's truck faded into the distance, I looked at Thomas, and he at me, our eyes expressing what words could not. Something serious—and terrifying—had just played out in front of us.

I was still trying to fit all the pieces together when Mom walked into the office and up to Wally, whose eyes were wet with tears. She put her arms around him, eased his face onto her shoulder, and—as she did for me at the Quaker church—comforted Wally with an embrace.

CHAPTER

25

A YOUNG DEPUTY NAMED DEAN WINSLOW CAME OUT AND TOOK statements from Thomas and me about getting attacked, although he seemed bored by what we had to say, actually snickering when I mentioned the Casper masks. To make things worse, neither Thomas nor I could give a good description of the truck other than to say that it was old and had red paint beneath its layers of dirt and rust. I offered to take Winslow out to the scene and show him the tire tracks, but he pointed out that with the heavy rain, the tread print was probably gone already.

When Winslow left, we went back to work, and I filled Thomas in on who George Bauer was. It wasn't long after that when Bauer pulled into the lot and walked into Wally's house, his gait purposeful but his shoulders slumped as though weighed down by a powerful sense of loss.

Mom was at the Elgins' house when I went home to shower the remaining drywall dust out of my hair. She was still there when I finished, so I walked over, finding her and Jenna sitting at the dining room table, not a smile between them.

"Boys, come over here a second," Jenna said.

"Did we do something wrong?" Thomas asked.

"No, honey," Jenna said, smiling. "Not at all."

Mom said, "I told Jenna what happened. We're thinkin'—and

Wally agrees—that it might be best for you boys to take a couple days off—just till things calm down."

I waited for Thomas to object, and I think he was waiting for me to do the same, but neither of us said a peep.

Mom continued, as though she thought she had some convincing to do. "Wally's gotta find new hangers to replace Milo and Angus, so he'll be busy, and he won't be around to keep a lid on things."

"And in the meantime," Jenna said, talking more to Thomas than to me, "your father thought it would be a good idea if you boys went up to Columbia with him."

Charles stood in the kitchen, pulling coffee grounds out of their coffeemaker, his back tightening a bit when Jenna suggested that we join him on the trip.

"He's going up to see that handwriting expert," Jenna continued. "And we thought you two might go with him, maybe have a change of scenery."

Mom nodded her agreement without saying anything, as though not wanting to add another turn to the knot in Charles's back.

Thomas beamed at the suggestion. "Right on," he said, flashing me a big smile.

I smiled too, but out of the corner of my eye, I watched Charles give a sigh.

Mom and I stayed at the Elgins' house for supper that night, spaghetti and meatballs. Mom helped Jenna roll the meatballs, and the two of them talked in low voices. Charles retired to his study, and Thomas and I sat in the front room watching TV. From my seat on the couch, I could see into the kitchen, and though I didn't pay much attention to our mothers, there had been this one moment when I thought I saw my mom wiping a tear off her cheek. I pondered that small act and despite all that happened over the past few days, I felt pretty certain that it was Milo's treatment of Wally that brought that tear.

That night at supper, our parents took great pains to steer the conversation away from any mention of what had happened that day. Jenna kept the small talk flowing, and Mom chimed in on just about every topic. Jenna brought out a side of my mother that I had never seen before, as though Mom had been this wounded bird who suddenly found her wings and took flight. I think Mom talked more at that dinner than at any meal she and I had ever shared together.

At one point, Jenna asked about parish picnics, something she'd seen advertised in the paper. Every town big enough to have a church held a parish picnic, setting aside one Sunday each summer for a fund-raising party. Mom told Jenna about how the previous year, Wally had taken us to the one in Dry Creek. I had never been to a parish picnic before then, and the way kids talked about those things at school, I figured I'd been missing out on the coolest event of the season.

I remember wondering, at the time, whether Wally had invited us as a way of dating my mom. It didn't make sense, but that didn't stop me from thinking it. They sat together every day in the office, and if they wanted to be a couple, they didn't have to go to a parish picnic to take that next step. My concerns were further assuaged when we arrived at the picnic and within a few minutes, George Bauer showed up. The three of them hung out together while I ran around spending my money on things like the ring toss, the grab bag, and the dunk tank.

As Mom told Jenna about the picnic, it dawned on me that Mom must have known about Wally and George that day. She had been Wally's co-conspirator, playing along so that he could be with George—in public—in a way that hid the truth from judgmental eyes. Then I thought about the caring way that Mom held Wally after Milo left, and I suddenly felt foolish for thinking that Wally ever had designs on my mother. That hug she gave him was so tender—a sister holding a brother whose world had just fallen in on him, his life destroyed by the likes of Milo Halcomb. It seemed like every time I turned around that summer, I saw something new in my mother.

After supper, Mom went home and I stayed behind to help Thomas with the dishes—Mom's idea, not mine. After dishes, I said my goodbyes.

Outside, on the western horizon, the tail end of the storm broke above the hills, and the setting sun exploded against the clouds in waves of gold and purple and red. As I took a moment to admire the colors, I heard the screech of Hoke's front door.

Figuring he probably hadn't heard about all that happened, I made my way over to tell him about the attack, laying the story out in great detail because Hoke, more than anyone I knew, appreciated the small details. He studied my expression during most of the retelling, but toward the end he let his gaze wander out to the woods, looking at nothing in particular, just slowly moving his head from side to side.

When I finished, he gave a sigh and said, "I'm sorry, Boady."

"What are you sorry for?" I said. "You didn't do nothin'."

"I should have warned you...about the danger," he said. "Remember when we talked about folks trying to feel like they belong by putting others down? Us versus them?"

"Yeah."

"Well, it runs much deeper than that." Hoke leaned back in his chair, fixing his eyes on something far away, the way he always did when he was about to get deep. "In a perfect world, ignorant notions should die a quick death. A thing like racism, if it can't find a kindred spirit...it's like a dog barking at a stone. But if you can find just one other person who thinks like you...well, even the most irrational belief can grow roots. Small-minded people feed off each other, and before you know it, you have mobs, and you have burning crosses, and lynchings."

"But we didn't do nothin' to them. They had no cause to come after us the way they did."

"Men like that, they don't need much in the way of cause. All it takes is a couple guys angry over something, looking for someone to blame. It's like Dr. King said: 'Nothing in all the world is more dangerous than sincere ignorance.' Sometimes I think that's the truest thing a man's ever said."

"He was swingin' for my head like he wanted to kill me."

"Boady, you ever heard of a boy named Emmett Till?"

"Is he from Jessup?"

"No. Emmett Till was a black kid from Chicago. He was fourteen back in 1955, when he took a trip down to visit some relatives in Mississippi. While he was there, he talked to a white woman. Not long after that, a couple good ol' boys with guns took Emmett from his uncle's house—just took him. Three days later, they found the boy's body in a river with a cotton gin fan tied around his neck. Those men beat that boy beyond recognition, and then shot him for good measure."

"Jesus."

"And all because they didn't like the way he talked to a white woman."

"But that was a long time ago—before I was even born. They put a stop to all that because they passed those civil rights laws."

"Boady, the men who beat and murdered those people for all those years, do you think they simply disappeared because someone passed a law?" A quiet sadness wrapped around Hoke's words as he spoke, as though he held himself responsible for the sins of people who came before him. "Do you think those folks just figured out that they were wrong and went home?"

"No, but things are different now, ain't they?"

"I wish to God they were, but that stuff still happens. Maybe not in the same way as what happened to Emmett Till, but it's out there—always will be."

"Not always. People change."

"People can change if they *want* to, but the sad truth is that humans are hardwired to be prejudiced. It's passed down from ancestors who were just trying to figure out what to fear and what to hunt. We learned to separate things into good and bad, and that particular human frailty is alive and well in every one of us. It's not a matter of *if* we have prejudices—we do. It's a matter of understanding those instincts and fighting against them."

Hoke pulled out his pipe and worked through the ritual of packing tobacco into it. I wanted to argue against what he had said, but frankly his story about Emmett Till scared the crap out of me. And I began to contemplate the short walk between getting hit with a broom handle and getting beat to death with it.

After he lit his pipe, he took a deep draw and let the smoke roll out between his lips. Once it cleared away, he said, "You'll never change what a person thinks in their head or what they feel in their heart by passing a law. If a man doesn't want to look at who he is deep down, he's not going to much care what the law says about it."

CHAPTER

26

I'D NEVER BEEN TO A COLLEGE CAMPUS BEFORE, BUT THOMAS had, and as we sat in the back of Mr. Elgin's Imperial on the way to Columbia, he took great pleasure in telling me about the visit. The thing he remembered most was a preacher who stood on the steps of one of the buildings and lectured the people passing by about the dangers of premarital sex. It came across as something of a comedy routine, because the preacher spent most of his energy assailing the seductive power of James Taylor music.

We didn't see any preachers on our visit; in fact, we spent most of that beautiful day buried in the archive room of a newspaper office. It was Thomas's idea.

Mr. Elgin had an appointment with a document expert who worked in the Ellis Library. The walk there took us across Francis Quad, an expansive lawn in the middle of campus surrounded by a dozen buildings made of brick and granite, serious-looking structures that commanded reverence. In the middle of the quad stood these six enormous columns, just out there for no good reason—or so I thought, until I read a plaque that said the columns were all that remained of a building that had burned down in 1892.

And as much as I appreciated the fine architecture surrounding me, that wasn't what caught my eye the most—it was the girls.

Charles walked in front of Thomas and me as we crossed the quad, passing students lying in the grass in groups of two or three, some talking, some studying, and others just lying out in the warm sun. The girls were pretty and wore shorts and jeans and T-shirts, not uniforms like at St. Ignatius.

There were these two girls walking toward us as we neared the end of the quad, they both wore really short shorts; one had on a tank top, the other, a halter top. We passed them, and I swear neither one wore a bra. I did my best not to look, but what could I do? The one in the halter top caught me ogling and gave me a smile. After they passed, Thomas turned to me with the biggest grin on his face, a silent ovation to the wonderful thing that had just happened.

At Ellis, Charles had us follow him up to the third floor, where he repeated his instructions to meet him out front at noon. As Thomas and I made our way back toward the exit, we passed an overlook where you could see down into the library's massive reading room. It looked more like the grand ballroom of a castle than a library, with a ceiling that had to be nearly three stories high and windows big enough to drive a bus through.

For the briefest of moments I felt like I understood the draw of going to college—hell, just being there made me feel smarter than I was. As I took in that view, Thomas started laying out the plan that he'd concocted on the drive up. We were going to dig up the story on Hoke Gardner.

Our quest began by asking the reference librarian at Ellis where we could find old newspapers from Columbia. She talked really fast, and I didn't understand half of what she said, but Thomas seemed to get it. In the end, she sent us to the morgue—that was the term she used—at the office of the *Columbia Missourian* newspaper.

We only had to walk a couple blocks because the *Missourian* was a product of their journalism school. There we met a nice woman named Sandy who took us to a room where they stored all the old newspapers.

"You can look up old editions on microfilm, or in these bound volumes," she said. "We don't have any kind of index, but if you know when the things you're looking for happened, I can get you started."

I thought back to Hoke's conversation with Sheriff Vaughan. "In 1966," I said. "We're lookin' for some kind of accident that happened in May of 'sixty-six."

"Well, let's see." She went to a drawer and pulled out a spool of microfilm, threading it into a machine with a screen. "This is May and June of 'sixty-six. One of you can start here."

Thomas sat at the machine and started reading.

Then she walked to the other side of the room and from a shelf pulled down a big red book, laying it on a table. "This is the hard-copy edition of every newspaper for that month."

Because Thomas started his search at the beginning of the month, I opened my book to the fifteenth of May, which led with a story about students being required to take an exam for the military draft. I scoured every article for that day, and the only accident report I found told of a skydiver who broke his leg when he messed up his landing east of town.

I skimmed through three more editions before I came to an article with the headline: "WOMAN DISTURBS NEIGHBORHOOD." I was about to move on but the picture of a man next to the article, one of those photos that businessmen keep handy in case their name makes the newspaper, caught my attention. Something about the man's eyes reminded me of Hoke Gardner, albeit a much younger and less ragged version.

In the story, police were called out because a woman had been seen pacing back and forth in front of a house, yelling obscenities.

She held something in her hand that one neighbor said looked like a gun. When they got to the scene, police found an intoxicated woman raising a ruckus outside the home of a man named Hoke Gardner.

"I got one," I said.

"Story about Hoke?"

"Yeah, but it ain't no accident; it's about a woman who was mad at him."

"What's it say?"

"Gimme a second."

Thomas waited while I read. When I finished, I did my best to summarize the article.

"This woman named Mariam Fisk went to Hoke's house late one night and was cussin' him out—wantin' to fight him. Someone said she had a gun."

"Who's Mariam Fisk?"

"His sister-in-law. Hoke used to have a wife named Alicia."

"Mariam wanted to kill Hoke?"

"That's what it sounds like. The eyewitnesses said that when Hoke didn't come out, Mariam said she was gonna go in and get him. But then she heard the sirens and threw the gun, or whatever she had in her hand, through Hoke's picture window. After the police got there, Hoke came out...he'd just been released from the hospital—here it is—following a car accident where his wife had been killed. Hoke told the police not to arrest Mariam because she was grieving."

"Does it say when the car accident happened?"

"Um...yeah, May fifth."

Thomas went back to his microfilm and began scrolling ahead.

I continued. "It says that Hoke refused to press charges—he said there wasn't no gun. Said she threw a rock through the window."

Then Thomas piped up. "I found the accident." He read to himself, his finger moving under the lines of print. "Hoke drove off the road and hit a tree. The car caught fire, but they think Hoke was thrown from the car. His wife, Alicia, and...his daughter, Sarah, both died."

"Daughter, Sarah?"

"Yeah," Thomas turned to look at me. "She was five years old."

I thought about the burn scars on Hoke's hands and arms. Had he tried to save his family? Or did that happen as he fought to save himself? Then I thought about Sheriff Vaughan's heavy sarcasm as he all but accused Hoke of having an affair with Lida Poe, the way he put an emphasis on the word *accident* as if to suggest that it had been anything but an accident. I struggled to square all this new information with the man I sat next to on his porch.

Lost in my thoughts, I had all but stopped listening to Thomas. "I found the obituary."

That perked me up.

"Says that Hoke was a criminal defense lawyer." He paused to read further. "He and Alicia were childhood sweethearts. Both from Dry Creek. That's where his wife and daughter are buried...at the St. Peter Cemetery."

Thomas and I read through the rest of May's newspapers and found nothing more on Hoke Gardner, or on Mariam Fisk. We thanked Sandy for her help and walked back to the quad, both of us more subdued than we'd been on our first trek across campus. The sky was still sunny, and the girls just as pretty as before, but I found myself staring at the columns in the center of that lawn, my thoughts stuck on Hoke Gardner and the load of secrets that lay hidden behind his quiet smile.

CHAPTER

27

M R. ELGIN SEEMED UNUSUALLY HAPPY WHEN WE LEFT Columbia, and he never struck me as the kind of guy who wore that description easily. I figured his meeting must have gone well. Whatever it was that put him in that good mood also set him to whistling to the songs on the radio as he drove.

It's not that Mr. Elgin was mean or anything. I think his work, and all those problems at Ryke, stayed on his mind around the clock. He told Thomas once that he had to work from home a lot because he didn't trust the staff at the factory. "They were Halcomb's people," he said. "Always trying to get a peek at the stuff on my desk, or listen in on my phone calls." Once things settled, he planned on cleaning house and starting fresh.

Our drive back to Jessup took us through Jefferson City, where Charles stopped at a little shop called Zesto and bought us each an ice cream cone. From there, our route twisted and hopscotched south down a chain of two-lane highways that cut through all kinds of little towns. We had just passed through one of those towns when Mr. Elgin looked up into his rearview mirror and muttered, "Are you kidding me?"

Thomas and I both turned around and saw the lights of a squad car.

Charles pulled over, rolled down his window, and put his hands on the steering wheel like it was a practiced move. The cop—a deputy sheriff from whatever county we were in—was a chubby man with a buzz cut on top and jowls below that worked to give his head the shape of a shoebox. He stopped near the rear of the car, and said, "Both hands on the wheel, please."

"They already are, Officer," Mr. Elgin said.

Then the deputy walked up to the driver's door, put a hand on the roof of the car and leaned down. "Can I see your driver's license?"

"I'll need to take my hands off the wheel for that," Charles said. "Is that okay?"

"Don't be smart," the deputy said. "Go ahead and get it."

Charles leaned forward, pulled his wallet out, and began working the license out of its plastic cover.

The deputy leaned down a little more and gave a look to me, then Thomas, and then back to me again and said, "You all right back there, son?"

I didn't understand the question, so I looked to Thomas, who had his eyes forward, looking at the back of his dad's head. I said, "I'm fine, sir."

Charles handed his license to the deputy. "Can I ask why you pulled me over?"

The deputy studied Charles's driver's license, flicking his eyes back and forth to compare the picture to Mr. Elgin.

"I wasn't speeding," Charles said.

"Is this your car?" the deputy asked.

"Yes, it is."

"Can you show me the registration?"

"It's in the glove box. I'll need to slide over."

The deputy put a hand on the grip of his gun and said, "Go ahead."

Charles slid to the middle of the bench seat and leaned to reach into the glove box. Sitting back up, he handed a piece of paper to the deputy. "I'd still like to know why you pulled me over."

"Got a complaint of someone in a car similar to this one drivin' erratically."

Charles closed his eyes and took a deep breath, his fingers squeezing the steering wheel and then relaxing, but he said nothing.

When the deputy finished looking at the vehicle registration, he handed the paper back to Charles and said, "Mind you, we don't like people drivin' carelessly through here. A big car like this could do some real damage, so let's keep 'er calm, okay, Mr. Elgin?"

"I understand," Charles said in a tone as flat as glass.

The deputy returned to his squad, pulled a U-turn, and drove away.

The rest of our trip was a pretty quiet affair. Charles Elgin didn't whistle anymore as we made our way back home, and we didn't talk much either.

Our mothers were on the Elgins' porch when we pulled up, and Jenna came down the steps to meet us. "Well?" she said.

Charles tapped the packet of papers he carried and said, "It was just as I thought. I'm calling Vaughan."

I think Jenna expected more of a conversation, and I suspect Charles would have preferred that as well, but getting pulled over by that deputy seemed to put him in a mood—and I can't say that I blamed him.

Jenna went back and joined Mom on the porch swing; and Thomas and I went up to his room to hang some black-light posters. Through the window, I could see Hoke sitting on his porch writing in one of those black books again. *Exorcising ghosts,* wasn't that what he called it? He'd been writing in those books for as long as I could remember, and all the while he'd been hiding his past from me. But now that I'd had a peek into that past—a dead wife, a dead daughter, and a sister-in-law who tried to shoot him—all those years of his writing made me wonder more than ever what those pages held.

Thomas and I went to work hanging posters. He had one of Jimi Hendrix and another of a large peace sign that we tacked up side by side on one wall. The third poster, the one I admired the most, showed a black panther with glowing white fangs and claws. We hung that one above the head of his bed and made plans for me to come over after dark to see how it looked under the black light.

It was about then that I glanced out the window and saw Sheriff Vaughan's car parked on the road out in front of the Elgins' house. Thomas and I made our way downstairs and could hear Charles and Vaughan going at it already. They stood on the sidewalk half-way between the house and the road. We slipped onto the porch and took up a position on the front steps.

"The expert said that Cecil Halcomb signed those invoices," Mr. Elgin said. "He tried to make it look like it wasn't his signa-ture, like someone else forged it, but the expert found markers consistent with Halcomb's handwriting. Look here, you see how the loop in the *L* has this bow in it? And the curve of the capital *C* is the same in both. Cecil also wrote with the same letter height and slant—"

"Mr. Elgin, I don't wanna contradict your *expert*, but if you were the one stealin' money from Ryke and ya wanted to frame Cecil Halcomb, wouldn't ya try and give the signature a few of those markers you're talkin' 'bout?"

"That's the point, Sheriff. Those markers aren't things you fake; they're things you do out of habit."

Hoke Gardner stepped off his porch and started toward the Elgin house.

"Did this expert of yours say he'd take the stand and testify—one hundred percent—that Cecil Halcomb wrote those invoices?"

"You know it's not a hundred percent, but he can say that it's most likely Cecil's handwriting. And if that's the case, then Cecil was also involved in that woman's death. Why can't you see that?"

"Mr. Elgin, there's a lot y'all don't know about this case—"

"You keep saying that, but what could you possibly have that stops you from even looking at Cecil Halcomb?"

"Well, for starters, Cecil Halcomb couldn't have killed Lida Poe. We know that for a fact."

Hoke stopped his approach about ten feet shy of the two men. "How could you know that?" Hoke asked.

Vaughan stepped back and looked around at the audience that had gathered, apparently noticing for the first time that Hoke had walked up on him. He hesitated for a moment, as if weighing his reply, and then said, "Okay, fine. Let's go through it. Lida Poe took a hunnert and fifty-eight grand out of her bank account—cash—on a Friday afternoon...right around four o'clock. That's easy enough to know cuz of the bank records. She was reported missin' by a friend on Sunday mornin'. So we know she disappeared sometime between Friday and Sunday. Well, Cecil Halcomb was out of town. He and his boy Jarvis left Jessup around five on Friday. They were in Dallas all weekend with an airtight alibi."

"How do you know that Cecil left at five?" Hoke asked.

"Not that it's any of your business, but I asked him, and he told me. We also have a receipt showin' that he bought gas in Springfield at seven. I drove down there myself and talked to the clerk, and he remembered Cecil because Cecil spat tobacco juice on the floor as he paid for his gas."

"But you still have a window of opportunity," Hoke said. "It only takes a couple hours to drive from Jessup to Springfield. If she drains her account at four, and Cecil buys the gas at seven, that leaves an hour unaccounted for. Plenty of time to kill Ms. Poe and still make it to Springfield."

"Except, Lida Poe's neighbor saw her drivin' her car as late as nine o'clock that night—saw her pull into her driveway, sit there a minute, and then pull out again, like she forgot somethin' and had to leave. And when she left, Poe backed into a neighbor's car and took off—a hit and run. They called it in."

"Nine o'clock at night," Hoke said. "Did the neighbor see Lida Poe, or just the car?"

"It was Lida Poe's car in Lida Poe's driveway. Who the hell else would it be?"

"Don't you think you're being a bit too quick to rule out other possibilities?" Charles said.

"Get this through your heads," Vaughan said. "Cecil Halcomb didn't have nothin' to do with the death of Lida Poe. I go where the evidence leads me, and it ain't leadin' me to Cecil Halcomb. That's all there is to it."

"Is that really all there is to it?" Hoke said. "So this has nothing to do with the fact that you and Cecil are cousins?"

Charles's eyes grew big, and the sheriff's cheeks flushed red.

Hoke continued, "Turns out, the good sheriff here's a second cousin of the man who rightly should be a suspect in all this mess."

Vaughan's breath puffed shallow in his chest. "What I am to Cecil Halcomb has nothin' to do with it," Vaughan said.

Thomas and I leaned forward on the porch steps, rapt by the back-and-forth of accusations that cut through the air like swords.

"In fact," Hoke continued, "why isn't the state patrol down here? You shouldn't even be working this case. It's almost as if you're hanging on to it to keep the waters good and muddy."

"What are you implying?"

"I'm not implying a thing—I'm saying it outright. Your conflict of interest isn't even a close call. I have contacts in the criminal division up at the state patrol and I think it's high time they take a look at what's going on down here."

"I don't need the state patrol," he said. "We got it under control."

"Do you?" Charles quipped.

"Yes, we do. We're runnin' down leads as we speak," Vaughan said, looking coolly at Hoke. "We believe Lida Poe was datin' a white man, and we think he was her accomplice. Got Poe to withdraw all her money, killed her, buried her, and then pro'bly hit the road in that green Gremlin of hers."

Thomas and I looked at each other with eyes as big as hen's eggs. I was the one who said what we were thinking. "Did you say...a green Gremlin?"

CHAPTER

28

I RODE WITH SHERIFF VAUGHAN OUT TO WHERE THOMAS AND I had found the Gremlin, going from blacktop to gravel, to a thin trail that gnarled its way into the woods. Mom, Hoke, and the Elgins came behind us in the Imperial. Vaughan made us stay at the top of the ravine as he floundered his way down to the smashed car, and when he came back up, he sent a call out over the radio for reinforcements. "I've located Lida Poe's car," he said.

Deputies started arriving within fifteen minutes, and after an hour, there were four of them down in the ravine, along with a couple guys from the highway department who came out with a front-end loader. They hooked chains to the car's frame and rolled it onto its wheels.

Once they got one of the doors pried open, Vaughan and Deputy Winslow crawled in and started digging around. Those of us on the top of the hill waited anxiously as they carried what they found up to Vaughan's squad car, spreading it out on the hood. At first, it looked like the kind of stuff you'd expect to find in a car: ice scraper, road maps, tire tool. Then Vaughan laid the car's ashtray on the hood, a lone cigarette butt rattling around inside. Next to the ashtray, he laid a silver Zippo lighter.

The lighter struck a familiar chord in me, so I inched forward to get a better look, shuffling closer until I could see the worn image on the side—a silhouette of a naked woman swimming through stars. I knew that lighter; I'd once held it in my hand.

"That's Milo Halcomb's lighter," I blurted out.

Vaughan looked at the Zippo and then at me. "What are you talkin' 'bout?"

Mom walked up beside me so she could get a better look. "That's Milo's lighter, all right," she said. "I've seen him use it a thousand times."

"Look at that butt," I said. "Is it a Viceroy?"

"Viceroy?" Vaughan asked.

"That's what Milo smokes," I said.

Dean Winslow picked up the cigarette butt, looked at it, and nodded to Vaughan.

Then Hoke said out loud what we were all thinking. "Milo left his lighter in Lida Poe's car when he ditched it here."

Sheriff Vaughan waved a hand in the air as if wanting to stop us from going any further down that path. "There's probably a ton of lighters like this out there. It don't mean—"

"Sheriff Vaughan." Hoke interrupted him. "I'm going to be calling the state patrol in the morning. You can dance around all you want, but I've—we've—had about enough. If you won't look at the Halcombs...then we'll get someone on this case who will."

Vaughan straightened up and puffed out his cheeks like he was holding back a whole mouthful of slander, then he pointed at Hoke, his finger shaking slightly. "Y'all need to clear out—right now. This here's a crime scene." He turned to his deputy. "Dean, escort these folks back to the highway and don't let nobody down here that ain't wearin' a badge."

The deputy looked at us somewhat apologetically, shrugged, and gave an open-palmed gesture to herd us back to the Imperial. He didn't need to follow us out.

On the drive back to Frog Hollow, Hoke and Charles solidified their resolve to bring in the state patrol. You would think that unearthing Lida Poe's car—and then finding Milo's lighter inside it—would have sent Vaughan tearing down the road, his siren blasting, looking to arrest Milo Halcomb, but it didn't happen that way.

The following morning came with no announcement of an arrest, as did the morning after that. A full three days passed before I heard the news that Milo had been arrested—not for murder, but for possessing a stolen car and for being an accessory of some kind. And to hear Mr. Elgin tell it—which we did because Thomas and I hid behind my propane tank when Charles told Hoke the news—we were lucky to get that much.

"They got him for dumping the car," Charles said. "His fingerprints were all over the interior. When they went to arrest him, they asked if he knew Poe or had ever been to her house, and he said no. When they asked about the car, he denied ever being in that car, but then he must have smelled a trap because he clammed up. The good news is, they sent a guy down from the state patrol, a Detective Royce. He stopped by the office to give me a briefing this morning. Said he's pushing to convene a grand jury."

"That's the logical next step," Hoke said.

"Thanks for making that call, by the way. Royce seems to be lighting a fire under this thing. Said he might have enough to charge Milo with conspiracy for Ms. Poe's death, but it's weak."

"It's circumstantial," Hoke said. "His cigarette lighter in the car puts him in the middle of everything, but it doesn't prove he killed her. It makes sense that dumping the car goes hand in hand with the murder, but it's not proof beyond a reasonable doubt."

"Royce said the same thing. But he also said that Milo Halcomb is at his wit's end. Started crying when they put the cuffs on him. Went back and forth between anger and fear. They're hoping to get a high bail and keep him behind bars while the grand jury takes a look at it."

"Royce is a good man," Hoke said. "Had a few cases against him back in the day. He knows his stuff. All we can do now is wait."

I didn't tell anyone, but after hearing that Milo had been arrested that day, I stayed up late into the night waiting for trouble. I pictured the men in the Casper masks driving their truck down Frog Hollow, building up a head of steam at the top before cutting the engine and coasting silently down to our neck of the woods. I listened for the crunch of gravel on the road outside of my window until I fell asleep, my head leaning against the screen.

I spent two more nights listening—although I did so from the comfort of my bed, straining to sort critter noises from footsteps, and getting nothing but tired. By the fourth night I dropped my guard and stopped listening.

CHAPTER

29

I T TOOK A WEEK FOR THINGS TO GET BACK TO NORMAL, IF THERE was such a thing as normal that summer. Wally Schnicker found a couple guys to replace Milo and Angus. Thomas and I went back to work, scrapping, sanding and anything else Wally wanted done, getting our first full paycheck on that Friday before the parish picnic in Dry Creek—eighty-four dollars each. Not bad given that my wounded arm wasn't fully up to snuff and Thomas still needed some training.

By Sunday, talk on the *Country Clatter* had turned from Milo's arrest to the coming bicentennial on the Fourth of July holiday, the country's two hundredth birthday. Word was, every town and hamlet had been saving up their pennies to put on extra-special fireworks displays that year; and as luck had it, the Fourth of July fell on the same Sunday as the picnic in Dry Creek. It felt like the stars were lining up for something big.

We lived closer to Dry Creek to our south than we did to Jessup going north—not by much, but enough that the school district had shipped me to Dry Creek for grade school. It wasn't a big town by any stretch; I think it only had about nine hundred people, which is just big enough to support a Catholic elementary school and a church. I'd never been to the school before, having been a product of the public school system back then, but I'd been in that church—or so my mom told me. The St. Peter Church in Dry Creek had been where they held my father's funeral. And across the road, in the St. Peter Cemetery, was where they laid him to rest.

The school and church were a single structure built on the side of a hill, like everything else in that part of Missouri. Looking at it from the uphill side, the church seemed no fancier than any other church in Missouri. But from the downhill side, the school climbed two stories up the slope before you even got to the church. And with the church sitting on top, and its two gothic steeples reaching skyward, the edifice looked like one of those German castles I'd seen in pictures.

At the very bottom of everything lay the parking lot, which served as a playground during the school year and, for one Sunday each summer, a festival grounds for the parish picnic. From the back edge of that parking lot, you could throw a rock far enough to clear the bluff, below which curled the river, where the fireworks would be shot off from a barge once the sun went down.

By the time we got to the picnic, the festivities were in full swing. I paused at the entrance to let the hot rush of smells—cotton candy, barbecue sauce, kettle corn—wash over me. Just ahead, a heavyset man taunted the crowd from his perch above a dunk tank. He wore a T-shirt that had been so thoroughly soaked he could have just as well been naked from the waist up. Halfway through an insult, a softball hit the plate-size target, dropping the big man into the tank, sending a splash of water into the air.

Thomas stopped with me to scan the crowd, while Mom and Jenna passed by us, heading for the craft booths. Then Thomas and I walked the opposite direction, weaving past a throng of people waiting in line to buy beer at the beer garden—the picnic's second biggest moneymaker after bingo. I scanned the crowd for Jarvis as we walked, but didn't see him—or the Boob Brothers for that matter. I did see a couple deputies wandering the grounds, though, and that set me at ease.

Because we'd just gotten paid, we had our own money to spend, and we launched into playing games, competing to see who could land a Ping-Pong ball on a small plate, or drop a ring on the neck of a Coke bottle. Thomas had a particular talent for the ring toss, and before too long we had to find Jenna and get her car keys so we could deposit four six-packs of Coke in the trunk.

Neither Wally nor Charles joined us that day—and Hoke never went to things like that. Charles excused himself, saying that he had to stay home and read job applications because he'd fired a bunch of people at Ryke—Cecil's spies, he called them—and he needed to find replacements.

Wally also begged out because of work, or so he said, but I don't think anyone bought it. Something inside of him had broken that day with Milo, and like a damaged spring that causes a watch to lose time, what Milo said to Wally had robbed him of something important. He still went through his routine, but his smiles seemed forced, and his eyes carried a weight that hadn't been there before. Mom said that a couple of his regular contractors had dropped him. She didn't need to tell me why—we both knew.

After spending a few hours and better than twenty bucks playing silly carnival games, Thomas and I found ourselves in a line to buy food at the barbecue pit, a semicircle of grills manned by sweaty men in stained aprons. They cooked up all kinds of meat from hot dogs to pork steaks to ribs—most everything slathered with a heavy dose of barbecue sauce, which made my mouth water.

As we stood in line, a man up front, holding a half-empty pitcher of beer in his hand, lost his balance while clowning around with his buddy. He fell backwards at the head of the line, sending the rest of us bumping into each other like boxcars on a stopping train. I stumbled backwards into someone who squeaked as I hit her. I turned to find Diana.

"Hey, Boady," she said.

I had no idea she knew my name. She stood next to another black girl, slightly taller, but just as skinny.

"This is my cousin Sheila." She pointed at the other girl. "Sheila, this is Boady and..."

"Thomas," I said, pointing.

"I'm Diana." She held out her hand to Thomas and he shook it. Then he shook Sheila's hand, giving her a slight bow as he did.

I'd never seen Diana outside of school, and she looked different in her denim sundress. At school she always wore her hair in a single braid that fell between her shoulders. Add to that a blue-and-white uniform and a pair of saddle shoes, and you couldn't help but see something of a little girl in her. But at the picnic, she'd pulled her hair up on the top of her head, knotting it slightly off-center so that it fell long and full over her left shoulder. I think it was that, and the sight of her exposed shoulders under that sundress—something forbidden in the halls of St. Ignatius—that made her look older to me. Whatever the reason, the effect tied my tongue up in knots.

I wanted to tell Thomas that Diana was the only black kid at St. Ignatius. I wanted to put them together and let them talk—get it all out there—so that if he chose to attend St. Ignatius in the fall, he'd at least know what lay ahead. I had so much that I wanted to say, but all that came out was "You in line for food?" A lunkheaded comment at best. Then I stuck my hands into my pockets and shut up.

Sheila spoke next, her eyes and smile fixed squarely on Thomas, who carried one of the Cokes he'd won. "Can I have a sip of y'all's sodie? A girl'd like to die of thirst waitin' in this line." She had a stronger accent than someone from Jessup.

"It's warm," he said, holding out the half-empty bottle. "I won it at the ring toss."

"As long as it's wet," Sheila said, taking the soda and sliding up closer to Thomas. "We been walkin' 'round for hours, and I'll be darned if we can find a bit of shade."

"Sheila's from Memphis," Diana said to me, almost as if Sheila and Thomas were in another room instead of standing right next to us. "She's never been to a parish picnic before."

"Neither has Thomas," I said. "He's from Minneapolis. His family lives next door to me."

"Minneapolis?" Sheila shrieked, as though that were the most interesting thing I could have said. "I've always wanted to see Minneapolis."

"What a coincidence," Thomas said. "I've always had a thing for Memphis."

I wanted to throw a bucket of water on the both of them.

As we continued our slow march toward the grillers, Sheila wedged her way even closer to Thomas's side, putting me in back to walk beside Diana, which didn't bother me at all.

"Ya goin' to the dance?" Diana asked.

"Who's playin'?" I said, as if that mattered.

Parish picnics normally ended with a dance inside the gymnasium, usually dominated by high school kids. Word had spread that the dance would be halted when the fireworks started. Mom and Jenna told us that we could go to the dance as long as we met them at the car to watch the fireworks—and home from there. I honestly hadn't planned on going to the dance, being as I didn't know how to dance and couldn't see paying two dollars to sit on some hard wooden bleacher and watch someone else do it.

"It's a DJ," Diana said.

"I'm not sure," I said.

I tried to act natural, but I became overly conscious of every little detail about my appearance. I'd been sweating, but did it show? I casually glanced down at my pits, and didn't see any offending stains, but then I noticed that my partially untucked shirt fell awkwardly across my hips. Should I keep my hands in my pockets or pull them out to tuck in my shirt? Or maybe I should just let my arms hang free at my side? *God, I'm a basket case,* I thought.

We bought hot dogs—Diana got an extra one for her mother—and then we all walked to the condiments table, where I covered mine with a little of everything. Diana took a thin line of ketchup on each of hers. I didn't see what Sheila and Thomas did; they had their backs to us like we weren't even there.

"Come on, Sheila," Diana said. "I gotta give Momma her hot dog." Then Diana looked at me, gave me the sweetest smile, and shrugged. I found myself reading everything in to that one simple smile, and it tied up my tongue again.

"We'll see y'all at the dance," Sheila said as she turned to join Diana.

"Yeah," I managed to say. "Maybe."

Then, before they got out of earshot, Thomas hollered, "Count on it."

CHAPTER

30

After we finished our hot dogs, I told Thomas to follow me, and we charged up the steps to the front of the church and onto a street lined with muscle cars: Camaros, GTOs, Corvettes, Novas, all with their hoods popped open. We snaked through a group of gearheads and made our way to the front gate of the cemetery, pausing there for a second to make sure that no one was watching—the cemetery being off-limits to prevent teenagers from sneaking in there to make out.

With no one paying us the least mind, we slipped in and followed a path that took us toward the heart of the cemetery, where a life-size statue of an angel stood with her wings spread and her hands open as if to beseech us for pity. I scanned the gravestones as I walked, weaving in and out of the rows.

"What are we looking for?" Thomas asked.

"Hoke's family—his wife and daughter. That obituary said they're buried here."

"That's right." Thomas moved a row away and began to search as well.

We stepped lightly over the graves, as if not wanting to disturb the inhabitants sleeping below, and it brought to my mind the trips my mother and I used to make to visit my dad's grave on his birthday. Mom would sit in the grass over his resting place and cry as she brushed dust off the polished face of the granite. She would talk to the stone, telling it how much she missed him, how it seemed like each day without him came harder than the day before. Her heart had been so badly broken that sometimes it seemed like breathing itself caused her pain.

I was young then, but not so young that I couldn't add things up. I watched as my mother poured out her grief to a piece of stone, while I stood a mere arm's length away. Somewhere along the way, I came to believe that both my parents had died when my father fell—but only one of them had stopped breathing. As I grew older, I stopped going to the cemetery. It had been four years since I'd been there, and as I passed row after row of headstones, those old memories swirled around me in the breeze.

But then I remembered being out at the Quaker church and Mom putting her arms around me and hugging me. I always told myself that Mom and I were more like partners in some short-term venture, that we didn't have the kind of relationship where hugging was a thing. We didn't need to be close. But maybe I was wrong about that. Maybe the hugging part had been there the whole time, though neither of us knew it. It was as if we found something that day at the Quaker church, some-thing I didn't remember losing. And just like that, I wanted to smile.

"Here it is," Thomas called out.

He had stopped in the shadow of the angel and faced a large granite monument with the name Alicia Gardner carved in it. The marker stood a few feet away from a much larger headstone for Agnes and Robert Fisk, her parents. Alicia's headstone didn't mention that she'd been married to Hoke. It read LOVING DAUGH-TER, DEVOTED MOTHER. Next to Alicia was Sarah's marker, with a teddy bear etched on it. I don't think I had ever seen anything sadder than that gravestone with the teddy bear on it.

"Man, could you imagine losing your whole family?" Thomas said.

I pointed to Alicia's stone. "They didn't say that she was a wife—just a mother and a daughter."

"That's cold," Thomas whispered.

"And there's no space next to Alicia for another grave—no place for Hoke when he dies. It's like they cut him out for all eternity."

"I hate cemeteries," Thomas said. "It's like you can feel the sadness just by walking through. Kind of creeps me out."

"My dad's buried here," I said.

Thomas dropped his eyes. "Oh, sorry, man. I didn't mean it like that."

"It's okay, I know."

"Where's he at?"

I led Thomas deeper into the cemetery, to the back edge where the bluff opened up to the river. Dad's gravestone, a simple thing barely knee-high, read: JOHN MICHAEL SANDEN, NOV. 30, 1940– OCT. 28, 1966. I looked down at my father's grave and noticed fresh flowers on the ground next to it, probably purchased by Mom at one of the booths at the picnic. I pictured her bringing Jenna out to the grave shortly after we arrived, and I wondered if Mom cried this time.

For no good reason, I felt my throat tighten and tears start to build. I turned and walked to the bluff, taking a seat on the rock ledge; Thomas joined me there. Below us, a barge loaded with fireworks lay anchored in the water, waiting for sunset. A stone's throw away, two buzzards floated lazily in an updraft. On a large rock beside us, dozens of young lovers had carved initials into the sandstone, many of those initials later crossed out with anguished knife slashes.

We sat there in silence, me with my legs dangling over the edge of the rock, Thomas with his knees pulled up to his chest. Then, he asked, "How old were you when your dad died?"

"Five," I said.

"Do you remember him?"

"I think I do—a little. Sometimes I close my eyes and I think I can see his face—but I can't be sure if it's a memory or somethin' I made up. Sometimes I'll walk into a room and smell somethin' or hear somethin' and remember...I don't know what I remember exactly, but I know it's there—maybe a feelin' that I had when I was with him."

The look on Thomas's face told me that I wasn't making sense, so I tried again.

"I think I remember him when I smell Old Spice, or freshly cut grass. And there's somethin' about eatin' mulberries that makes me think of him. I don't know why, but I do. I can see his footprints in my mind. He used to till Mrs. Dixon's garden in the spring, and he must've let me walk behind him cuz I remember his boot prints in the dirt. They were spaced so far apart, I had to jump from one to the next."

I looked at Thomas again and this time saw pity in his eyes.

"I sound stupid, don't I?"

"You sound like you miss him."

I shrugged.

Thomas didn't say anything after that, not until the sound of music came wafting from somewhere beyond the church. "Is that the dance?" he asked.

"I think so."

"So what'd you think about Sheila?"

"I think she's into you in a big way," I said.

"I just love the way she talks. And that other girl...what's her name?"

"Diana."

"Yeah, Diana. She's cute. You should ask her to dance."

"I . . . don't—"

"I think she likes you."

"Naw . . . I don't think so. We sat by each other in history, and she never said a word. If a girl likes ya, she should at least talk to ya."

"You really don't know much about girls, do you?"

"I know about girls," I said, lying through my teeth. "What I don't know about . . . is dancin'."

"Dancing's easy."

"Yeah, right."

"Just think of it like marching—you step on the beat, right? But, instead of marching forward, you move side to side."

"That don't sound easy at all," I said.

"When we get in there, just watch me and do what I do."

"So we're really goin'?"

"That's where the girls are," he said, getting up from the bluff.

To me, this dance stuff had calamity written all over it, but Thomas had his mind set, so we headed back through the cemetery and out the front gate. As we crossed the street full of muscle cars, I saw Jarvis Halcomb's truck parked down at the end of the row. He and the Boob Brothers sat on the tailgate talking with some girls, not paying any attention to us as we crossed the street.

Thomas and I hit the steps leading down to the picnic, and I gave Jarvis one last look—and I was pretty sure I saw Bob's head turn my way just as we disappeared below the retaining wall.

CHAPTER

31

THE LINE TO GET INTO THE DANCE RAN TWO ABREAST AND A dozen deep, and when my turn came, I begrudgingly handed two dollars to the woman at the door and followed Thomas in.

Bleachers lined one long wall where people sat in small groups watching the dancers, of which there were only a handful so far. Most of the onlookers—kids my age—collected in the open space between the entrance and the dance floor, as though they hadn't fully committed to being there.

The song playing wasn't a particular favorite of mine, but it had Thomas bebopping as we made our way through the crowd, his head swiveling around, scanning the room. I knew who he was looking for, and they weren't hard to find, being the only other black kids in the whole gymnasium. He spotted them, pointed, and made a beeline for the bleachers, where they sat together on the bottom row.

Sheila saw us coming and nudged Diana, who waved and smiled. Then Sheila scooted away from Diana, opening up a gap between them where Thomas and I could sit, a move that put Thomas next to Sheila and me next to Diana—a move that, I was willing to bet, had been worked out in advance.

Thomas and Sheila immediately launched into a conversation about their respective home cities, each trying to best the other on who had the better culture, a conversation that left Diana and me on the sidelines, given that Jessup had all the culture of a fat man scratching his butt. I stared at my feet, and then at a cluster of girls line dancing in front of us, and then back at my feet, trying to come up with something to say. I wanted to thank Diana for helping me with my history final, but I didn't want to open the door to her part in helping me cheat on a test. Instead I just sat there sweating.

And good God, was it hot in that gym. The sun had already crawled its way behind the hills to the west, but the heat decided to stay behind and torture us. Tall, thin windows had been pulled open but offered little relief from the midsummer heat. Four large fans, one in each corner, shot slivers of air toward the center of the room but did nothing to stop the sweat from gathering on my temples.

Then, just when I thought things couldn't get any more uncomfortable, Thomas and Sheila jumped up and charged onto the dance floor, leaving me alone with Diana.

To call Thomas a decent dancer would be like calling the Rolling Stones a passable rock band. The kid had moves that seemed to disconnect his ribs from his hips, sliding them in opposite directions, his legs and arms slinking and snapping like the business end of a bullwhip. What he did bore no relation to marching side to side like he'd told me to do.

"He's a good dancer," Diana said.

"I'll say," I replied.

"You like dancin'?"

I looked around the room at the crowd milling and standing and judging. They would be watching me as I clucked and pecked like a drunken chicken out there. My mouth dried up just thinking about it.

Diana followed my gaze to a pack of spectators, kids who were in our grade at St. Ignatius. Some of them were looking at us and talking, one even pointed as she whispered into her friend's ear.

"I see," Diana said, her eyes dropping to the floor.

"What? No," I said, trying to swallow the dust off my tongue. "It's just that..."

"It's okay, Boady."

Some of those kids were among the ones who'd laughed at me the day Coach Thayer hit me with that eraser. The heat of my embarrassment from that day still smoldered in my chest.

But then I thought about Diana. She had been the only one who didn't laugh. And here we sat with her thinking that the reason I didn't want to dance had something to do with her—that I somehow found her lacking. She deserved better than to be stuck with a chickenshit like me.

Out in front of us, the song ended, and Thomas nodded and waved to try get me onto the floor. Sheila also tried to coax us out, although Diana had her eyes cast down, looking at the toe of her shoe, and didn't see it. Another song began—a song that I liked.

I started watching other dancers, not Thomas—because you really shouldn't try juggling knives until you've mastered tennis balls. One of the guys, a cowboy with a beat-up straw hat, seemed to know what he was doing. I moved my feet in front of me to mimic his steps, my eyes locked in on his boots. I stepped to the right...brought my feet together...stepped left...together...repeat. What do you know; it was kind of like marching side to side.

"You like this song?" I asked.

"I love this song."

"Yeah, me too." I tried to say more, but nothing came out.

Then after a pause, Diana said, "It's one of those songs that's easy to dance to."

"I s'pose," I said. "But I gotta tell ya something…I don't know how to dance."

She looked in my eyes as if trying to spot a lie.

"I mean it—I ain't never done it before…but if you want to dance with me, I'm willin' to give 'er a go."

She smiled and nodded, the twinkle in her eyes saying, *About time.*

We took an open space near Thomas and Sheila and started dancing, my steps rigid and off the beat, my hips bouncing up and down—not side to side like everyone else. I didn't look at Diana at all, preferring instead to keep my eyes on the cowboy. He held his arms close into his side, so that's what I did too. He turned in a spin—I did not do that.

When I felt like I had managed the fundamentals, I looked at Diana, and her smile tripped me up—and just like that, I was off the beat again. I looked down at her feet and managed to get back into rhythm. By the time the song ended, I could hold my own without watching the cowboy, but I still couldn't look at Diana.

The DJ rolled into the next song—another good one—without giving us a pause to leave the dance floor. Diana leaned in to me and said, "You're a really good dancer."

I knew that to be a lie, but one I could live with. If she didn't mind my flopping around, who was I to care? I spent that second song perfecting my one move: right, together, left, together, repeat. Pretty soon I felt like a kid who just learned to ride a bike, and I had to suppress the urge to whoop at my accomplishment. By the time that second song wound down, I had come to the realization that I might actually like dancing.

Then the DJ threw a new challenge at me. All music, throughout human history, can be broken down into two types—fast songs and slow songs. Just as I got a handle on the fast ones, the DJ said, "Now for a change of pace we're gonna slow things down a bit." I had no reference point for this. I had seen slow dancing on TV but never paid any attention to how they did it. I paused to allow Diana the opportunity to leave the dance floor. She did not. Instead she stepped in to me, her eyes asking, *Should we?*

Holding a girl for a slow dance looked so easy on TV, yet I had no idea what to do. I held my left arm out to the side, the way I'd seen Jimmy Stewart do in all those old movies. Diana placed her hand in mine, and I gently held it, reaching my other hand to her side where it came to rest on her waist. As I did that, she stepped in even closer, putting her hand on my shoulder.

We stepped slowly in small circles as the music swelled around us, dislodging the nervous crust from my joints. I looked into Diana's eyes and held my gaze there for the first time since we had entered the dance floor. My goodness, she was pretty. She leaned her body in to mine, slid her right hand out of my hand and reached both arms up around my shoulders. I followed her lead, wrapping my arms around her waist.

She smelled...I want to say nice, but it was so much more than that. Her presence in my arms seemed to erode the walls of my senses, and I could smell the very softness of her skin, taste the mingle of her perfume and sweat and apple shampoo. The effect made me almost dizzy. She swayed and I followed—the tiny muscles of her back rippling against my fingertips. The tickle of her hair on my arm made me ache to hold her tighter.

Then she raised herself up on the tips of her toes so that her lips were next to my ear and whispered, "I know what ya did."

Her words confused me, and I stopped dancing for a beat or two.

"Mrs. Lathem told my mom 'bout that boy wantin' to throw his puddin' on me. Said you knocked him down and stopped him." Diana touched her lips to my cheek and kissed me, the corner of her mouth pressing against the corner of mine. She held the kiss there for an eternity before pulling back to look into my eyes. "Thank you," she said.

I forgot all about stepping and rhythm and beats. I simply held Diana and moved. Nothing in the world existed at that moment outside of the two of us. I slid my hand gently up the curve of her back, feeling the roundness of her shoulder blades, her body tight against mine. Spinning lights from the DJ booth swept across the dance floor in delicious chaos, removing us from the rest of the world. I closed my eyes and immersed myself in a feeling more powerful than anything I had ever felt before.

I wanted to stay in that place for as long as I could, but all songs must end, and when the music stopped, it left me wobbly. I waited for the next song, hoping for another slow one. Instead, the DJ announced that he was putting the dance on hold so that everyone could go outside and enjoy the fireworks.

I'd never been more disappointed to go watch fireworks in all my life.

CHAPTER

32

THE FOUR OF US LEFT THE DANCE TOGETHER, THE GIRLS peeling off to go watch the fireworks with their families, our goodbye drawn out in a way that felt good and bad at the same time. After that, Thomas and I parted ways as he turned left to find our mothers, and I turned right, heading for a row of port-a-potties, ducking into one that seemed somewhat clean.

While inside, I heard the first round of fireworks explode over the river. When I came out, the sky was lit up in bursts of red and gold and white, enormous plumes that cast fluttering shadows as the sparks fell back to Earth.

Distracted as I was, I didn't see Jarvis until he grabbed a handful of my shirt and yanked me toward a strand of trees, throwing me up against one. "I saw you out there dancin' with that jigaboo," he said. "It all makes sense now. Your little butt-buddy's got you screwed up."

I could smell the alcohol on his breath and hear the slur in his words. Behind Jarvis, Bob and Beef were casting furtive glances around, apparently more concerned by who might be watching than was Jarvis.

"Trippin' Bob the way you did. Runnin' from us. And then ya go and get my uncle arrested. Just couldn't keep your mouth shut about that lighter, could ya?"

I squeaked, "How'd you—"

He pulled me away from the tree and slammed me up against it again. "We know everything!" he said. "We're everywhere."

Bob started laughing, but Beef stepped away from us, sliding into a shadow and disappearing toward the picnic grounds.

"You're a damned nigger-lover. Been one from the start, ain't ya. You ain't one of us; you're one of them."

One of them. At school, getting called *nigger-lover* was about as bad as it got. Of all the insults a guy could throw at you, that one and *faggot*—hit the hardest. They held supremacy over all others, and demanded retaliation—at least those were the rules.

But I thought about Wally Schenicker. Calling him a hateful name didn't change the fact that he was as decent a man as I'd ever met. And what about Thomas? I was supposed to be outraged that Jarvis accused me of being his friend? Should I have been repulsed for feeling what I felt when I danced with Diana? *Faggot, nigger-lover*—those words had become so powerful to me, chasms dividing good from bad, heaven from hell, us from them. But in the end, they were nothing but words.

I summoned what little grit I had in me and answered Jarvis. "I sure as hell *ain't* one of you."

I never even saw his arm move. His hand flew up open-palmed, fingers spread wide, and he slapped me on the side of my head so hard that I was sure he loosened some teeth. He struck my jaw, my cheek, and my ear all in one blow, leaving me in a soupy haze. I could still see his mouth moving, feel the spit of his anger on my face, but I couldn't hear the words on the other side of the hum.

A blast from the fireworks penetrated the fog before anything else, the flash of white, red, and blue reflecting off Jarvis. After that, I started to hear his words again.

"If ya ain't scared of me, then ya ain't smart," he said, pulling the sleeve of his T-shirt up to expose the CORPS tattoo on his shoulder. "You know how ya get one of these?"

"Jarvis! What the hell ya doin' there?"

Both Jarvis and Bob looked to see who said that. Behind them, that young deputy, Dean, walked up with a smile on his face and his thumbs shoved into his utility belt. Jarvis let go of my shirt.

"Hey, Dean. Just havin' a little chat with my friend Boady here. Ain't that right, Boady?"

Dean said, "Someone told me St. Ignatius done messed up and gave you a diploma. Tell me that ain't so."

Behind Dean, Beef made his way back to where he'd been standing before, shuffling a few inches at a time as though he'd never slipped away.

"Yeah, who'da figured," Jarvis said with a big grin. "Not only that, but I got me a scholarship to wrestle up at Warrensburg."

"Is that a fact?"

"Wait," I said. "You saw him hit me, right?"

"I never hit you," Jarvis yelled. "I was just havin' a little fun."

Dean said, "Maybe it's time you let the boy go enjoy the fireworks. They're mighty impressive this year."

"Really?" I said with as much incredulity as I could muster. "That's it?"

"Yeah, boys," Jarvis said. "Let's go watch us some fireworks."

The three of them, along with Deputy Dean, made their way back to the line of muscle cars up in front of the church.

As I watched them leave, I wondered how far Jarvis might have gone had Dean not shown up—had Beef not gone and fetched him. I also wondered if I'd have a bruise in the morning, and I contemplated what—if anything—I would tell my mom, or Thomas. They wouldn't be able to see it in the dark, and I decided to sleep on it and see how it looked in morning.

At the car, Mom and Jenna sat in the lawn chairs they'd

brought, while Thomas and I lay on the windshield. The fireworks were the best I'd ever seen, yet with so many other things pinging around my head—and the side of my face throbbing in pain—I found my thoughts wandering back to Jarvis and what he'd said. "If ya ain't scared of me, ya ain't smart."

CHAPTER

33

I RELIVED MY CONFRONTATION WITH JARVIS OVER AND OVER AS I struggled to find sleep that night; eventually, I forced that memory out of my head by thinking about my dance with Diana. I could still feel her lips on my cheek, her dress under my fingers, the tickle of her hair where it touched skin, her arms around my shoulders. If I breathed in slowly enough I could smell the mix of her perfume and body heat.

I must have drifted past the point where thoughts became dreams, because soon Diana was in my arms again, dancing in the shade of an old willow. In my dream, I had grace, my feet gliding from step to step never truly touching the ground, soft music looping around us, lifting us as we moved.

But somewhere in that bliss, the violin struck a sour note, one that sounded oddly familiar. When it happened again, I recognized Grover's whine. I opened my eyes to the light of a half moon drifting in through the open window, my dog standing at the foot of the bed, his nose pressed against the screen.

Grover rarely left Mom's side once they got tucked in for the night, so it was strange to see him there. I stirred, and he briefly looked at me before turning his attention back outside, the night air barely ruffling the curtain as it drifted in.

Crawling to the foot of my bed, I gave Grover a pat on the head and took a look outside. Hoke's house was completely dark, and over at the Elgins', a thin light shone from the single bulb that Jenna kept on at the top of the stairs. I was about to go back to bed when I heard the sound of gravel crunching under running feet.

Grover barked and bounced on his paws as though wanting to go through the window. I put my hands around his mouth and strained to hear. The footsteps grew softer and more distant, but I could still hear them between Grover's muffled barks. I gave a harder look and saw something moving, a shadow—a man—running toward the bottom of the road, disappearing past Hoke's place. That's when I noticed a new light, tiny like the flame of a candle, flickering in the grass in front of the Elgins' house.

"Mom!" I yelled, grabbing a pair of pants and falling through my bedroom door into the hall. "Mom, somethin's goin' on at the Elgins'." I jammed my legs into my pants and tumbled out the front door.

Stepping barefooted across the gravel, I yelled my fool head off, hoping to awaken Hoke and the Elgins. The flame burned along a rope lying in the middle of the lawn, the stink of smoke and kerosene filling my nose as I closed in. Beyond the flame stood a cross, eight feet tall, thin and straight, the whole thing wrapped in what looked like burlap.

I was about to yell again when—*BOOM!* The fuse touched off the burlap and it erupted in a pillar of fire. I fell backwards to the ground, the heat from the blaze licking at my chest and face. As I crawled away from the fire, two large hands grabbed my arms as Charles pulled me back.

Jenna stepped out onto the porch, her eyes sharp with anger. Thomas walked over and joined me. Mom, in her housecoat, came up the walkway and stood behind us.

"God damn them," Charles cursed as he rushed to grab the garden hose.

Hoke was making his way over to us, and next to him, Grover, who had been sniffing a zigzag in front of the Elgins' property, popped his nose up, looked down the road, and took off running. That's when I remembered the man I'd seen from my window.

"He's down there!" I yelled, pointing in the direction of Schenicker's.

"What?" Hoke asked.

At the same time, Charles asked, "Who?"

"The guy! I saw him!"

No sooner had the words left my mouth than the roar of a truck engine pierced the darkness, coming from that shadowy section of road between Hoke's house and Schenicker's. It choked and sputtered to gain a head of steam, and I recognized the sound; the last time I had heard it was when a man in a Casper mask tried to bash my head in with a broomstick.

Mom put her hands on my shoulders and drew me in to her, a gesture that felt far more natural than I would have thought. And there we stood, the group of us, frozen by the roar of that truck, the noise growing louder like a charging hellhound. Headlights flashed on, blinding us as it neared. When it passed, a man's voice hollered out from the driver's seat, something that sounded like "Go home, nigger!"

I strained to see past the headlights, hoping to glimpse a face or license plate, but it all remained cloaked in darkness. I couldn't even tell if the cab of the truck held more than one man.

And I didn't see the rock. Nobody saw it, a silent missile launched by someone in the pickup. It sailed through the night air, silently arcing, in search of a victim. We had been standing close enough to one another that it was bound to find a target.

I heard the rock hit, the sickening sound of tearing flesh and cracking bone somehow finding its way past the noise of the pickup. Then Mom's hands went limp on my shoulders, and she fell where she stood, her body crumpled, motionless at my feet.

"Mom!" I yelled, dropping to her side.

Jenna joined me there and immediately started feeling around Mom's head, drawing back a hand painted with blood. She began yelling orders.

"Thomas, get me a flashlight and some towels."

In the thin glow of the porch light I could see a small dark pool gathering beneath Mom's head.

"Charles, call an ambulance—and the sheriff."

Hoke eased himself down to his knees and lifted Mom's legs to elevate them a few inches.

Thomas came out of the house with his arms full of cotton towels and a flashlight, laying everything on the sidewalk beside Jenna.

"Go grab some blankets from the linen closet," she said to Thomas, and he scurried back into the house.

I watched in silence as Jenna moved with confidence, gently pressing a towel to a wound on the side of my mom's head. Thomas returned with some blankets, and Hoke rolled one into a bundle to put under Mom's feet, keeping them raised. The other he spread over her torso.

Charles came back out of the house and stood over his wife. "The ambulance is on the way and so is—"

When Charles didn't finish his sentence, I glanced up and saw his eyes locked on something down the road. As he walked out to get a better look, I turned and saw a glow lighting up the treetops down by Schenicker's. Charles stepped into the road and hollered, "They set his house on fire."

Charles took off running down the road with Thomas hauling ass to catch up to his father. Hoke stood and made his way toward the Elgins' house, telling Jenna that he was calling the fire department.

Everyone seemed to be buzzing and zipping around me, while I did nothing beyond lifting Mom's wrist and gently rubbing the back of her hand. For all those years we lived in the same house, existing in each other's lives like shadows, always there, sharing the same space yet never really touching—and now, all I could do was hold her hand and let the weight of all those wasted moments press down on me.

Hoke rejoined us after calling the fire department. "She's going to be okay," he whispered. "The ambulance will be here any minute."

Half an hour. That's how long it took for the EMTs to arrive—the longest half hour of my life. But once there, they moved with an urgency that gave me hope. The sheriff came next, driving past us and going down to Wally's house, the flames shooting up into the night so high that I could see them licking the sky above the tops of the trees.

They put Mom on a gurney, and after I watched the two men roll her away, I noticed something lying next to the sidewalk a few paces away from where my mother had fallen. It was the rock that had hit her in the head. When I bent down to take a closer look, I had to swallow back a wave of panic that welled up in me. I recognized that rock—the size of a baseball, white with glassy striations across its surface. It was the rock that I had thrown at that pickup and at the men wearing the Casper masks.

The efficiency of what our attackers had done that night became clear. They burned the cross to scare the Elgins. They torched Schenicker's house to punish him for being who he was. And the rock—that was payback for what I had done to them. I had poked them in a way that they couldn't let stand, and so that night, that rock had been meant for me.

CHAPTER

34

B Y THE TIME I CLIMBED INTO HOKE'S CAR TO FOLLOW THE ambulance to the hospital, neither Thomas nor Charles had yet returned from the bottom of the road. I had no idea what happened to Wally Schenicker. Before leaving, I showed Jenna the rock that hit my mother and explained how it was the same one I'd thrown at the men in the Casper masks. She would be the one to pass that information on to Sheriff Vaughan.

At the hospital, a doctor and a nurse came out to help the EMTs, the nurse grabbing the gurney and pulling it through the doors while the doctor walked alongside. The emergency room doctor seemed too young for the important task that lay ahead of him, somewhere in his late twenties, with hair pulled back in a small ponytail. They wheeled my mother past the check-in and disappeared behind a second set of doors.

I wanted to follow, but Hoke put a hand on my shoulder, guiding me to the waiting area and a row of orange chairs. The room had no music or television to fill the heavy silence, so I set my focus on a large clock on the wall and watched as it slowly ticked its way toward one a.m., the thin second hand lingering unmercifully on each dot before moving on to the next.

I glanced at the entrance every so often, wondering whether another ambulance would arrive with Wally, burned but alive. As we neared half an hour of waiting—with no other ambulance showing up—I became hopeful that he'd escaped the flames, until it occurred to me that there'd be no trip to the emergency room if he died in the fire.

At 1:45, the emergency room doors opened and a man walked through, mid-forties, beard, and a serious gait to his step. He walked past us without even glancing our way, disappearing behind the door where they had taken my mom. Hoke and I looked at each other, Hoke shrugging his lack of an answer to the question I didn't ask.

We resumed waiting, and at some point I must have fallen asleep because I awoke to the sound of footsteps, my head leaning on Hoke's arm. The young doctor with the long hair walked toward us looking grim.

"I'm Dr. Draeger," he said, shaking hands with Hoke and ignoring me. "Mrs. Sanden is in stable condition. The blow she took caused a fracture in her temporal bone." He pointed to the side of his own head to show us.

Hoke either didn't understand what the doctor said or he had frozen his expression to hide his concern from me, nodding calmly like he was listening to a list of lunch specials. But I couldn't hold my thoughts back.

"A fractured skull?" I whispered.

Draeger heard me, but he again spoke to Hoke. "It's never good to have a fracture of any bone, but in this case, there's an upside. With a head injury there's usually swelling—that's one of the biggest dangers. A fracture can actually work to ease some of the pressure on the interior of the skull. We had to perform surgery to—"

"Surgery?" I said.

Now Dr. Draeger looked at me when he answered. "We brought in one of our surgeons, Dr. Kanner. He's really good—one of the best. He did an operation to relieve the swelling. She came through it just fine. Her vital signs look good. We've sedated her and cooled her to keep the swelling down. I also did a preliminary GCS protocol to test her responsiveness—"

"GCS?" Hoke asked.

"A Glasgow Coma Scale."

"Coma!" My knees buckled, forcing me to sit in one of the chairs. I thought about a girl named Karen Quinlan who had fallen into a coma at a party and couldn't come out of it. We'd read about her in my Current Events class because her case went to the Supreme Court that spring. What I remembered most about the story was how they made it sound like she was both alive and dead at the same time.

"What's your name?" Draeger asked.

"Boady."

"This is Mrs. Sanden's son," Hoke added.

The doctor sat beside me. "Listen, Boady—your mom is unconscious. That's a good thing. When a person sustains a trauma…a bad hit to the head like your mother did, the body will shut down to protect itself. We've given her some medication to keep her unconscious until we see if the swelling goes down or not."

"Will she wake up?" I asked. "Will she be all right?"

"Your mother will get the best treatment possible."

He didn't answer my question. Part of me wanted to hear him say that my mother would be just fine, but another part of me appreciated that he was doing his best to be honest. Hoke placed his hand on my shoulder, and I could feel tears start to well up in my eyes. I fought them back, swallowing them down inside me.

"Can I see her?"

The doctor looked up at Hoke for guidance, and Hoke must have signaled his okay because Dr. Draeger said, "You can see her for just a little bit."

We walked deeper into the hospital to a dimly lit room where Mom lay in a bed, white gauze wrapped around her head, a tube taped to her mouth, an IV in her arm. A nurse stood beside her bed, repositioning some wires that disappeared beneath the edge of her blanket. Mom looked pale and weak, but better than she looked lying on the ground in the Elgins' front yard.

Dr. Draeger said, "We're going to keep a close watch on her all night. In the morning, Dr. Kanner will be back to follow up. He did his residency in Chicago and is kind of an expert in head trauma. We're lucky to have him. There's not much more to do for now except keep close tabs on her and watch for any signs of swelling or infection."

Hoke said, "Should we wait...here...or?"

"I'd recommend that you go home, get some rest, and come back around, say, nine. Dr. Kanner will have had time to give her an examination by then."

Hoke looked at me as if waiting for my consent. I nodded.

"I think you should stay with me for a spell," Hoke said.

I nodded again.

We walked back out to find Sheriff Vaughan standing, hat in hand, in the waiting area. "Y'all got a second?"

The three of us sat down.

"Is Wally okay?" I asked.

"Yeah," Vaughan said. "Mr. Schenicker wasn't home. He was...visiting a friend...a guy named George Bauer. His house is gone, though. How's your ma?"

Hoke explained what Doc Draeger told us, and Vaughan asked us to give an account of the truck and the rock and anything else we could tell him. Neither of us was of much help.

"But it was the same truck," I said. "I'm sure of it. You need to get the tire tracks. There'll be parts of the tread missin'."

"We have that," Vaughan said. "The Elgin boy found them for

us. He said it was the same tread that you two saw that day y'all got hit. We'll be lookin' for trucks with that tread print, but it's like lookin' for a needle in a haystack."

"You should start with the Halcomb clan," Hoke said. "I don't know which of them did it, but you know they're knee-deep in what happened out there—well, except for Milo."

"Except for Milo?" Vaughan asked.

"He's in jail," Hoke said. "He's the one Halcomb you can rule out."

Vaughan looked at us as though deeply confused about something, then he said, "Mr. Gardner, Milo Halcomb bailed out of jail yesterday morning."

CHAPTER

35

THE LIGHTS WERE OFF AT THE ELGINS' PLACE WHEN WE GOT back home. There were still fire trucks and squad cars at the end of the road—stamping out embers and looking for evidence, I suspected. On Hoke's suggestion, I stopped at my house to grab a sleeping bag, a change of clothes, and some essentials, and then headed over to his place.

Hoke lived in a modified A-frame cabin; the upstairs was a single bedroom with a balcony that overlooked the living room below. Hoke slept in a bedroom on the main floor and had turned the upstairs bedroom into a library with hundreds of books on simple pine shelving lining the two longest walls. A small reading table stood against the far wall, above which the room's only window looked out over the treetops.

Hoke laid down three couch cushions from downstairs for me to use as a bed and retrieved a pillow from a closet. As he left the room, Hoke walked over to the reading table and removed a photo frame, silver and hinged, that opened like a book. It held two pictures, and I stole a peek before he could close it—black-and-white photos of his wife and daughter, faces I recognized from the obituary.

Hoke held the frame behind his leg and looked around the room one last time. "Well, if you need anything," he said, "I'll be downstairs." With that he left me alone.

I turned off the light and waited. Once the house fell silent, I snuck over to the reading table, turned on the small lamp, and began looking for signs of Hoke's past life—finding none: no pictures on the walls, no mementos on the table, no indication that he held any connection to another human being. What he did have were books, lots of them. On one side of the room, he kept an extensive collection of literature that included Shakespeare, Homer, Whitman, Faulkner, and a ton more. On the other wall his books seemed more educational, beginning with the Talmud, the Qur'an, the Upanishads, histories on the Buddha and Christ, along with books on philosophy like Aristotle, Socrates, Sir Francis Bacon, Schopenhauer, and Leibniz. I had heard of some of those names, but most were foreign to me back then.

At the end of the shelf, tucked behind the legs of the reading table, I saw a trunk that looked like a pirate's treasure chest only smaller. It had two buckles and a clasp on the front with a padlock on it. I had to sit on the floor to get to the trunk because Hoke had it slid so far back. I slowly pulled it out from under the table, being careful to not make a sound, and ran a finger across the opened buckles and the lock, which hadn't been clicked shut.

I had a feeling that I knew what that trunk held. Hoke kept all of his books in that room, but where were the black books with the red spines—the ones he'd been writing in all those years? I listened for Hoke and heard only silence. I knew that I shouldn't go through his things, but he knew everything about *me*—all those years of sitting on his porch, pouring out the details of my life while he kept everything about his own life a secret.

It didn't take as much effort as you might think to justify my invasion of Hoke's privacy. Sheriff Vaughan had said that Hoke should have gone to prison for something. How could I let that go? We lived next door to this man; we had a *right* to know—and that was all it took. I lifted the hasp and eased the trunk lid open, a thin *creak* escaping the hinge. And there inside I found Hoke's books.

I leaned the trunk lid up against the wall and listened again. Silence. I tiptoed to the front of the loft and peered down. The house lay as still as morning dew. I went back to the trunk and moved my fingers across the spines of ten books, each with a year written on it, starting in 1966 and ending with the year 1975. The volume for 1976 must have been downstairs with Hoke.

I tenderly pulled the first book out, handling it as if it were a relic so fragile that it might fall apart if exposed to human touch. I opened it to its first page and read: *Dear Mariam, I am writing this letter to explain why I haven't yet killed myself.*

Mariam Fisk? It had to be. I flipped forward through the pages to see how long the letter went on and saw that it continued, all the way to the end of the book. I pulled the second volume out of the trunk and opened it to find the same. All those years, Hoke had been writing one long letter to his dead wife's sister—the woman who'd wanted to kill him back in 1966. I went back to the first volume and began reading again.

Dear Mariam,

   I am writing this letter to explain why I haven't yet killed myself. I know that my continued existence is a loathsome and cowardly thing in your eyes, and I won't argue otherwise, but you deserve to know why I still live—while my daughter and my wife do not. It is my hope that after reading this, you will come to see that my decision not to kill myself had a purpose.

   That night you came to my house and threw your father's revolver through my window, I heard what you said, what you screamed at me—that I killed your sister and my little girl. You were right on both scores, I did kill them. I killed them just as surely as if I put a gun to their heads. Your sister begged me not to drive that night, but I could be bullheaded, even downright mean when the scotch kicked in. Of course you know that already.

Before I get to the purpose of this letter, I need you to know that on the night of the accident, I did everything I could to save my family. There is not a day that goes by when I don't curse whatever twist of fate caused me to be thrown clear. I was the one who should have died that night.

I know that you will choose to believe what you want to believe, and that's okay, but I have no reason to lie anymore. By the time you read this, I will be dead, my memory all but gone from this world. I just need you to know the truth about that night before I tell you the rest.

In the end, I will not ask for your forgiveness—to the contrary, your condemnation of me is well placed. I condemn myself for what I did. I only write this so that you may know that my continued existence on this earth is not as selfish an act as you may believe it to be.

A creak of a board from somewhere downstairs stopped my heart. I waited for another sound, something that might tell me if Hoke was ascending the steps. When I heard nothing more, I crept to the rail at the end of the loft and peered down again. The house below remained silent and still. When I crawled back to the book, I brought the lamp down off the table, set it on the floor beside me, and covered myself and the lamp with my sleeping bag.

Comfortable that I had blocked enough of the light from escaping the loft, I returned to the book to read about Hoke Gardner—and me.

CHAPTER

36

R EADING THAT FIRST VOLUME FELT LIKE DESCENDING INTO A
cold, black pit. Hoke, a man who reveled in small details,
wrote so meticulously that I could see and feel every step of his
journey. Maybe that was the whole point of the letter—to draw
Mariam in so that she would understand. Whatever the reason,
Hoke's words filled my head and heart with grief and brought me
down to a place so bleak that it seemed no light should survive.
And just when I believed that the depth of Hoke's grief would
never find a bottom, I found it.

On a bone-chilling night in the fall of 1966, Hoke Gardner
drove from Columbia to Dry Creek, parking near the entrance
to the St. Peter Cemetery. Reaching into his glove box, he pulled
out the Colt that had once belonged to his father-in-law—a
gun that came to him when Mariam Fisk threw it through his
picture window, a final gasp of anguish on the night she'd hoped
to kill him.

His left arm lay limp across his leg, the weight of his lifeless
hand holding the gun against his thigh so he could inspect it one
last time. He wasn't afraid, yet his fingers trembled as he pulled
the hammer back to half-cocked. He opened the loading gate and
turned the cylinder—six bullets, but all he needed was one. Even
in this moment of desperation he fixated on the details.

Hoke opened the car door and embraced the frigid drizzle that fell sideways in the wind, the tiny half-frozen water droplets needling his face and neck, the cold penetrating his flesh, and seeping deep into his bones and muscles. *If there was such a thing as perfect weather for a deed such as this*, he wrote, *this was it.* He drew the collar of his jacket up tight around his unshaved neck, the windbreaker far too thin to keep out the cold, but that wouldn't matter for much longer.

He looked around the cemetery to make sure that he was alone. He was. No sane person would go to a cemetery on such a miserable night. He walked to the statue of the angel, her outstretched hands imploring Hoke not to do what he was about to do, yet her stony eyes offered him no comfort. Near her feet, he found Alicia's grave, and next to her, his sweet Sarah. He sat on the wet grass and rubbed his fingers over their names.

"Daddy's a good driver," he wrote. Those would be the last words that Sarah would ever say, a five-year-old's attempt to stop the argument her parents were having. Alicia hadn't wanted Hoke to drive. She knew he'd had too much to drink. Hoke wouldn't listen, though, and ordered Alicia into the car. Twelve minutes later, he would drive his car into a tree. Twelve minutes later, Sarah and Alicia would be dead.

Hoke leaned down, kissed both headstones and whispered, "I'm sorry."

He lifted the Colt from his pocket, laid it on his lap, and wiped the drizzle from his eyes. He had spent five months fighting the pain, and every day it grew stronger, eating away at his heart, at his mind, until it had grown so large that only a bullet could stop it—a bullet from a cold, wet revolver.

I raised the barrel to my lips, touched it to my tongue, tasted the bitter edge of gun oil and sulfur.

But the barrel slid against the roof of his mouth when he put his thumb on the trigger. Was the roof of his mouth the best place to aim? He moved the barrel under his chin, but didn't trust that, either. It might hit his jawbone, or a tooth, and alter the bullet's course. He brought the gun up to his temple and decided that would be the spot, in that soft place beside his right eye.

It wasn't fair, and I knew it. One simple bullet and I would be free of the pain. It seemed too easy.

He looked at the sky, watching the lightning as it stabbed at the horizon across the river. Then he closed his eyes, and pulled the hammer back with his thumb. His heart fluttered in his chest; his breath fell shallow; his forehead dripped with sweat and rain. He pinched his eyelids shut, whispered, "I'm sorry" again, and pulled hard on the trigger.

CLICK!

The gun didn't fire. A wave of panic swept over Hoke, and he cocked the hammer back again and—*CLICK!*

"Damn you!" Hoke cried out like a wounded dog, his eyes raised to the sky. He tried a third time. *CLICK!* His arm slumped under the weight of his failure, his head tipping down until his chin rested on his chest. *CLICK!* "Why won't you let me stop this? I just want it to be over." He pulled the trigger once more, and this time it fired.

Hoke awoke in the hospital—the second time that year—his head bandaged and an IV in his arm. It took a few minutes for his memory to come back: the cemetery, the rain...the gun. He had allowed it to dip lower with each misfire. By the time the worn firing pin found enough primer to cause a spark, the gun had fallen to such an angle that the bullet must have glanced off his skull.

He had a vague recollection of a man—a priest—kneeling at his side in the rain, but they weren't in the cemetery. Hoke must have stumbled to the steps of the rectory, which meant that the gun might still be in the cemetery, waiting for him.

The clock on the wall showed three thirty, and the sunlight coming in through the window told Hoke that he'd been out for hours, if not days. It was all Hoke could do not to scream out his anger. Instead, he pulled the IV out of his arm, found his clothes in the small closet, put them on, and then quietly slipped out of the room, determined to finish what he had started. Before he could get to the exit, though, a commotion arose in the corridor behind him. He heard a nurse call out that he was missing.

Hoke spotted a police officer coming in from outside, as of yet unaware of the hunt for the man with the head wound. He thought about charging past the officer, making a break for it, but in his weakened state, it would have been a short race before the cop caught him. He looked around and found himself standing outside of the hospital's chapel, so he slipped inside and took a seat in the last pew, putting his head down, pretending to pray.

There, he carefully unwrapped the gauze from his head, listening to the voices in the corridor in the hope that the staff might assume that he had made it out of the building. When he finally looked up he saw a young woman kneeling in the front pew, her hands folded together so tightly that it squeezed the blood from her fingers, her knuckles pressed to her chin, her lips moving in silent prayer. Tears poured from her closed eyes and rolled down her cheeks.

Before long, a doctor walked into the chapel and Hoke dropped his face back into his hands to hide. But the doctor passed by Hoke and walked slowly down the aisle, touching the woman's shoulder, pulling her out of her prayers. She turned toward the doctor, who squatted so he could look at her as he told her his news.

"I'm sorry," he whispered. "John didn't make it." He started to say more, but the woman turned pale and collapsed, the doctor catching her and easing her head down to the seat of the pew.

That's when Hoke saw the little boy wandering along the side wall of the chapel looking at the faux stained-glass windows. The boy hadn't noticed the doctor come in, nor did he see his mother collapse. As the boy moved from window to window, he came near the back pew where Hoke knelt. When he saw Hoke, the little boy approached him with a mixture of caution and curiosity. He stared at Hoke for a bit then spoke.

"What happened?" he asked.

Hoke did not want to speak at first, but the little boy's big brown eyes—eyes that held no clue that his life had just been turned upside down—touched Hoke. In that moment, Hoke saw his silence as an act of selfishness, so he answered.

"I had an accident," Hoke said.

"So did my daddy," the little boy said.

"What's your name, little man?" Hoke asked.

"My name is Boady," I told him.

CHAPTER

37

A S THE FIRST TRACE OF MORNING BLED ITS WAY INTO THE eastern horizon, I was still working on the fourth volume of Hoke's letter to Mariam. I leaned against one of the shelves with the book on my lap, my sleeping bag still draped over my head, and the lamp warm at my side.

Hoke's writing had opened my eyes to a world that lay hidden in plain sight; it was as though I had been staring at a mirror all my life and that mirror suddenly turned into a window. I'd grown up with Hoke next door to me, the limp arm, the scar that ran up the side of his head—a scar that came from a bullet meant to end his life—but now I understood that Hoke didn't just happen to end up on Frog Hollow. He'd sought us out.

So many insignificant turns in my life, events I believed to have been random chance, had actually been orchestrated by Hoke—like getting Grover. It was all a setup. Hoke had been watching me wandering through the woods alone and decided that I needed a dog. So he bought a coonhound puppy, knowing that I'd take to the dog in a way that would force my mother to let me keep him—and it worked just as Hoke had planned.

All those skills that he taught me, catching fish, using a whetstone, changing oil—the kind of things that a father teaches a son—he came to Frog Hollow to teach me those things, to fill the void left behind by my father. I had no idea. He'd been so quiet in his method, so unobtrusive, that it never occurred to me that it had all been part of a plan.

But Hoke's generosity didn't stop with my mother and me. The books told about how Hoke enlisted accomplices to help him carry out his altruism. One worked for the county social services, and every Christmas she gave Hoke the names of families who were struggling. Hoke would then sneak gifts: sleds, tricycles, diapers, and sometimes a little cash, to those families, usually leaving the presents on their porch in the middle of the night.

The other accomplice was a nurse at the hospital who contacted Hoke whenever a child fell seriously ill. Hoke secreted money to those families so that mothers and fathers could take time off work to be at their child's side in those dire times. Those parents went to their mailboxes and found unmarked envelopes full of money and a note, which read: *For you and your child in this time of need.*

Growing up, I'd read stories about the Anonymous Angel of Jessup, as the *Jessup Journal* called him. The stories told of gifts that came when they were most needed; it was an answer to a prayer, they would say. One of those families, the Jensens, had spoken at our school assembly back in February. Leslie Jensen, the little sister of one of my classmates, rode her sled out into the street and was hit by a car. She lingered in the hospital for over a month before she died. I remember how her father broke down, telling us how much it meant for him to be at her side when she took her last breath. He never knew—no one knew—that Hoke Gardner gave him that gift.

I had just finished volume four when I heard sounds coming from downstairs, Hoke moving around. I held my breath as footsteps shuffled across the hardwood floor below. I clicked the lamp off and slipped out from under the sleeping bag, ready to drop the book into the chest and shove everything back to its hiding spot under the table. But the footsteps stopped near the bottom of the steps, paused there, and then continued on to the front door.

Through a window on the front gable, I watched as Hoke turned to go to Schenicker's. I put volume four into the chest and skipped ahead to last year—1975—opened it, and thumbed past the everyday activity that Hoke took so much pleasure in writing about. Soon I came to a page where he wrote about Mom.

I never knew it, but Hoke made a point of being on his porch every day when Mom walked home for lunch. He would offer a friendly hello, and sometimes she walked over and joined him on the porch.

One entry told of Mom looking lost and beside herself with worry. Once Hoke got her to open up, she told him about my getting caught smoking at school. She said she didn't know what to do and blamed herself for not being a strong enough parent to keep me out of trouble. She lamented that I'd go downhill once I entered Jessup Public High School. Hoke had been the one to suggest sending me to St. Ignatius, but Mom told him that we couldn't afford it.

What I read next shifted the ground beneath my feet.

The summer before my freshman year, Mom received a letter from St. Ignatius telling us that I was eligible for a special scholarship designed to take kids from the country—troubled kids like me—and bring them to St. Ignatius, presumably to straighten us out. Mom applied for the scholarship, and to our surprise, they offered it to me. The news filled me with dread, but Mom said that it was "an answer to her prayers."

The truth of the matter was that there had never been a scholarship.

In his letter to Mariam, I read about Hoke's secret meeting with Simon Rutgers, the principal at St. Ignatius, where Hoke offered to make a sizable donation to the school provided that a small part of the money be used to create a special full-ride scholarship. He then attached two additional conditions. First, the inaugural scholarship had to be awarded to me; and second, my mother could never find out the truth about the source of the funds. Hoke was paying for me to go to St. Ignatius.

As the sun cleared the hills to the east, I put the lamp and the blanket away. I was about to return to reading when I heard Hoke—the Anonymous Angel himself—come in the front door. I put 1975 back into the trunk, carefully slid the books back to their hiding spot under the reading table, and went downstairs, stopping first in the bathroom to check my face. Jarvis didn't leave as much of a bruise as I expected. It would pass as a smudge of dirt if anyone noticed.

Hoke stood at the fridge, pulling out the fixings for breakfast. "How many sausage links do you want with your eggs?"

"Two or three," I said.

I couldn't seem to make eye contact with him. I had read his letter to Mariam; I had stolen something from him, and I felt ashamed about it—but at the same time, I knew that if I had it to do over, I would read them again.

"Sleep okay?" he asked.

I wondered if the exhaustion showed in my eyes. "Yep," I answered.

"I thought we might head into the hospital first thing this morning—after breakfast, of course."

"You think Mom's still unconscious?"

"Probably, but that was the plan, right? They want to keep her sedated. I'm sure they'll tell us more when we go in."

We ate eggs and sausage, and potatoes cooked in butter. Hoke told me that he'd slipped out to visit Schenicker's place and found Wally there, rummaging through the debris, looking for photos and keepsakes. "He thinks Milo Halcomb had a hand in what happened. He's got no evidence other than the fact that Milo threatened him with that very thing."

"Does he think Angus helped?" I asked.

"Wally didn't say. What do you think?"

"I don't think he'd do somethin' like that unless Milo pushed him to it. Angus ain't like his old man—at least not as I see it."

"You may be right about that."

We finished the meal and were taking our plates to the sink when a knock at the door pulled our attention. Hoke answered it and found a man in his late forties, wearing a suit and tie. "Dillon Royce," the man said, holding out his hand for Hoke. "State Patrol."

Hoke slipped outside and closed the door, their voices turning into a mumble so low I couldn't make heads nor tails of it. I went and sat down in one of Hoke's living room chairs, the one closest to the door, and from there I could just barely make out what they said.

"We've met before," Hoke said.

"I wasn't sure you'd remember," Royce said. "I was still cutting my teeth back then."

"You held your own better than most. I hear you're working the Lida Poe case now."

"Assisting. It's still Sheriff Vaughan's show, but I'm pitching in. That's what I'm here about. I was just down at Mr. Schenicker's place, and I understand the Sanden boy is here."

Hoke lowered his voice. "I thought it'd be best if he stayed here awhile—with Milo Halcomb being out on bail."

"You think Milo Halcomb was involved in what happened last night?"

"I think that's where I'd start. Halcomb and his brother run with a bunch of good ol' boys, call themselves the CORPS. It could be one of the Halcombs, or maybe one of that group. You can bet that some Halcomb's got a finger in this thing one way or the other. Did you question Milo?"

"That's the thing, Mr. Gardner," Royce said. "Milo Halcomb's missing. His brother bailed him out yesterday and no one's seen him since."

"Christ almighty." Hoke spat words.

"We thought you... and the boy should know." Royce lowered his voice so quiet that I had to crawl to the door to hear. "What I'm about to say is confidential. I'm only telling you this because... well, there's a boy involved, and he's an important witness in all this. You see what I'm saying?"

"Is Boady in danger?"

"We had a snitch tell us about a phone call he overheard Milo make from the jail. He said that Milo told someone that if that person didn't bail Milo out of jail, he'd blow everything up."

"Blow everything up?"

"Those were his words. Then he said, 'I'm getting out of here one way or another—it's your call.' The next thing you know, his brother Cecil comes in with the bail money."

"Blow what up?"

"And then last night, you folks out here get attacked. I honestly don't know what to make of it, but we can't find Milo now, and no one's talking to us. I'm not saying that the Sanden kid's a target, but I'll sleep better knowing you're keeping an eye out."

"I appreciate the heads-up," Hoke said.

I could tell Royce was getting set to leave, so I scrambled back to the chair and picked up a newspaper, flipping it open just as Hoke came in. He looked at me kind of funny-like and said, "You should go get cleaned up so we can head into town."

I nodded and then noticed that the newspaper in my hands, the one I pretended to read, was upside down.

CHAPTER

38

HOKE DROVE ME TO THE HOSPITAL, THE ENTIRE ELGIN FAMILY following in the Imperial, all of us anxious. When we arrived, we learned that they wanted to limit Mom's visitors to three at a time, so Jenna, Hoke, and I went to Mom's room, leaving Thomas and Charles in the waiting room.

I think Mom looked worse in the sunlight than she did when Hoke and I had seen her hours earlier, her eyes ringed by dark shadows, and her face more swollen and pale than before; but they had stopped giving her the sedative and her eyes struggled to open when she heard us.

"Boady?" Her voice cracked as she whispered my name.

"Yeah, Mom, I'm here."

She smiled a weak smile and reached her hand up to hold mine. I gave her fingers a light squeeze.

"I can't . . . stay awake," she murmered.

The doctors told us that she'd be groggy. They also told us that she had no memory of what had happened or why she was in the hospital, so we avoided that subject. Jenna talked to her about the tomatoes they had coming up in the garden. I told her about staying at Hoke's place. None of the conversations amounted to a hill of beans, but some of the things we said made her smile. When she grew too tired to keep up her fight for lucidity, she went back to sleep and we went to the waiting room.

It was decided that Charles would take Thomas home, leaving the three of us there to keep vigil and wait for another chance to visit her. I suspect that Mr. Elgin was fine with that, the way he jittered the whole time he'd been there. It wasn't long after Charles and Thomas left that Dr. Kanner came out to see us. He said that the preliminary tests were good—no sign of brain damage so far—but it was too early to know for sure, and the sedatives made it impossible to test her motor skills. They would need to keep Mom in the hospital for a few days, but then, she might come home.

Kanner talked to us about the long-term problems that can follow a traumatic brain injury, things like memory loss and a lack of dexterity. These were nothing more than possibilities, but he wanted to prepare us for the worst.

"When she gets back on her feet, I'm going to send her to University Hospital in Columbia. They have these tests they can do called the Halstead-Reitan Battery. It'll give us a look into how much damage occurred and where we may need to focus our attention."

"You think there might be permanent impairment?" Jenna asked.

"That's always in the cards. Her coma scale puts her in the low to moderate range, and that's a good start. Her traumatic amnesia..." He looked at me as if that needed a translation, which it did. "Not being able to remember what happened last night—that's common and doesn't mean anything. We'll know more in a few weeks when she goes up to Columbia."

After Dr. Kanner left, we retook our seats in the waiting room, my thoughts lingering on the darkest of Kanner's words: *long-term problems, loss of memory, lack of dexterity.* Mom might need help for some time to come—years—maybe forever. Then I thought about my plan to leave Jessup, just eight months away, all my preparations upturned by what Dr. Kanner had said. I should have been mentally stomping in circles, angry at the interference in my plan. But I wasn't angry, not even a little bit.

I tried to remember the last time that I'd thought about leaving Jessup, an undertaking that had once been my great preoccupation, the song that I couldn't get out of my head. But as I sat there, I couldn't remember when that notion last stirred in me. Was it possible that I had come to accept—maybe even like—my life on Frog Hollow?

As I pondered that notion, the weight of having stayed up all night caught up to me. Steeped in thoughts of my mother, Hoke, Wally, and the Elgins, I fell into a deep hibernation, one of those sleeps where you feel like you melt into the fabric beneath you, which for me was the vinyl cushion of a waiting room couch.

When Jenna woke me up sometime later, it took me a moment to remember where I was and why I was there. Jenna said that the doctor had authorized another visit. I blinked hard to work the sleep out of my eyes, and then followed Hoke and Jenna back to Mom's room.

She looked better on this visit than she had earlier. She no longer had to fight to keep her eyes open, although her left eye drooped unnaturally. She smiled a wary smile, as if she knew that she had been rescued from the brink of something terrible. She could move her hands and arms, and when we walked in, she was practicing touching her thumb to the tips of each of her fingers on her left hand—and faltering when it came to her pinky.

Jenna gave her a light hug, being careful not to touch the bandages on Mom's head. "You're looking good, sister," she said.

"I feel...numb," Mom said in slow, measured words. I could see the care she took to formulate her sentence, yet her consonants remained slurred despite the effort. "What happened?"

Jenna looked at Hoke, who stepped up beside the bed.

"You had an accident," he said.

Mom looked puzzled, so Jenna said, "I'll tell you all about it when you come home. Charles and I were talking, and we'd like you and Boady to move in with us—just until you're all better."

That was the first I'd heard of that plan. Jenna looked at me, I think to get my opinion on the matter, and I nodded.

"Boady can share a room with Thomas, and we're going to turn Charles's study into a bedroom for you. You'll have your own bathroom."

Mom smiled again, distracted from the question of how she came to be in a hospital.

CHAPTER

39

HOKE DROVE US BACK TO FROG HOLLOW, WHERE THOMAS and Charles were already in the throes of rearranging furniture at the Elgins' house. I cleaned my stuff out of Hoke's library, lamenting that I hadn't finished reading Hoke's letter to Mariam.

The Elgin house had enough bedrooms that I could have had my own room. They offered to shuffle things around for me, boxes and stuff left over from the move, but I declined. I liked the idea of sharing space with Thomas. He had set up a cot and offered to let me have his bed—a move that likely came at the direction of his father—but I was happy to take the cot. Thomas emptied out three of his drawers for me, and I brought some clothes over to fill them. When we had finished moving things around, his room still had more walking-around space than mine did across the road.

The Elgins went out of their way to make me feel at home that day, and I did my best to be the polite guest, offering to help cook and clean. I even suggested that Thomas and I go pull weeds in the garden that evening, which ticked Thomas off because he'd been doing his best to avoid that particular chore. By the time we went to bed, I was so tired that I could have slept on a pile of bricks, so the cot didn't bother me in the slightest.

On the second day, Wally stopped by after breakfast and asked if Thomas and I still wanted to work for him. I said yes without hesitation, but Thomas looked to his mother before answering. She gave a slight nod, and Thomas passed that nod on to Wally. I had wondered how Wally was handling the destruction of his house, and I have to say, if he had any anger or sadness about it, he did a good job of keeping it locked away. But then, I suppose Wally had become something of a master at keeping things hidden.

Later that morning, when we walked into Schenicker's office, I was surprised to find George Bauer sitting in my mom's chair. My expression must have been transparent, because George immediately said, "Don't worry. I'm only keeping the seat warm until your mom is back." I shrugged as if that hadn't been my thought.

Wally didn't send us out on a job that day. No sanding. No scrapping. Nothing like that. Instead, he had us clean up the debris of his burned-down house, filling up the one-ton with charred wood, appliances, and the like, and hauling it all down to his dump. I suspected that Wally didn't send us out to a jobsite because of Milo—with him having vanished like a ghost the way he did. I didn't put much stock in the idea that Milo might come out of hiding just to go after me or Thomas, but Wally wasn't about to take that chance.

Jenna, Hoke, and I went in twice a day to visit Mom, and she looked stronger every time we came in. Her ability to speak had improved dramatically in just a couple of days, and on Wednesday, Dr. Kanner told us that we'd be able to bring her home at the end of the week.

That evening, we moved Charles's desk out of the office and into the pantry, where it blocked a row of cupboards. Charles grumbled some, but seeing no other place to put it without having to lug it up the stairs, he gave in quickly. Besides, Jenna had put her foot down on that score and said that Mom couldn't climb steps, so she'd be staying in the study. I helped take Mom's bed apart and carry it across the road. And as we got it put back together, Charles said, "This should work out well," a statement made, I think, to let Jenna know that he had caved to her will on the subject.

On Thursday, after Thomas and I worked until near sundown hauling debris, we were sitting on his porch when a car pulled up and parked in front of the house. I recognized the man stepping out of the car as Detective Royce. He gave a nod as he passed by us and knocked on the door.

"Good to see you again, Detective," Charles said when he answered.

"Mr. Elgin, could I have a word with you...and Mr. Gardner?"

"Sure, let me get my shoes on."

Royce stepped inside, closing the door behind him.

"Come on," I whispered.

I pulled Thomas off his butt and we hustled across the road to my house. In the carport, I poured some kibble into Grover's bowl and checked his water, keeping one eye on the front door of the Elgin house. When Charles and Detective Royce came out, they walked toward Hoke's place, just as I figured they would.

I signaled for Thomas to follow me over the side of the carport rail, and we ran around the back side of the house, waiting at the corner for Royce and Charles to mount the steps to Hoke's porch. We couldn't see them, but we heard the knock at Hoke's door, which gave us our signal to scamper over and hide behind the propane tank.

"Hello, Detective," Hoke said.

The squeak of chairs told me that they were settling in on the porch.

"The grand jury issued an indictment for Milo Halcomb," Royce said. "We filed it this afternoon. I thought you two should know."

The porch went silent for a while, and then Hoke asked, "You got a good case?"

"Pretty solid," he said. "We had some new evidence come in at the last minute that locks it up for us."

"What evidence?" Charles asked.

"Milo's brother, Cecil, came forward and told us that Milo had been having an affair with Lida Poe."

"Really," Charles said. "I didn't figure Cecil Halcomb to be the kind of guy to turn on his family like that."

"I asked him about that," Royce said. "Claims he couldn't go on covering up for his brother—especially after he got screwed when Milo jumped bail. Blood may be thicker than water, but money is always thicker than blood."

Hoke said, "So Milo was having an affair with Lida Poe and gets her to embezzle a bunch of money...and when things get hot, he kills her and takes the money? Is that the theory?"

"Makes as much sense as anything," Royce said.

"What about the handwriting expert," Charles said. "That points to Cecil being involved."

"I've never been a fan of handwriting experts. They have some validity, but they're not perfect. Besides, did you have your guy look at Milo's handwriting? Maybe Cecil and Milo have similar tendencies. Or maybe Milo was trying to make it look like Cecil's handwriting and was copying his signature."

Hoke said, "Detective Royce, you don't know Milo Halcomb, but...by all accounts, he's as dumb as a stump. I can't see him thinking that far ahead."

"And what about that phone call at the jail?" Charles added. "All that stuff about Milo blowing things up?"

"Keep in mind, it's a jailhouse snitch. Maybe he got it wrong."

"Any idea where Milo might be?" Hoke asked.

"That's the other thing," Royce said. "We got a hit on one

of Milo's credit cards. He used it Monday night in Laredo, Texas."

"You think he's in Mexico?" Charles asked.

"Pretty sure of it," Royce said.

"Did he empty out his bank account before he left?" Hoke asked.

"No, but he only had a couple hundred bucks in there. He bailed out on a Sunday morning. The attack here happened pre-dawn on Monday, long before any bank opened. He might have suspected that one of you could identify him from that attack on Mrs. Sanden, so he took off. Didn't have time to get to the bank and close out his account. Besides, if he *was* Lida Poe's accomplice, he's got enough cash to get by."

"So that's it?" Charles asked. "Put a warrant out for Milo Halcomb and sit back and wait—see if he comes back from Mexico?"

Royce said, "I know it's not the outcome you were thinking, but that's what it looks like. And with this new information from Cecil, it's a good theory. There's nothing more to do right now. We've disbanded the grand jury. It's the end of the trail."

There was a long pause before Hoke spoke again. "Well, we appreciate what you've done, Detective. At least we have the indictment on Milo."

"We'll keep our eyes and ears open," Royce said. "If anything new pops up, we'll be happy to take a look."

Charles gave no statement of agreement or parting salutation as Detective Royce's boots scuffed their way down the steps. After Royce left, Charles and Hoke went inside, their conversation blocked by the walls of the cabin.

CHAPTER

40

MOM CAME HOME TO THE ELGINS' HOUSE A LITTLE unsteady and a bit confused, but looking healthier than she did lying in that hospital bed. The first thing Jenna did that day was to style Mom's hair in a way that covered most of what the doctors shaved off for the surgery. It lifted Mom's spirits immensely. We all waited on Mom hand and foot—even Charles did little things like pull her chair out for her at mealtime and hold her arm if she faltered. Mom protested all that attention, but it fell on deaf ears.

She improved a little more each day, tiny steps moving toward a big goal. The cognitive testing had been scheduled for three weeks out, and Mom set her mind to using every second of that time to render those tests moot. She worked crossword puzzles, practiced dexterity exercises, and read books aloud to sharpen her tongue.

With the word out that Milo had skipped to Mexico, Thomas and I started lobbying Wally to let us go back to sanding houses. He stuck to his guns for most of a week, but then heard that Angus took a job at a tire shop in town. Wally went by and asked Angus to come back to work, but Angus said he couldn't—that it wouldn't look right to the family.

When Wally asked about Milo, Angus said that he hadn't heard from his father since the day he got out of jail. I think that answer, more than anything else, convinced Wally to put Thomas and me back to work. It felt good to be out on the jobsites again, felt like things had come around full circle. Thomas and I had even taken to the woods again, celebrating our days off by climbing trees and fishing in the pond.

When the week came for Mom to go to Columbia for her tests, she seemed to be back to the woman she had been before she got hit, although she spent some afternoons in bed because of headaches. She negotiated with Jenna to let her move back home—not that Mom needed Jenna's permission—and they'd agreed that if the tests went well, we'd move back across the road. I liked living at the Elgins', but I also missed my little house and my little room.

The logistics for Mom's trip to Columbia came together with input from just about everyone. Charles had gotten a batch of Milo Halcomb's time cards from Wally, and offered to drive everyone to Columbia so he could visit that handwriting expert again—he hadn't given up on seeing Cecil Halcomb behind bars. Jenna wanted to go with Mom to offer moral support, and Hoke—who stayed home—insisted that he be allowed to pay for a hotel, as they would need to stay overnight.

As for Thomas and me, we had been invited to go to Columbia, but begged off, saying that we wanted to stay behind and finish hauling Schenicker's house to the dump. Mom and Jenna weren't on board with that at first, even though Thomas and I were alone and unchaperoned all day long working for Wally. Charles came down on our side, pointing out that Milo had skipped to Mexico. But the clinching argument was that Hoke would be within earshot at any given moment. That became the final piece that tipped things in our favor.

In all honesty, though, working for Schenicker wasn't the only reason that we didn't want to go to Columbia. We planned to work on Schenicker's project, true enough, but the real reason that we wanted to stay behind had nothing to do with work.

I had been sitting on the Elgins' couch, flipping through the newspaper, when an advertisement caught my eye. The Jessup drive-in was showing a movie called *The Pom-Pom Girls*. It only took a few seconds for an idea to bloom in my head.

I took Thomas out to the barn and showed him the ad. "We should go to the drive-in this weekend," I said.

He looked back and forth between me and the newspaper a few times, and then said, "I hate to burst your bubble, but I see a couple flaws in your plan, not the least of which is neither of us is old enough to drive a car."

"We don't need to drive a car," I said. "We're gonna hike there."

"Hike? To a drive-in?"

"It's on the south edge of Jessup—just on the other side of those woods." I pointed in the direction of town. "A three-hour hike if we move fast. We can pitch a tent on this side of Gunner Creek. Once the sun goes down, we stroll across the old tractor bridge, and the drive-in's right there. We can sit in the weeds alongside where the cars park."

"But we won't be able to hear it."

"It's *The Pom-Pom Girls,* not Shakespeare. We don't need to hear it."

Thomas smiled as he thought about my idea. "It might work," he said finally.

"Sure it will," I said, holding out my hand. He slapped me some skin to seal the deal.

As the day for Mom's trip approached, Thomas and I set to the task of perfecting our plan so that we could spring into action the minute the Imperial disappeared around the bend. I snuck my duffel and sleeping bag to the Elgins' house, hiding them under Thomas's bed, where we stored most of our camping supplies. We filled the canteens with water, put fresh batteries in the flashlight, and made a list of everything we'd take, leaving no room for error.

When the day for the Columbia trip finally arrived, Thomas and I remained nonchalant, working for Schenicker until four o'clock, showering after work, and then playing catch with a baseball in Thomas's yard, our casual demeanor hiding the excitement churning inside.

Around five o'clock, Charles came out of the house carrying Mom's and Jenna's overnight bags, placing them in the trunk of the Imperial. A minute later, Mom and Jenna stepped onto the porch, arm in arm—the way Jenna preferred to walk when helping Mom down steps. Both women were giggling as if one had just cracked a good joke.

Thomas burned a fastball to me and I caught it in the palm just below my middle finger, sending a stinger through my hand. I pulled my glove off to shake away the pain and Thomas seemed to think that was funny as hell—which it kind of was. I hadn't turned my glove the way Hoke had taught me to do. I glanced at his house and saw him watching us from his porch, a smile on his face as if to say, "See? I told you."

I looked around me at that moment and tried to take it all in—fix it in my mind like a snapshot. There had been a great many hard times that summer, but there had been some good ones, too, and that day, that minute of happiness, made for one of the best.

If a guy could freeze time and hold a moment inside him, forever unchanged, that one would have been the kind of memory to hold on to. But memories aren't like photographs; they can't halt the passing of time. Instead, they lay like footsteps along a path, each determined by the step that came before and colored by the ones to follow.

Over the years, I would try to go back to the memory of that afternoon, pull it from the ruins and clean away the stains, but some things just can't be done.

CHAPTER

41

THOMAS AND I SPRANG INTO ACTION AS SOON AS OUR PARENTS rounded the bend, packing our camping gear with the speed and efficiency of a couple marine recruits assembling rifles. With three hours of hiking ahead of us, we didn't have time to horse around.

Grover had gotten used to sleeping in the carport since Mom and I moved in with the Elgins, and that worked out great because we didn't want him tagging along on this trip—the last thing we needed was to have Grover wander into the drive-in and give away our mission. Once packed, we slipped quietly out the back door of Thomas's house, being careful not to attract Grover's attention.

Our hike took us down the tractor trail, past the pond, and into the deep woods that cut Frog Hollow Road off from the rest of civilization up in Jessup. We walked at a steady pace, following paths and fence lines that I knew well, talking more on the downhills than on uphills, so as to preserve our energy. Being hell-bent on our mission, we made better time than I had expected, reaching the ridge above Gunner Creek well before sundown. The south edge of Jessup lay just beyond the creek.

"That line of stores is Osage Plaza," I said, pointing at the back side of a row of buildings that ran atop the bluff on the other side of the floodplain. "That's the plaza with the record store in it."

"The one across the street from the IGA?" Thomas asked.

"That's it." I moved my finger to the right, to where the bluff eased into a hill with a manageable slope, allowing for cars to drive down into the bottom land and the drive-in. "That shed on top of the hill is the ticket office for the drive-in. You can't see the screen from here, but it's behind those trees."

"What about that creek?" Thomas had his eyes fixed on Gunner Creek, a run of water that might pass for a river in some states.

"There's a tractor bridge upstream a bit. We'll cross there and cut along the bottom of the bluff. The weeds are high enough that we can crawl right up to the side of the drive-in."

"Crawl?"

"Well, I suppose we could wait until dark and just walk over, but you might miss out on some of the plot."

"You're a funny guy, you know that?"

To the west, a big white cloud with a gray belly hovered above the horizon.

"Are we going to get wet tonight?" Thomas asked, looking at the cloud.

"We got nothin' to worry 'bout," I said. "It ain't gonna rain."

"Is that your woodsy intuition talking again?"

"No, it's the weatherman," I said. "I watched the news last night."

I was lying about that, but I wasn't about to come this far only to be halted because Thomas feared a few raindrops.

He pitched the tent while I started the fire and cooked some hot dogs. We ate, doused the fire with canteen water and dirt, and then struck out for the drive-in, taking a flashlight so that we'd be able to find our way back after the movie.

When we got to the bank of Gunner Creek, we followed a dirt trail upstream until we came to a rickety old bridge that had probably been built sometime in the last century. After crossing the bridge, we headed back downstream, fighting through the dense brush and thorns to make our way to the base of the thirty-foot bluff on the back side of Osage Plaza. The drive-in lay in the hollow just a couple hundred feet ahead.

We paused at the base of the bluff to rest, hiding among some enormous cedar trees. The sky had grown dark enough that the floodlights from the plaza up above us cast a dim glow down, causing the shadows of the trees to dance around us as the wind picked up. Ahead of us, previews started playing on the drive-in's screen.

"What now?" Thomas asked.

"Follow me," I said.

We crouched low in the weeds, like soldiers invading foreign soil, working our way close enough to hear the murmur of sound coming from the tinny speakers. With forty feet to go, we dropped to our hands and knees and crawled to a spot just off the driveway, where a row of thornbushes separated us from the gravel parking lot. There, we settled in to watch the movie.

The drive-in held a smattering of cars, a dozen or so parked with an honest view of the screen, and three more in the back of the lot, where shadows offered more privacy. The movie started with a group of scantily clad girls practicing a cheerleading routine on a beach. A faint echo from the old speaker system floated our way, just loud enough to tease us with dialogue. Between that and reading lips, we could make out some of what they were saying.

"I told you this'd work," I whispered.

And then, as if on cue, a crack of lightning lit up the sky to the west. The night breeze turned cooler and began to grow in force, raising the hair on the back of my neck. Thomas turned to me with a mixture of disbelief and I-told-you-so, and before he could say a word, a raindrop the size of a jellybean careened off his nose.

"Oops." I shrugged.

"Oops this!" Thomas leaned over and slugged me square in the arm.

I rolled against the thorns, hugging my biceps. "That didn't hurt," I squeaked. "You hit like a girl."

"So, weather boy, what are we going to do now?"

The rain began to tap faster.

"It might pass."

Lightning flashed, followed by an immediate roar of thunder.

"But then again, it might not," I said.

"Son of a bitch," Thomas yelled. "I knew it. I knew it was going to rain."

"If you knew it, why'd you follow me down here?"

"Because I'm an idiot." The rain started coming down at a steady pace, big heavy drops that peppered us good—and it was just beginning. "You got any money?"

"Yeah, why?"

"We're going up to the IGA, and you're going to buy me a raincoat or a garbage bag, or something."

Thomas stood up and took off running up the driveway that led to the ticket office, and I followed, the rain starting in earnest as we ran past the ticket booth.

CHAPTER

42

A T THE TOP OF THE HILL, THE ENTRANCE TO THE DRIVE-IN opened onto Jefferson Boulevard, a four-lane stretch of blacktop teeming with cars, most driven by those high-schoolers old enough to drive. To our left, the stores of Osage Plaza were already closed for the night. Across the street from the plaza, though, the IGA shined like a mirage. We waited for a gap in the traffic and charged across the boulevard, stopping at the door of the IGA to catch our breath and to watch the lightning as it flashed in quick bursts, silhouetting the hills beyond Gunner Creek, where our campsite was getting drenched.

The IGA didn't sell raincoats, of course, but they sold large black garbage bags, and I bought a box of them. I also treated Thomas to a candy bar, my way of apologizing. Outside again, we each pulled out a bag and I used my dad's pocketknife to cut slits for our heads and arms. Looking like a couple of hobos, we remained under the shelter of the store's awning, ate our candy bars, and waited for the rain to lighten.

"Well," Thomas said, "if you do go to college, we can cross meteorology off the list. You obviously have no gift for it."

"I told you, I ain't smart enough for college."

"Oh, you're smart enough," he said. "You figured out that tire tread thing before anyone else did. Maybe you should be a cop."

"Like Vaughan? I don't think so. I'd rather be on the other side, like Hoke was."

"Yeah, I can see that."

I didn't say anything, but there was a small part of me that could see it too.

I think reading Hoke's letter to Mariam, his careful, thoughtful way of understanding life, had started me thinking that maybe something lay ahead for me that didn't involve Sheetrock. I hadn't told Thomas about reading Hoke's books because sharing what I had stolen seemed a greater sin to me than the theft itself. I also didn't tell Thomas that his constant talking about college had given birth to a tiny voice in my head that repeated the question *Why not?*

Truth is, I didn't want to get Thomas's hopes up—or mine, for that matter.

"I think it's calming down," Thomas said. "Should we make a run for it?"

Rain still fell but not like before, although the lightning continued to crisscross the sky. I nodded, and we jogged across the parking lot, holding up at the edge of the boulevard to wait for a break in the steady stream of goat ropers and gear heads racing back and forth.

"After that truck," Thomas said, pointing to a gap in the cars.

I recognized the truck as it passed us, big and red. Jarvis's truck, with Jarvis behind the wheel—and he recognized me, too.

Thomas had already run two lanes out when the truck hit its brakes, the high-pitched squeal of tires skidding on wet asphalt piercing the night.

"Run!" I yelled, charging into the street to catch up with Thomas.

"What?"

"Run!" I yelled again.

Jarvis burned through a U-turn, his tires spitting angrily as they tore at the wet pavement. Other cars had to lock up their brakes to avoid a crash. Thomas saw the truck but had no way of knowing the danger inside its cab—yet he ran like he understood.

We charged through the empty parking lot of Osage Plaza, heading for the back side. I looked behind me and saw the pickup bound into the lot, its headlights bouncing wildly as it caught a piece of the curb. The roar of the truck's engine exploded through the chilly night air behind us.

Thomas ran faster than me, taking the lead, but he didn't know where he was going. At the back side of the plaza he turned right, sending him down the truck access behind the stores, when he should have turned left toward the drive-in. I yelled, but my voice fell mute behind a clap of thunder. I chased after him, calling his name. When he finally heard me, we were halfway to the other side of the plaza, as much distance ahead of us as we had behind us, a solid concrete wall on our right and a bluff on our left.

"We gotta go this way!" I yelled, pointing in the direction of the drive-in ticket booth in the distance.

We had barely turned around when the truck's headlights lit the corner in front of us, cutting off our retreat. We had no choice but to race farther down the truck access, our path lit by a few floodlights lining the back side of the stores. We were almost to the other end when two figures came running around the corner—Bob, holding a piece of pipe, and Angus, holding a tire tool.

We stopped cold.

Jarvis drove toward us at a pretty good clip. Thomas ran to a stack of pallets and pulled the pile down to block the truck, forcing Jarvis to skid to a stop, his truck nosed into the building to block most of the alley.

Thomas ripped his garbage bag off and raised his flashlight as a weapon. I did the same, pulling my dad's pocketknife out, unfolding the blade, and holding it in front of me for Jarvis to see. When we held up our weapons, Bob and Angus stopped their approach. We backed up to the guardrail at the edge of the bluff but could do nothing more than wait for our attackers to come at us. We were trapped.

Jarvis got out of his truck and walked toward us at a slow, deliberate pace.

"What do you want?" Thomas yelled. I think he was trying to sound angry, but I could hear the fear in his voice.

"Hear that, Bob?" Jarvis hollered as he slowly eased his way down the alley. "Boy wants to know what we want."

"Leave us alone, Jarvis," I said. "This is getting outta hand."

"Oh, it's outta hand aw-right," Jarvis said through a drunken slur. "It's been outta hand for too damned long—ain't that right, Angus?"

Angus didn't answer. He seemed unsteady as he looked back and forth between me and Jarvis and Bob, who stood there tapping the pipe against his leg.

Jarvis pointed at me. "Because of you, Milo's gone." Then to Thomas, who had one leg over the guardrail, he said, "And this boy here—y'all got some nerve comin' to my town and messin' with my family. You got a lot to learn 'bout how we do things down here. And I'm gonna teach y'all what happens when ya mess with a Halcomb."

They started closing in slowly, Jarvis from our right and the other two from our left. Thomas stepped fully over the guardrail, where three feet of limestone separated him from the edge of the bluff. Out of the corner of my eye, I saw him peering down into the darkness.

"That's right, boy," Jarvis said. "Jump! Not as clean as a bullet to the head." He raised a finger to his forehead and tapped at a spot between his eyes. "I know that for a fact. But it'll do."

Between the eyes. The exact place where I saw the bullet hole in Lida Poe's head. Something shifted and a revelation flashed in my head that scared the hell out of me.

Thomas yelled, "Boady, jump!"

I turned just in time to see Thomas disappear over the edge of the bluff. I leapt over the guardrail and looked down, expecting to see his broken body. Instead I saw an enormous cedar tree—its top about six feet shy of where I stood—shaking violently as Thomas tumbled through its branches.

Jarvis, Bob, and Angus must have been shocked by Thomas's suicidal dive, because they froze where they stood. Then Jarvis ran at me, and I turned to the bluff, tossed my dad's knife out to a spot just beyond the girth of the tree, and jumped.

I sailed feetfirst into darkness, hitting slightly ahead of dead center, pounding through the wet branches with a velocity I hadn't expected. It took everything I had to keep from getting tossed out of the tree. I closed my eyes, the needles tearing at my arms as I groped to catch a limb. I bounced off a branch, twisting face-first into the tree. Another limb, a sturdy one, jammed into my ribs and knocked the breath out of my chest. I managed to right myself just before I came to a stop—four feet off the ground.

I eased myself down and curled around the pain in my side. I didn't feel any blood, which was good. My heart pounded hard against the walls of my chest, the pulse thumping loudly inside my ears, but I had made it to the ground in one piece.

"Boady, come on!" Thomas half yelled and half whispered his plea, crouching beneath the next tree down. I crawled to the edge of the branches to look for my dad's knife. I wasn't leaving it behind. Above me they were yelling and cursing. A chunk of asphalt slammed into the stony ground a few feet away, but I remained safe under the tree, crouched on all fours, looking for the knife. It had to be close. A couple more pieces of asphalt hit the ground, then the tire iron.

That's when I saw the reflection—the blade of the knife—in the weeds a couple yards out. I was about to make a dash for it when the tree began to shake as if it were being ripped down its center. I looked up to see a large mass silhouetted against the light from the alley, a man's body shooting headfirst through the branches. I rolled left to avoid being crushed under the juggernaut. As I did, the tree catapulted the man into the air, and he smacked into the earth with the sound of breaking celery.

I scrambled to my feet, expecting a race, but the body remained still. I hesitated. Watched. The body didn't even twitch. I crawled to where he lay, Jarvis, motionless, his head twisted unnaturally on his shoulders, his mouth open, eyes staring at the ground. I didn't have to touch his neck or feel his chest to know he was dead.

For a moment, I couldn't take my gaze away from him. Those eyes that had stalked me through the halls at St. Ignatius were now cold and hollow, staring into a tuft of weeds, his enormous wrestler hands no more threatening than the wet moss beneath them.

"Jarvis!" Bob called out from above. "Jarvis, you okay?"

Angus ran toward the end of the bluff where it turned into a slope, probably looking to find a way down. Bob followed, and the two of them disappear into the night.

A mess of cuts, scrapes, and bruises crisscrossed my skin. My side shrieked with pain, but my legs worked just fine—so I picked up my dad's knife, and I ran.

CHAPTER

43

"W HERE'S THE FLASHLIGHT?" THOSE WERE MY FIRST WORDS
TO Thomas. Not *Are you okay?* or *Jarvis Halcomb is dead,*
but *Where's the flashlight?*

"It's broke," he said. "What the hell happened?"

"They're comin'—we gotta book."

I rushed into the scrub brush and stickers, blind to what lay
ahead of me but propelled by what lay behind. We needed to cross
the bridge before Bob and Angus made it down into the river
bottom. Lightning flashed in large arcs above us. Thorns scraped
against our jeans and tore at our arms as we pushed through
the scrub.

When we got to the bridge, I turned to look back. A bolt of
lightning lit the field, filling the valley with shadows and movement. I thought I saw someone chasing after us, but then again, it
could have been nothing more than a sapling dancing in the wind.
We crossed the bridge and followed the cow trail downstream,
taking a knee at the base of an oak tree to find shelter from the
rain. As Thomas knelt down beside me, I noticed that he held his
left arm against his stomach.

"You okay?"

"I think I broke my wrist," he said. "It hurts like hell and I can
barely move my fingers."

I tried to examine his arm, but the flashes of lightning made everything crooked.

"What happened back there?" he asked.

I bit a hole in my T-shirt just below my rib cage and tore the bottom half of the shirt away to make a sling for Thomas.

"Jarvis tried following us down the tree. He's dead."

"Dead? Are you sure?"

I lifted the sling over Thomas's head, carefully maneuvering his arm into place. "I'm sure," I said. It felt so real, so permanent, saying the words out loud.

Another lightning flash lit the world around us, and I was sure that I saw someone standing on the bridge. I sank lower into the weeds, and Thomas matched me.

"What is it?"

"I don't know."

"Are they following us?"

"It's too dark. I can't tell."

"Is there another bridge? Can we get back to town?"

"That's the only one I know of. Can you travel?" I asked.

"Not fast, but I can keep up with you."

"Let's go."

I kept looking behind us as lightning illuminated the creek bottom in short electric bursts, creating shapes and silhouettes that took on the forms of Angus and Bob—and then nothing, the figures disappearing like objects in a fun house.

We were supposed to have a flashlight on the return trip, so I hadn't memorized the way as well as I should have, but I remembered a fallen tree that stuck out over Gunner Creek. When I found that tree, I knew we were close. Just up the ridge and into the clearing, and we should find our tent.

We climbed through thick scrub, the low branches and thorns ravaging my shirtless abdomen and arms. By the time we emerged into the clearing, I was shivering to beat hell, and Thomas seemed as weak as a half-drowned cat. The moonless night forced us to move like blind men feeling our way to the tent. When we crawled inside, Thomas hobbled in like a three-legged dog, holding his wounded arm tight against his ribs.

"How you doin'?" I asked as I wrapped our sleeping bags around us.

"I feel like my arm's about to explode," he said. "The only parts that don't hurt are the numb parts."

"Should I make a splint or somethin'?"

"You know how?"

"How tough can it be? A couple sticks and some string."

"You're not making a fishing rod out of a cedar switch. That's my arm you're talking about."

"Don't matter anyway, cuz I can't see a thing."

"I have a penlight in my backpack—in the small pouch on the back. It's not much."

I groped around the backpack until I felt the zippered pouch, and inside found a small light the size of my finger. I clicked it on and it lit up the tent enough that we could see each other. I focused the light on Thomas, taking a good look at his arm. He ran his right hand over his wounded left wrist, his fingers moving slowly, stopping near a lump on the pinkie side of his wrist.

"Whoa, that's ugly!" I said, leaning back against the hard frame of Thomas's backpack—which gave me an idea. I put the penlight in my teeth, pulled my pocketknife out and started cutting the nylon straps that held the aluminum frame to the backpack.

"What the hell are you doing?" Thomas objected.

"Makin' a splint."

Thomas opened his mouth as if to object again, but I destroyed the pack before he could say a word.

I held the aluminum tubing against Thomas's arm to get an

idea of the length needed, and then bent the tube back and forth until it snapped, repeating this until I had three sections of frame all straight and firm and of equal length. I took off my socks and used them to cover the rough ends of the rods so they wouldn't cut Thomas's arm. The sturdy nylon cords, which had held the backpack together, worked well to bind the splint. Although I'd never ever seen a splint up close before, I thought I did a pretty good job.

"You had to break my backpack for this?" Thomas said as he looked at my work.

"Does it feel any better?" I asked.

"It's a splint, not morphine," he said. "It hurts like hell...but at least I won't bend my wrist."

Thomas lay back, staring at the circle of the penlight where it reflected off the side of the tent. The rain had stopped, and the lightning had moved in to the distance. Yet with each muted flash, I saw shadows moving outside our tent, my imagination conjuring up Bob and Angus sneaking through the trees. And with each new flash, I had to convince myself that there was no way they could have followed us there.

I also saw Jarvis in my mind's eye, his unblinking stare cast to the ground. I remembered how he came at us, backing us up to the edge of the bluff. I saw him tapping his finger to his forehead, and I remembered the thought that shot through me just before I jumped into that tree.

"I think Jarvis Halcomb killed Lida Poe."

"What?"

"If he didn't kill her, he was there when it happened."

"You think so?"

"Back at the Quaker church, when I went to yell at Vaughan about the tire tracks, they'd already moved the dirt off Lida Poe's face. I saw it, all tight and gray. She had a bullet hole right here."

I touched my finger to the spot where the bridge of my nose met my forehead. "That's exactly where Jarvis pointed when he said that thing about you takin' a bullet to the head. What'd he say? 'Wasn't as clean as a bullet to the head—'"

"'I know that for a fact.'" Thomas finished the line. "That's what he said. He said, 'I know that for a fact.'"

"Why say that unless he saw it happen?"

"But he had an alibi?"

"They had a whole hour where they coulda killed Lida Poe and still been in Springfield at that gas station by seven. And remember, Vaughan said someone saw her car driving around but they didn't see her. What if Milo staged things to give Cecil and Jarvis their alibis—hid the body, made sure people saw Lida Poe's car that night, and then dumped it in that ravine?"

"That explains his lighter being in the car."

"Exactly. And that's why he made that call from jail. When he said he'd blow things up, he wasn't talkin' about Schenicker's house; he was talkin' about the alibi—the plan. That's what he was gonna blow up. He knew what happened cuz he helped. He was gonna rat on Cecil and Jarvis if they didn't bail him out of jail."

"But Jarvis had no reason to kill Lida Poe, did he?"

"I ain't put it all together yet, but he was there. How else would he know 'bout that bullet between her eyes?"

"So what do we do now?"

"We have to get you to a doctor," I said as I slipped my shoes back on. "Then we'll call Royce and tell him what we think."

Thomas shined the penlight at his arm and wiggled his fingers slightly. "I think I'm good to go," he said.

With that, we crawled out of the tent and set out for home.

CHAPTER

44

THE PENLIGHT MADE A HUGE DIFFERENCE, ITS THIN GLOW catching enough of the world that we could skirt around some of the more prickly obstacles that lay in our way. Then, about halfway back to Frog Hollow, the moon peeked out from behind the clouds, bright enough that we could see our way just fine. Thomas found a sturdy stick to help with his balance, and the last half of our hike moved at an impressive pace, considering how beat up we were.

The relief that washed over me when the woods opened up near the pond made my knees go flimsy. We were almost home. We passed the leaning tree and followed the tractor path that led to the back side of Thomas's house. My wet, pruney feet squished inside my old sneakers—fresh socks were just a few hundred yards ahead. We planned to put on some dry clothes and then go wake up Hoke and tell him everything, not only about Jarvis's death and Thomas's broken wrist, but about what we thought happened to Lida Poe. He'd know what to do after that.

The tractor trail ascended gradually along the side of the hayfield, and when we came around the old cow barn, a glint of light drifting from inside the house whispered to us, calling us home.

We headed around to the front porch where the Elgins kept a key under a planter. I did the honors seeing as Thomas only had one good hand, and when I turned the key it rolled easily, almost as if the door wasn't locked at all. I pushed the door open and stepped aside to let Thomas go by.

Thomas had barely passed me when a shadow moved inside and Thomas disappeared into the house as if he had been sucked into a vacuum. Then two hands grabbed me, yanked me in, and threw me to the floor so hard I bounced, my attacker slamming his weight on top of me and twisting my left arm behind my back.

"I got him!" the man on my back hollered. It was Bob. I kicked at him, but he wrenched my arm to the point that I thought he might snap it out of its socket.

I could hear Thomas screaming in pain as he fought with shadows on the other side of the room. A large man, older, with a full beard, held Thomas against the stair rail. Even in that dim light, I recognized Cecil Halcomb, having seen his picture in the newspaper, tall and thick with the same crazy eyes that Milo had. He had shoved Thomas's arms through the spindles of the stair rail, and Angus squatted on the steps behind Thomas, tying them together.

"You know who I am?" Cecil hissed at Thomas through gritted teeth.

Thomas did not answer.

"I'm the father of the boy y'all killed tonight."

Thomas said, "We didn't—"

Cecil punched him in the ribs. "Shut your mouth, boy. You don't get to say a goddamned word. My son's dead, and someone's gonna pay for that."

Bob knelt on my back, his attention on Cecil, his right hand holding my twisted left arm. Something at that moment made me think about Emmett Till. I wondered if he fought for his life or stayed quiet in the hope that they might let him live. If we stayed quiet, took the beating they had in mind, and didn't mouth back, would they let us live? I wanted to believe that Cecil might stop short of killing us, but deep down, I knew better. He'd made a point of making sure we could identify him—not the kind of thing you do if you're going to let a fella live.

I decided that I would not go quietly.

A few feet away, I could see a fireplace poker leaning against the hearth. Could I shake free and reach it? No, Bob was too heavy and too strong; even if I got away, he'd be on me before I could swing it. What else?

They finished tying Thomas to the stair rail and Cecil stepped back, his hands trembling as he spoke. "Where there is evil, it must be purged," he said. "I will repay what's appropriate—an eye for an eye."

He was going to kill us. Fear began to crawl up my spine, and I fought to push it away. There had to be something I could do. I refused to just lie there and wait for Cecil Halcomb to kill us.

Then I remembered my father's pocketknife. My right arm remained free at my side, and I slowly slipped my fingers toward my pocket, careful not to draw attention to my action. Bob kept his eyes on Cecil as the man turned in small circles like he was lost somewhere deep inside his own head. I slowly tilted my hips to get two fingers into my pocket. I could feel the metal rivets against the tips of my fingers. I pinched the knife between my index and middle fingers and slid it out.

Cecil stopped turning and without looking up from the floor said, "Angus, Bob, you boys are about to earn your badges."

Bob tensed up, almost as if Cecil's voice—or his words—scared the hell out of him.

I found the groove in the blade and propped the handle against my leg, opening the knife with a click that I thought for sure Bob heard. But he hadn't. I tucked the knife in my hand, the blade hidden beneath my wrist, and slowly crept my arm up until it lay near my head.

"You boys been wantin' your tattoos...well, tonight's the night." Cecil reached behind his back, lifted his shirt, and pulled a gun out of his belt.

Holy shit!

Cecil waved for Angus to join him. "It's time to show what you're made of, boy. See if you measure up the way my Jarvis did. You ain't no soldier of mine if you can't do what needs doin'."

And just like that, I understood why Jarvis killed Lida Poe—to please his father. The tattoo on his arm, the one he showed me when he wanted me to vandalize the Elgins' house, that was his badge—proof of his father's approval, proof of his standing in the CORPS, proof that he could do *what needed doin'.* I also understood Jarvis's words from the picnic in a whole new light. *If ya ain't scared of me, then ya ain't smart.* And when he showed me the tattoo again: *You know how ya get one of these?*

Angus didn't take the gun, until Cecil shoved it into his chest. Even then he carefully wrapped his fingers around it like it was something that could bite him.

I had my arm out in front of me with the blade still hidden beneath my wrist. If I could get Bob off me, then what? I thought about running to Hoke's, but that would guarantee Thomas's death. If I could get to Angus, maybe I could wrestle the gun away before he shot me. I tried to come up with a third plan, something that didn't end badly in my head, but try as I might I could see no better option. I had to attack. I had to get the gun or die trying.

I silently begged Thomas's forgiveness in case I made a mess of things. Then I turned the blade skyward and swung my arm over my head with as much force as I could.

Bob squealed as the knife sank into the meat of his thigh,

causing him to tilt and let go of my arm—but he stayed on top of me. I rolled and swung again, this time at his chest. He leaned back to dodge my attack, and I buried the blade into his hip.

When I pulled the knife out for a third go, I saw that the tip had broken off, embedded now in Bob's pelvis. Before I could stab him a third time, he dove off me like he was being attacked by wasps. I was free.

I sprang to my feet. Angus and Cecil watched with looks of stunned confusion on their faces. I charged at them, but quickly fell. Bob had my ankle in his grip. I stomped at his face with my free foot, hitting him twice in the nose and breaking his hold.

I stood again, but Angus no longer held the gun; Cecil did, the barrel pointing at me. I saw rage in his eyes as an evil grin pressed up into his cheeks. My last thought before the room exploded with the sound of Cecil's gun was *I have failed.*

CHAPTER

45

I T FELT LIKE A PUNCH, THE BULLET HITTING ME. IT WENT IN under my left collarbone, and threw me back against the wall near the front door. I thought I might be able to make it outside, until I tried to raise my arm to open the door—and couldn't. Dizzy, I slid down the wall, my legs splaying out in front of me, a wave of pain filling my chest and turning my arm numb. That's when the burning started. And holy hell, did it burn.

In that split second before he pulled the trigger, I knew Cecil was going to shoot me—I knew it—yet when it happened I couldn't believe it. No warning or nothing—he shot me just as calm as a man picking meat out of his teeth.

The world seemed to be moving through water, noises muffled, movement slowed. I tried to stand but couldn't find the energy, and even the slightest effort fed the fire in my chest and arm. Over my shoulder, a trail of blood stained the wall where I'd slid down. On the front of my shirt, blood spread dark and red across my chest. My attempt to save Thomas had been wasted.

I blinked away the fog that filled my head and saw Cecil still pointing the gun at me. When he realized that I couldn't move, he handed the gun to Angus. "Finish him off," he ordered.

Angus took the gun and looked at me, and back at Cecil with unsteady eyes. Cecil saw it too.

"Shoot him, goddammit!" Cecil yelled. "He killed my boy. He killed Jarvis."

"I didn't kill Jarvis," I said. "You were there, Angus. You know I didn't."

"Dammit, Angus, do your duty. I gave an order, and you're gonna follow my damned order. I'll not have you leavin' here with nothin' on me. You understand? Either you kill him or, by God, you'll stay here with him."

Rivulets of sweat trickled down Angus's forehead as he brought the gun up and fixed the sight on me.

"Don't do it, Angus," I pleaded. "We're friends, you and me. Don't—"

"This is the one who set the law on your daddy. It's because of him that your daddy's on the run for murder."

"You ain't like them, Angus. You ain't no killer."

The nose of the gun drooped as my words found a foothold.

"Goddammit, Angus, you shoot that boy right now or I *will* shoot you. Don't you think that I won't!"

The barrel of the gun twitched, and Angus blinked hard as if to clean sweat from his eyes.

Cecil raised his voice another notch as red blotches bloomed in his cheeks and neck. "I mean what I said, soldier—you ain't leavin' here alive if you don't pull that trigger. You ain't havin' nothin' on me. Now shoot the little prick and be done with it."

Angus's chest pumped like a panting dog as he raised his left hand to steady the gun, but the weapon continued to tremble.

"Do it!" Cecil yelled.

Angus squinted as he brought the front sight in line with

the rear sight. He closed his left eye, aimed with the right, and tightened his finger around the trigger.

Then his right eye lifted and looked past the gun sights—at me. He stopped panting, the muzzle of the gun settling until it pointed at the floor.

Cecil grabbed Angus by the shirt and began shaking him. "You goddamned coward! I told you I'd—"

That's as far as he got when the front door exploded open and Hoke came storming into the room, a black revolver in his right hand thrust out in front of him. He ratcheted the hammer back and pulled the trigger.

Click—it didn't fire.

Cecil seemed stunned, watching this crazy old man marching toward him with a revolver in his hand. Then Cecil grabbed the gun from Angus.

Hoke ratcheted the hammer back again—*k-k-k*, pulled the trigger and *click*—another misfire.

Cecil fired at Hoke, the bullet tearing through Hoke's gut and slamming into the wall beside me.

Hoke stopped in his tracks when the bullet hit him, and again *k-k-k*—but this time Hoke's gun fired. The bullet caught Cecil in the upper chest, sending him stumbling backwards.

Hoke kept trying to fire his gun as though Cecil's bullet had never touched him. *K-k-k—click, k-k-k—click.*

Cecil shot again, this second bullet tearing through Hoke's crippled left arm, doing no damage as Hoke pulled the trigger for the sixth time. *K-k-k—click.*

Cecil's third shot hit Hoke in the chest, dropping him to one knee, his revolver slumping toward the floor.

Cecil must have thought that he had finished Hoke off, because he aimed his gun back at me, dead center of my chest. I closed my eyes, but when his gun fired I felt nothing. I opened my eyes to see Hoke once again on his feet, standing between Cecil Halcomb and me, his arms heavy at his sides, his knees shaking to hold him upright. Hoke had taken the bullet meant for me.

I heard the click of Hoke's hammer being ratcheted back, and with one last heave, Hoke swung his arm up and fired.

The bullet punched through Cecil's neck, a fan of blood spraying out. Cecil dropped his gun and grabbed the wound with both hands, his eyes wide in disbelief.

Hoke fell to his knees, his head dropping forward. He tried to raise his gun again, but couldn't.

Cecil gaped like a dying fish and ran for the door, half tripping over Bob as he fought to get out of the house. I reached out with my good arm, hoping to grab his leg, but all I did was awaken the pain in my chest, causing me to grit my teeth so hard that I thought I might break my jawbone.

Hoke fell to the floor in a crumpled heap and I rolled to my side, squirming my way to get to him, my whole torso on fire.

Bob tried to get to his feet and follow Cecil, but his right leg didn't work on account of the knife wounds I'd put there. He gave up on standing and used his good limbs to drag the useless one toward the door.

I thought I might have it in me to kill Bob that night, but when we passed each other on the floor—him slinking one way and me the other—I saw his eyes wet with tears, and the part of me that wanted to drive my knife into his throat lost its starch.

Hoke had fallen onto his back, blood covering his whole body, his chest jerking as he fought to breathe. I curled my arm around his head.

When he saw me, he whispered, "I'm sorry."

"I'm okay," I said.

Blood bubbled up past his lips, and his eyes rolled shut. He tried to breathe, but it all caught in his throat and came out in a gurgle. I didn't know what to do.

And then in a voice so weak I could barely make it out, he said, "I'm...sorry" again. And with those words—for the second time in my life—I lost a father.

CHAPTER

46

MUCH OF WHAT HAPPENED NEXT PLAYED OUT IN A HAZE. I remember lying on the floor next to Hoke as Thomas pressed a piece of cloth against my wound. I didn't know how he came to be at my side until he told me later—that Angus had cut him loose from the stair rail. Thomas called for help while Angus sat in a dark corner of the room and cried. The ambulance ride to the hospital is gone from my memory, but I still have a vague recollection of doctors standing next to my bed, talking about surgery. I tried to listen and understand what they were saying, but a persistent and demanding need for sleep forced my eyes closed.

Next, I remember waking up in a hospital room with Mom and Jenna and Thomas—his arm in a cast—sitting in chairs at my bedside. I would learn later that Thomas had called the hotel where they were staying to tell them what had happened. After some hugging and crying, I asked about Hoke. They looked at each other, and Mom cried so hard she couldn't talk. Jenna told me what I already knew—still, I had to ask.

Thomas had been the last of the wounded to leave the scene—Bob having been taken away in the second ambulance and me in the first. And Thomas made sure that Sheriff Vaughan knew the details of the attack. Thomas told me that the last thing he saw before they carted him off to the hospital was Sheriff Vaughan putting handcuffs on Angus Halcomb. Thomas said more after that, but I couldn't keep my eyes open and I fell asleep again.

I stayed in the hospital for three days. On the second day, Vaughan and Royce visited me to get my version of events—they were reopening the Lida Poe case. I don't think I added much more than what Thomas had already told them, but it felt good to give a rundown of what Thomas and I had come up with.

When they let me go home, I returned to my little house and my little room. Charles had moved Mom and me back—Mom's idea. She told Jenna that she wanted to take care of me at home, and it felt good to be back in my own bed. Two days later, Thomas came by and said that Detective Royce was at their house and wanted to talk to everyone—wanted to let us know some stuff before it made its way on to the evening news.

I had my arm in one of those slings that holds the arm tightly to the chest, keeping the stitches from moving. Mom still wore her hair parted on the side to hide her scars. We were in tough shape as we walked across the road, yet I couldn't help but look at the empty chair on Hoke's porch and think of how that man's last act was the only reason I was alive.

At the Elgins' house, I stopped on the porch, frozen by fear, my breath beating quarter notes as I relived what happened on the other side of that door. Mom waited with me as I pulled myself together. And then, walking through the door, I thought I might pass out. In my mind, I saw Cecil Halcomb pointing his gun at me, and Hoke struggling to step in front of the bullets. I saw Thomas tied to the spindles of the stair rail.

I closed my eyes until the visions turned to smoke. When I opened them again, I saw the plaster patches on the walls where the bullet holes had been. I saw new carpeting where my blood and Hoke's blood had pooled. And I saw the Elgins and Detective

Royce sitting at the dining room table, their expressions mirroring my own doubt that I would be able to fight past the ghosts and make it to a chair. Charles came to my rescue, holding my arm and leading me to the dining room and to a seat.

Royce started by saying, "There's been some movement in the... well, in everything. We're issuing a press release this afternoon, so I wanted to tell you first. We know what happened to Lida Poe."

I thought back to the conversation Thomas and I had in the tent—our theory about Jarvis, a theory that we'd both passed on to Royce. Thomas and I looked at each other, and I suppose he too wondered if we had gotten it right.

"We charged Bob Decker—the boy that you...the boy that got stabbed here—we charged him with some serious felonies. It's going to be a long time before he sees the outside world again."

"Did you charge him with murder?" Charles asked.

"No, Mr. Elgin, we did not. That's one of the things I wanted to explain before you read it in the paper. Decker's parents got him a lawyer right away, so we weren't able to get a statement from him. But then we showed his lawyer how strong of a case we had for a crime called felony murder—"

"I'm sorry," Jenna interrupted, "but aren't all murders felonies?"

"Felony murder is a murder that happens during the commission of another crime—another felony. So it doesn't matter what Mr. Decker thought might happen when they came here. They broke in with the intent to assault these boys—that's a felony, so he's responsible for any death that occurred."

"But he's not being charged with that," Charles said.

"No. We offered him a deal, which includes convictions for burglary, arson, and assault—both for what happened here and for the other attacks. Decker admitted that he and Jarvis Halcomb did the drive-by when they hit you with that broomstick. They also burned down Mr. Schenicker's house and threw that rock."

He nodded at my mom. "Cecil put 'em up to it, but they were the ones who carried it out. So, Mr. Decker's going to be in prison for a long time—regardless of the murder case."

"And what about Angus?" I asked.

"He's going down for the assault here, but that's all. I believe him when he said he wasn't involved with the other attacks. I get the feeling that his family didn't trust him with secrets."

I don't know if I was supposed to feel relief about Angus not getting charged with murder, but I did. He was no match for Cecil and Jarvis, yet when push came to shove, he didn't shoot me.

"Did Jarvis kill Lida Poe?" I asked.

Royce paused as though I'd stepped on the speech he'd prepared, but then said, "Yes. And we know this because of Bob Decker. That's part of the reason we gave him the deal. Jarvis confided in Mr. Decker, so we know that Cecil used the Poe killing as a rite of passage for his son. Honestly, though, I think Poe's murder had nothing to do with her skin color and everything to do with Cecil having someone to take the blame for that money he embezzled."

"So it *was* Cecil Halcomb who embezzled the money," Charles said, with a hint of I-told-you-so in his voice.

"We executed a search warrant out at Cecil's farm and found most of Lida Poe's money there. We're pretty sure Cecil was the white man that Lida Poe was seeing on the sly—her accomplice."

"He used her," Jenna said. "Got her to steal all that money and then just threw her away."

"That's about the size of it," Royce said. "Jarvis may have pulled the trigger, but Cecil orchestrated everything. She was the perfect scapegoat."

"But then he pointed the finger at his own brother?" Charles said.

"To protect his son, yes," Royce said. Then his expression turned a notch more somber. "We found Milo Halcomb's body buried in a shallow grave under the floorboards of one of Cecil's sheds."

Mom gasped at those words. Then, almost to herself, she said, "Cecil killed Milo?"

Royce nodded. "We think Cecil changed his plan once we found Lida Poe's car with that lighter inside. Milo probably sealed his own fate by calling Cecil from jail and threatening to blow up their scheme if he didn't get bailed out. Made it easy for Cecil to turn on his brother—make Milo the new scapegoat.

"But keep in mind, Milo's not innocent in all this," Royce continued. "He's the one who hid the car and gave Cecil and Jarvis their alibis. That's the piece that Angus gave us. After he learned that his uncle murdered his father, Angus couldn't wait to talk. He told us that after you found that car, he overheard Cecil and Milo arguing. Cecil blamed Milo for not hiding Poe's body and her car any better than he did."

"But why did Milo get involved in the first place?" Mom asked. "That's what I don't understand."

"Money," Royce said. "We searched Milo's house and found twenty thousand dollars—money from Lida Poe's bank. The bills still had the paper bands around them, and we found her thumbprint on one of those bands."

Royce sat back in his chair and relaxed his posture the way a guy does when he's finished with the hard part of a conversation. "I'd say you boys pretty much hit the nail on the head."

I should have been proud for having figured out so much of what Royce told us that day, but I didn't feel proud. I had been the one to take Thomas out to the drive-in that night. I had been the one who led Cecil Halcomb to Frog Hollow, and for that Hoke lost his life. No, I wasn't proud at all.

There would come a day, years later on a trip home from college, when I confided my guilt to my mother. Her response was to tell me what I had told myself so many times—that I had no way of knowing that we would run into Jarvis Halcomb that night, that everyone thought the threat was over because Milo had fled to Mexico. She did her best to make me feel better, but the pinch of that guilt would remain.

Charles sighed heavily. "So now all you have to do is find Cecil."

Royce stopped relaxing and leaned back into the table, lacing his fingers together. "Yeah, about that...some boys running a trotline over on the Gasconade found a truck half submerged in the water. The tires match that tread pattern we've been looking for. There's no doubt, it's the truck they drove that night you got hit." He nodded again at Mom. "We also found that pattern in the mud the night Mr. Gardner died."

"It was Cecil's truck?" I asked.

"Not really. The truck belonged to a guy who used to work out at Ryke. The guy went missing back in 'sixty-eight. We're reopening that investigation. Near as we can judge, Cecil only used that truck when he needed a vehicle that couldn't get traced back to him—like for those attacks."

"What about Cecil?" I said.

"He wasn't in the truck. It rolled down a pretty steep ravine—must have dropped a good hundred feet or better, busted out every window and popped both doors off. There was so much blood inside...I can't imagine anyone surviving it. We have divers out there now, swimming up and down the river looking for him. We even set dogs on the trail to see if he climbed back up the ravine or walked away somehow. They haven't found anything so far. You mark my words, though, Cecil Halcomb is as dead as dead can be. We'll find him floating down the river or snagged on some fallen tree one of these days."

I pictured the blood spurting out of Cecil's throat as he ran from the house that night. Royce had to be right about him being dead. I wanted to believe him—I needed to believe him—but the body of Cecil Halcomb would never be found.

CHAPTER

47

THE STORY OF THAT NIGHT—THE NIGHT THAT HOKE DIED— made it into just about every newspaper in Missouri, even in the Kansas City and St. Louis ones. Because of that, we had reporters calling the house and a few that drove down Frog Hollow Road to take pictures. On the radio, a debate had been raging ever since the press release came out explaining the tragic death of Hoke Gardner and the understandable demise of Cecil, Milo, and Jarvis Halcomb. Half the town called in to praise Hoke for his sacrifice, and the other half clogged the airwaves with all sorts of crazy conspiracy theories to explain the government's deplorable attack on the Halcombs. I got so sick of the lies that I turned off the radio and kept it off.

Two weeks passed before we held Hoke's memorial. Sheriff Vaughan posted a deputy at the door to keep reporters and riffraff away. Still, it seemed like half the town showed up to pay respects to the man who gave up his life to save two boys. Principal Rutgers walked through, looking sadder than most, and it occurred to me that he wasn't just another gawker. He knew that Hoke had quietly paid for my schooling with a fake scholarship.

It made me wonder if the social worker and the nurse that I'd read about in Hoke's letter to Mariam were there as well. With all the news reporting going on, I half expected one of them to reveal

Hoke's secret to the press, but they never did. The Anonymous Angel of Jessup saved my life, and Thomas's life, and then died in my arms.

It tore me up to look at that drab little box that held Hoke's ashes, oak with no engraving other than his name and the dates of his birth and death. A box like that could just as well have been in some cluttered garage holding nuts and bolts. But this one held my friend Hoke, and he was gone, and I bawled pretty hard about that.

When it came time to leave, one of the strangers, a man in a gray three-piece suit, came up to Mom and held out a card. I expected it to be another reporter, but he explained that he was Phillip Waznewski, Hoke Gardner's attorney. He said he had some matters he needed to discuss with Mom and asked if she could stop by his office after the service. She looked at me and I shrugged my okay.

After we said our goodbyes to Wally and the Elgins, Mom and I got in the car and followed Mr. Waznewski to an office only a few blocks from St. Ignatius. Waznewski said that the business they had to discuss might take a while—maybe an hour—so I told Mom that I'd wait for her at the school.

St. Ignatius looked different without students buzzing around it—harmless, just bricks and windows. Grunting voices floated up from the football practice field, and I took a seat at the top of a grassy hill to watch the football team go through their summer drills below. I tried to focus on the practice, but my thoughts kept floating back to a slew of *what-ifs*. What if I hadn't cheated on that history test? I'd have gone to summer school, and then I wouldn't have been around for Jarvis and Bob to hit with that stick. I wouldn't have thrown that rock; Mom wouldn't have been hit...

Those thoughts were enough to drive me mad—a thousand

little turns, each exposing a new path that might have led away from Hoke Gardner dying. I was trying to find my way out of that labyrinth and back to thoughts that didn't so easily gnaw at my chest when I heard the sound of feet swishing through the grass behind me. I turned to see Beef walking my way.

I thought about running, but he had his hands in his pockets and his shoulders slumped forward—not the posture of a man out to beat me up for killing his friend. I turned my attention back to the football field below and waited.

Beef sat down beside me without saying a word—just plopped down and stared out into the distance like we'd been sitting there all day and simply ran out of stuff to talk about. I waited for him to speak, and after the seconds ticked into minutes, I broke the silence.

"Did ya know he killed her?" I asked.

Beef gave my question so much thought that I began to think he didn't understand what I asked him. I was about to repeat myself when he said, "Probably should've, but no, I didn't know."

I let the answer sit for a spell, not sure if I believed him or not, and as the silence grew heavy, Beef spoke again. "Jarvis and me...we've known each other forever. It's hard to believe that someone you grew up with could do somethin' like that, but...I guess, lookin' back, I knew somethin' was wrong. We weren't as close as we used to be. Things changed around sophomore year when his ol' man started diggin' his hooks into Jarvis—all that nonsense about the CORPS. Bob was happier'n hell to go along with that crap, but I didn't much care for it—and I told him so. We were still friends, but not like it used to be.

"One day I found him sitting in his truck before school. I went up to say hi, and I could tell he'd been cryin'. Of course, he denied it. He never told me what was up, and I just figured him and his ol' man were goin' at it again. Lookin' back now, I think that's about when that Poe woman went missin'. I kinda dropped the ball, I guess."

I said, "I appreciate what ya did out at the picnic. I saw ya sneak off to fetch that deputy."

Beef looked at me for the first time since he sat down. "You know...what you said to me that day in the restroom...about why I didn't try to stop Jarvis from beatin' you up, and how it wasn't all that complicated...that kinda got to me. Shamed me is what you did. Now I can't help but wonder if I coulda put a stop to it—maybe Jarvis would still be alive."

"I'm sorry he's dead," I said. I don't think I really meant it, but it felt right to say.

"Yeah, I'm sorry too."

The players on the field were running sprints back and forth, their grunts and moans climbing the hill and filling the gap as Beef and I fell silent again.

"You should go out for football," he said, finally. His words came out of the blue, and I thought he was joking, but the look on his face was nothing but serious. "I mean...once ya heal up, of course. I've seen ya run. You're fast. I'm helpin' coach the linemen this year. Be happy to put in a word with Coach Thayer."

My head was already too full of thoughts to take on any more, so I didn't say anything. When I didn't respond, Beef stood up, brushed the grass off his jeans and said, "Well, just give it some thought."

"I will," I said. And although the idea seemed absurd on its face, it was a better *what-if* to ponder than those that had been stirring around my head all day. "Thanks, Beef."

"Ronnie...that's my name. Ronnie Dupree."

"Well, then, thanks, Ronnie."

*   *   *

Mom's meeting lasted longer than an hour, and when I got in the car, her eyes were red from crying.

"You okay?" I asked.

She opened her mouth to answer, but the tears welled up in her eyes, and she shook her head. We drove to the Montgomery Ward parking lot and parked in a spot far away from everyone.

"What is it?" I asked again.

"Hoke left us his house—in his will."

Mom went on to tell me about the meeting she'd had with the attorney, about how, after he laid out what Hoke had left us—which was hard enough to take in—he said that Hoke wanted Mom to be executor of his estate, which meant seeing to it that Hoke's final wishes were followed. Mom full-out sobbed as she talked about all the people that Hoke wanted to help with his money. And then the conversation turned to his books.

"And I'm supposed to deliver some journals to a woman named Mariam Fisk—his sister-in-law. I didn't know he had a sister-in-law. Did you?"

I hesitated, and then said, "Yeah. I know about his family. I also know about the journals and Mariam Fisk." When Mom looked lost, I went through the details of the trip Thomas and I made to the newspaper archive in Columbia. I told her what we had learned about Hoke's past, and when I got to the part about the car accident, Mom turned pale.

She said, "That's why he wants his ashes scattered on Old Plank Road. That's probably where the accident happened. In the will, he said his life shoulda ended on Old Plank Road. I didn't understand what he meant."

"He wants his ashes scattered alongside the road?"

"To be honest, he didn't use the word scattered. He wrote that we were to 'dump' his ashes in the ditch."

"We can't just...dump his ashes," I said. "It ain't right."

"That's his last request."

"Mom, there's a lot you don't know about Hoke. You need to read his journals—it's one big letter to that Mariam woman. You have to read 'em and see—"

"Wait—you read his journals?"

I felt a ping of guilt enter my chest, but deep down, I was glad to have done it. "I read some of 'em, and you should too. You have to."

"Those are private." She looked at me like I had just asked her to knock the hat off the pope. "I can't read those and you know it."

"Did you know that Hoke was in the hospital chapel when the doctor told you that Dad had died?"

Shocked, she just stared at me.

"Did you know that he's the one paying for me to go to St. Ignatius?"

"Why would he..."

"Mom, please read 'em. You'll understand everything—and you'll see why we can't just throw his ashes away like that." Now I was crying.

We went back and forth for a little while longer, and although Mom never agreed to read the letter to Mariam, she backed away from her flat refusal. When we got home, I grabbed the trunk from Hoke's library and dragged it to my house, using my one good arm.

CHAPTER

48

I T TOOK MOM A WEEK TO READ ALL ELEVEN VOLUMES; THE FIRST day was the worst. She read in her room, and I could hear the sound of crying coming from the other side of the door as she discovered what I had—that Hoke Gardner had devoted his life to my mother and me. He had been there in ways that we'd never known, propping up the crumbling walls of our world, while we remained oblivious.

After that first day, she took to reading on the back porch, a box of tissues at her side. On the third day, I came home from hanging out with Thomas and found her sitting at the table reading about 1970. I hadn't read that one, but when I came in, she stood up and hugged me—for no reason at all. Then she took the book and went to the porch. I tried to remember what might have happened in 1970 that brought that on, but nothing came to mind.

After she finished the last book, we took a drive out to the cemetery in Dry Creek to visit the graves of Alicia and Sarah Gardner.

"He deserves to be here," I said.

"I know," Mom said, "but how can I ignore his last request?" She knelt down and touched Sarah's headstone. "How is that my place?"

"He saved my life, Mom. He's made up for whatever bad stuff he might've done."

"Don't you see, Boady? It's not our decision. We don't get to make that call."

A man in work clothes walked by a few rows over, and judging by the pruning shears in his hand I took him to be a caretaker. "Excuse me," I called out.

He stopped walking and looked at me, and I waved him over.

"You work here?" I asked.

"I do," he said. "What can I help ya with?"

"What's the rules on burying an urn—say right here." I pointed to a spot at the foot of Sarah's grave.

The man looked at the grass and then at the headstone. Then he paced off two steps and turned. "A standard casket's seven feet long," he said. "But this here looks to be a little girl—what, five years old when she died? I reckon she don't take up no more'n three foot, four if she was tall for her age. That leaves a good three foot of nothin' but dirt and rock. An urn—once you put it in its vault—well, that don't take up no more'n a foot. The sexton likes us to use the space as best we can, so won't be no trouble puttin' an urn here. But you'd need family permission. Then, yeah, we can do that."

"Thanks," I said, and the man left.

I looked at my mother, who continued to stare at the spot of grass where the man had just pointed, probably seeing—as I was—a small plaque with Hoke's name on it. She didn't say anything more, but I could tell that she was struggling. Hoke wanted his ashes to be tossed into the weeds, cast aside and forgotten in that place where he'd committed his greatest sin. He thought he didn't deserve better, but he was wrong.

We walked to the back end of the cemetery, to my father's grave, and Mom knelt down to pull a few untrimmed blades of grass away. She stared at the headstone for a long time and then said, "He'd have been proud of you."

Her words caught me by surprise, and I didn't answer.

"You've always been such a hard worker, kind, thoughtful. And all this—what you wanna do with Hoke's remains—you know it's the right thing to do, and that's how you set your course. That's the kind of man John was. He knew right from wrong, and found no gray betwixt 'em. I see that in you, and it makes me proud."

Mom rose to her feet and brushed grass from her knees. "You're right about this; Hoke deserves to be here with his family. If we need to talk Mariam Fisk into it, well, I guess that's what we'll do."

Mariam Fisk lived in Ashland, a little town just south of Columbia. Mom and I loaded Hoke's books into the car and drove there on a rare cool August morning. Mom had called before we went, telling Ms. Fisk that we were neighbors of Hoke Gardner, and that we had something to deliver to her. Mariam wanted to know what we had, but Mom dodged the question, saying that it was Hoke's final request, and we had no choice but to deliver it. "We'd prefer if you were there to take it so we don't have to leave it outside," she said.

When we arrived, Mom and I each grabbed a handle and carried the trunk up onto Mariam's porch, knocked on her door, and waited for Ms. Fisk to answer. She was pretty—or had been once, and I could see where the straggle of time had deepened the lines beneath her eyes and washed the shine from her hair. She looked on us with suspicion as she opened her screen door.

"What's that?" Mariam said, pointing to the trunk.

"This is Hoke's bequest to you," Mom said, using a word that the lawyer had given her.

That hadn't been Hoke's only bequest to her. Mom told

me—after reading Hoke's journals—that Hoke had been sending Mariam five hundred dollars a month, every month since the accident. He also left her ten grand in his will. She was the only person—besides Mom and me—to get any of his estate. All the rest went to a slew of charities.

"Can we come in?"

Mariam looked at us as though sizing us up, and then turned and walked into her house without answering. Mom drew a deep breath to summon her courage, and we carried the trunk in, showing Mariam the books. The disappointment on her face couldn't have been more obvious if she'd written it on her forehead with a felt-tip pen.

"Books?"

"They're his journals. It's really one long letter to you. He wanted you to have them."

"Why would I want to read anything *he* wrote? He killed my sister. Did you know that? Did he write about how he got drunk and crashed his car into a tree and killed his own daughter?"

"Yes, I know about that."

Mariam shot Mom a look that made it clear that she was itching for a fight, but Mom said, "I know it's hard for you. I know you're hurtin'. I looked for your name in the guest book at the funeral. I understand why ya didn't come."

"All those newspaper stories. I read 'em, but they don't know the truth. They don't know what he did to Alicia—to Sarah."

"I know that, Ms. Fisk, but you should read what he wrote. You might understand."

"What's to understand? What's to be gained by draggin' this all up again?"

Mom steeled herself and said, "Ms. Fisk, I'd like to bury Hoke with his family... in Dry Creek."

Well, that set Mariam Fisk off. "You will do no such thing,"

Mariam said. "You will not sully the ground of my sister and my dear niece with that man's remains. He's a cur dog, a no-good scum. I will not—"

"How dare you!" Mom hissed. "How—dare—you! That cur dog saved my son's life. He stepped in front of a bullet for my boy. You can hold all the hate you want in that black heart of yours, but don't you ever insult that man in my presence."

I stopped breathing. I had no idea that my mother had lungs like that, or the spine to hold them up. Good God, she was impressive.

Mariam's face went full-on red. "Y'all need to leave my house."

"Read the books," Mom snapped.

"I said leave!"

As we walked out the door and down to our car, I could see Mom's chest rising in short huffs. I half expected to catch a licking for talking her into this folly, but when we took our seats in the car, she said, "I'm so sorry for that, Boady. That woman's hurtin', and I shouldn't have yelled at her."

"But she deserved it," I said.

"No, Boady, she's just sad, that's all."

CHAPTER

49

THE MONTH OF AUGUST SLOGGED ALONG AS SLOW AS ANY month I'd ever known. With Thomas having a busted wrist and me having my shoulder messed up, we couldn't work for Schenicker, and trekking through the woods had become too much of a chore. We tried fishing, thinking that between the two of us we had one working set of hands. Climbing the leaning tree wasn't a problem, and we managed to get a line in the water, and even caught a fish, but the effort required to do the simplest of tasks took the fun right out of it.

Mom suggested that we grab a couple books from Hoke's library and kill time reading. It seemed a lame idea, but I figured I'd give it a go. I found a set of books by Sir Arthur Conan Doyle, who I knew wrote about Sherlock Holmes, and I pulled one out. Thomas read *Frankenstein,* by Mary Shelley; I'd seen the movie, but I didn't know they also wrote a book about it.

We took up places on Hoke's porch, me in my usual chair and Thomas in Hoke's. It felt strange having Thomas sit beside me instead of Hoke, no pipe smoke wafting in the breeze. But Hoke was gone, and it didn't make any sense to let the chair go to waste. I started my reading with *The Hound of the Baskervilles,* which only lasted me a couple days. I liked it well enough that I decided to read another. Before long, I'd finished the whole set.

In that third week of August, Mom, Jenna, Thomas, and I made another trip to Columbia to do Mom's cognitive testing—because she never got to finish it the last time on account of my getting shot. This time, our moms took Thomas and me along to keep us out of trouble, and while I didn't see that as being necessary, I supposed they had a point.

When the day came, Jenna drove us up to the university, where we stayed in a motel—Thomas and Jenna in one room and me and Mom in another. The next morning Jenna took Mom to the hospital for her tests, and Thomas and I walked around campus again, heading straight to the quad to lie in the grass and watch the girls walk by. But pretty soon a couple guys with long hair started playing a game where they kicked a beanbag back and forth, bouncing it off their knees, feet, heels—everywhere but their hands.

We watched in amazement, and when they took a break, Thomas asked where we might buy one of those beanbags. The guy called it a hacky sack and pulled a spare one out of his pocket, giving it to us. Well, that settled the question of what we'd do to kill time until Mom's tests were done—for two boys with busted wings, what game could be better? By the time afternoon rolled around, we'd gotten pretty good at the game. And somewhere in that afternoon of playing hacky sack and watching girls, I made up my mind to go to college—at least, I'd give it my best shot. If I wasn't smart enough, well, so be it, but I wouldn't fail for lack of trying.

At three o'clock we met Mom and Jenna back at the hospital as planned, and packed into Jenna's car for the drive back to Jessup. Mom said that her tests went well, and while there were some lingering effects of her injury, they should go away in time. That news called for a celebration, so we stopped at the Zesto in Jeff City for ice cream again.

When we got back to Jessup and Frog Hollow Road, we found a strange car sitting in our driveway. Mom parked in front of the Elgin place, as Mariam Fisk stepped out of the car. She opened her trunk and waited for Mom to cross the road. Mariam spoke first.

"Mrs. Sanden," she said. "I...I'm awful sorry for what...I shouldn't have spoken to you the way I did."

"You don't need to apologize," Mom said. "I was the one out of line."

"I didn't know. I mean...He sent me money all those years, but I just figured he did it to unburden his conscience. I never knew about you and your boy."

"Hoke Gardner was a complicated man," Mom said.

"I think you should have the books." Mariam lifted the chest out of the trunk and laid it on our driveway. "It's your story more than it's mine, but I thank ya for making me read 'em."

Mom stepped in and gave Mariam a light hug. "I'm sorry for the loss you suffered. Believe me, I know it's hard to lose someone ya love so dearly."

"Yeah, I s'pose you do know a thing or two 'bout that. And I want ya to know—I spoke to the folks out at the cemetery. I gave 'em permission to bury Hoke with Alicia and Sarah—that is, if you still have his ashes."

"I do—and thank you."

Then Mom looked at me and asked if Thomas and I could carry the chest into the house, which we did. When we came back out, Mariam Fisk was gone.

We buried Hoke Gardner's remains on the last Thursday before school started back up. It was a small gathering: me, Mom, the Elgins, and Wally Schenicker. Mom had invited Mariam, but she chose not to come. After the caretaker lowered the small burial vault into the ground, he left so that we could say a few words. Everyone said something, starting with my mom, who probably talked the longest.

I thought about what I should say, not sure how to sum up everything in a short speech. As I stood there thinking, I noticed that the evening sun, setting low, had cast the shadow of the angel statue so that her head was silhouetted in the grass next to my feet. It occurred to me that I stood where Hoke had tried to kill himself ten years earlier, and a final *what-if* came to me. What if Hoke had been successful that night?

Had Hoke's gun sent that bullet into his brain instead of just skipping across his skull, how very different would my life have been? He would have never found me in that chapel. He wouldn't have been there to teach me all those things. He'd been protecting us in ways we never knew. Mom and I seemed to live our lives on the brink of a great precipice, always one step away from falling, not knowing that Hoke had been there the whole time, standing between us and the edge. How do you say goodbye to someone like that?

When it came my turn to speak, all I could say was "Thank you, Hoke."

After that, our little assembly fell silent. And that's when my mother lowered her head, closed her eyes, drew in a breath...and sang.

Amazing Grace, how sweet the sound...

Her voice, full and sweet like honey, hung in the air around us. I had never heard my mom sing. I'd never heard so much as a hum or anything. But then I remembered the postcards my dad sent from Germany, and how he called her his songbird—and I understood.

That saved a wretch like me...

Jenna joined in with a low harmony, and the two together sounded like a single, beautiful voice.

I once was lost but now am found...

I have never been able to carry a tune, but I moved my lips that day and whispered the words just loud enough that I could hear them myself.

Was blind but now I see.

ACKNOWLEDGMENTS

I would like to thank the many people who have helped shape this novel, starting with Joely Eskens, Nancy Rosin, my agent, Amy Cloughley, and my editor, Emily Giglierano. I am also eternally grateful to all the folks at Mulholland/Little, Brown, including the editorial director, Josh Kendall; publisher, Reagan Arthur; marketing director, Pamela Brown; publicist, Maggie Southard; publicity assistant, Shannon Hennessey; cover designer, Lucy Kim; production editor, Mike Noon; and copyeditor, Alison Kerr Miller.

I also want to give a special thank-you to Jennifer Schoats Flack, Courtney Flack Salesman, Joni Gutknecht, Terry Kolander, and Sandy Schiefer for the technical assistance.

Allen Eskens is the *USA Today* bestselling author of *The Life We Bury* and five other novels, most recently *The Shadows We Hide*. He is the recipient of the Barry Award, the Rosebud Award, the Minnesota Book Award, and the Silver Falchion Award, and has been a finalist for the Edgar Award, the Thriller Award, and the Anthony Award. His debut novel, *The Life We Bury*, has been published in twenty-six languages and is in development for a feature film. Eskens lives with his wife, Joely, in outstate Minnesota, where he was a criminal defense attorney for twenty-five years.

READING GROUP GUIDE

Dear Reader,

While I'm known as a Minnesota writer, and have spent three decades here, I actually grew up in Missouri, a landscape that shaped me and my vision of human nature greatly. I've long wanted to write about my experiences, but could not have dreamed I'd do so at such a necessary moment. *Nothing More Dangerous* is a story of so many things—love, loneliness, friendship, redemption—but it is my greatest hope that this book joins our necessary conversation about what it means to be prejudiced. As Hoke says in the novel, "It's not a matter of if we have prejudice—we do. It's a matter of understanding those instincts and fighting against them."

I began writing *Nothing More Dangerous* in 1991, as a short story about a fifteen-year-old boy named Boady Sanden, who grew up in the hills of Missouri in the 1970s. The more time I spent with Boady, the more I came to understand that Boady had a journey to make, one that would mirror my own. You see, I grew up in a place and time where dark notions of us-versus-them roiled behind a thin veneer of respectability. The prejudices that I held in my youth were not the bold strokes that people associate with the Jim Crow era—separate bathrooms and the like—but rather subtle and subconscious notions, so pervasive that folks just took it for granted that one group of people held superiority over another.

I could see even back then that the attitudes of many in our country were changing for the better. But there was always that contingent who paid lip service to change while they cursed the "political correctness" that forced them into the shadows. The arc of history continues to bend toward justice, and I believe that our society will get there, but not if we continue to ignore those hidden notions that allow us to turn a blind eye toward ourselves.

I left Missouri when I headed north to go to college, eventually earning degrees in both journalism and law. Over the years, I clamored to understand that darker side of my past—the darker side of myself. *Nothing More Dangerous* was born out of that journey. This is a story that took me twenty-eight years to complete, but a lifetime to grasp. This novel is truly the story that I became a writer to tell, and I hope and pray that I have done it justice.

Nothing More Dangerous is a literary mystery and a coming-of-age-story. It is a story of redemption, loss, friendship, and forgiveness. But woven throughout *Nothing More Dangerous* is the journey of a boy struggling to understand and overcome his subconscious prejudices. In the end, I wanted to create a work that would not only entertain, but evoke emotion and contemplation. I want this story to join the conversation about the powerful hold that subconscious prejudices can have on all of us, to help to explain why the spark of old divisions can so easily become a flame when given a touch of oxygen, and to remind all of us that nothing will change unless we ask ourselves the right questions, even when they're tough.

I hope you enjoy it.

Allen Eskens

A CONVERSATION WITH
ALLEN ESKENS

What inspired you to write *Nothing More Dangerous*?

Nothing More Dangerous started out in 1991 as a short story about a fifteen-year-old boy named Boady Sanden, a boy who had more to him than what the rest of the world could see. I loved the good-hearted, yet naïve, nature of this character, and I wanted to do more with him than what I had done in the short story. So I expanded his journey, sending him down a path that I had once traveled, one that would teach him the depth and subtlety of racist notions. I wanted him to come to understand how prejudices can lie hidden in all of us, even if, like Boady, we are convinced that we hold no such beliefs. Boady's transformation takes place over a single summer in 1976, where mine was a journey of years.

This was my first story, and it was my desire to write this story better that compelled me to take up the study of writing. I spent the next twenty-eight years studying and rewriting *Nothing More Dangerous* until I felt that it was ready for the rest of the world to read. Now I feel it could not have come together at a more perfect time.

Tell us a bit about your own background. How did you come to be a novelist?

I was a terrible student in high school, but I became involved in theater and that gave birth to a passion that led me to college.

Once there, I found that I had an appetite for learning and switched my major many times, eventually getting degrees in journalism and law. Still, my creative side yearned to be exercised, so after law school, I took up writing as a way to reengage with that creative side. I wrote for my own enjoyment for twenty years before I set out to become a published novelist with my debut novel, *The Life We Bury*.

You're known for writing mysteries and thrillers. Do you see *Nothing More Dangerous* as different from your other books?

I write mysteries and thrillers because as a former criminal defense attorney, I am drawn to crime plots. But in truth, my mystery plots are there to serve as a vehicle to tell a more important story. When I start a novel, I always ask myself, *what is this story really about?* I want to bring my readers into a world of characters and relationships in a way that will hopefully evoke contemplation or stir emotion. My novels deal with themes like guilt, forgiveness, and prejudice, and those facets can be magnified when they are explored in the context of hunting a killer or solving a mystery.

Nothing More Dangerous is my most character-driven novel, and the mystery in it is more of a catalyst than a center post. Fifteen-year-old Boady does not set out to solve the disappearance of Lida Poe, but yet the missing woman becomes an integral part of his world. Placing Boady's awakening against the backdrop of that kind of evil forces Boady to confront his own prejudices in a blunt and honest way.

Many of your novels take place in Minnesota. What was it like to write about Missouri?

Writing about Missouri was a joy. Many of the vignettes in the novel come from my own adventures growing up in the Ozark hills. But much of what I wrote about had to come from my memory because the nearby city has expanded and encroached upon my beloved woods. For example, there is a scene in the book where the boys camp in an old moonshiner's hideout. That spot existed in my youth, but now has a highway built over it. The leaning tree, where Boady goes to find solace, is a tree that I used to climb in the woods near my home. That tree was cut down by developers a decade ago. But in the end, my strong memory of those places was easy to channel as I wrote the book.

What kind of research did you do to write *Nothing More Dangerous*?

There are conversations between Boady and Hoke about race that I wanted to make sure were intellectually honest, so I spent a lot of time studying those issues, adding the intellectual underpinnings to the memories I had growing up in that world. I also spent some time in Columbia so that those scenes were accurate to how the world was in 1976.

Are any of the characters in the novel based on real people?

The characters are all drawn from my imagination. But like Dr. Frankenstein building his monster, I pulled bits and pieces from many places, including from people I've known and from myself. There is one character, however, who is based on a real person. Mrs. Dixon, who only appears in the book as a memory, is based on a neighbor I had growing up in Missouri. She was a woman who lived a graceful and quiet life.

Did anything surprise you in writing this story?

I have to confess that what surprised me the most was that the central message of the novel—the prevalence of subconscious racism—still thrives to the extent it does. I wrote *Nothing More Dangerous* as a way to talk about that quiet racism that comes out in sentences that begin, "I'm not prejudiced, it's just that…"

My favorite novel of all time, *To Kill a Mockingbird,* examined a more overt and intentional form of prejudice, and as a kid, it was easy for me to exempt myself from the lessons of that book. I felt that, because I didn't believe in segregated schools or separate drinking fountains, I wasn't a racist. I could wrap myself in the comfort of believing that I held no prejudices, yet in the same breath, I could explain how the color of a man's skin impacted his ability to be a quarterback.

I wrote *Nothing More Dangerous* with the hope that I might entertain readers with a thrilling and powerful story, while quietly challenging them to question the ease at which people can be divided into us-and-them. I understood that such prejudicial urges exist in all of us, but my great surprise (and disappointment) was how easily those tendencies can again rise to the surface.

Why did you decide to set the novel in the 1970s?

I set the novel in the 1970s and in Missouri because that is a place and time that I am familiar with. More than anything else, I wanted this novel to be honest and authentic. I can speak from first-hand experience about how life was in that part of the world in the 1970s. I didn't see it then, but that's the point of the novel. Boady doesn't see the racism around him and within him because that is just how things are. It's when he starts to see the world through Thomas's eyes that he can honestly see himself.

Do you think things are different in our nation today? How has this story changed for you over the decades?

At one point in the novel, Hoke tells Boady the story of Emmett Till and he says:

> "Boady, the men who beat and murdered those people for all those years, do you think they simply disappeared because someone passed a law? . . . Do you think those folks just figured out that they were wrong and went home?"
>
> "No, but things are different now, ain't they?"
>
> "I wish to God they were, but that stuff still happens. Maybe not in the same way as what happened to Emmett Till, but **it's out there—always will be.**"

I wrote that line in the 1990s, and it seems as though the prescience of that statement has been borne out over the last few years.

As for the story changing, Boady's journey is basically unchanged from what I had first envisioned back in 1991. I could see back then that the attitudes of many in our country were changing for the better. But there was always that contingent who paid lip service to change while they cursed the "political correctness" that forced them into the shadows. The arc of history continues to bend toward justice, and I believe that our society will get there, but not if we continue to ignore those hidden notions that allow us to turn a blind eye toward ourselves. *Nothing More Dangerous* was written to spark that discussion.

What do you hope readers will take from the novel?

Nothing More Dangerous is a story of so many things—love, loneliness, friendship, redemption—but it is my greatest hope that this book will add to our conversation about what it means to be prejudiced. As Hoke says in the novel, "It's not a matter of if we have prejudice—we do. It's a matter of understanding those instincts and fighting against them."

Even good-hearted people, like Boady Sanden, can have blind spots, hidden ideas rooted in judgments tied to the color of a person's skin. Sometimes, it takes a little nudge for people to ask the right questions of themselves. *Nothing More Dangerous* was written to offer that gentle nudge.

QUESTIONS AND TOPICS
FOR DISCUSSION

1. Before you read *Nothing More Dangerous,* would you have considered yourself someone with prejudices? Do you feel differently about your own assumptions after reading? What does it mean to be prejudiced?

2. Discuss the setting of the novel—Jessup, Missouri. How does living in Jessup shape the characters? Would Boady be different if he lived somewhere else? How do our communities influence our worldviews?

3. What does Boady think he wants for his future? Do you agree that this is actually what he needs? How are his two desires in opposition? How does Boady try to rationalize this?

4. When you first met Hoke, did you think he was a good or bad guy? Why? Was there a point in the novel at which your opinion changed?

5. How is Boady's world challenged by having the Elgins in his life? How is Boady changed by his friendship with Thomas? Is this friendship different from the friendship Jarvis offers?

6. Discuss how *Nothing More Dangerous* explores racism. Is Boady prejudiced when the novel begins? Does he think he is? How does he come to see Jessup differently?

7. What is the difference between overt racism and prejudice? Is there one? How does Hoke help Boady to see his own prejudice differently? Do you think Hoke's vision of society is right?

8. Have the prejudices of Jessup changed by the end of *Nothing More Dangerous*?

9. Do you think the novel would be different if it was set in 2020 instead of 1976? Why or why not?

10. What does Boady mean when he says "It was as though I had been staring at a mirror all my life and that mirror suddenly turned into a window" (p. 225)?

11. Who is the villain in *Nothing More Dangerous*? Is there one? Do you think this villain would agree they're bad? Why or why not?

12. Hoke recites a quote from Martin Luther King, Jr: "Nothing in all the world is more dangerous than sincere ignorance" (p. 167). What does this quote mean? Why do you think the author chose this quote for this novel's title?